The Swing

Margaret Scott

AuthorHouse™ UK Ltd.
500 Avebury Boulevard
Central Milton Keynes, MK9 2BE
www.authorhouse.co.uk
Phone: 08001974150

© *2009 Margaret Scott. All rights reserved.*

No part of this book may be reproduced, stored in a retrieval system, or transmitted by any means without the written permission of the author.

First published by AuthorHouse 9/17/2009

ISBN: 978-1-4389-9436-9 (sc)
ISBN: 978-1-4389-9437-6 (hc)

This book is printed on acid-free paper.

To all my teachers

Acknowledgements

The publication of 'The Swing' would have been impossible without the help and support of several people. Firstly, I am indebted to Saul David's excellent book *Churchill's Sacrifice of the Highland Division*. His detailed research of the retreat to St Valéry, and its tragic outcome, gave me a source from which to construct the second part of the book.

The information about ENSA was supplied by Lillian Tertis, latterly my mother-in-law's closest friend. Without her I would have never known about SEMA, or that the classical musicians worked in groups of eight, that there was a solo and a chamber pianist in each group, or that they wore uniform. Lillian played the cello at Belsen, ten days after it was liberated.

When the script had been written, proof-reading was not only thorough but shared by experts whose advice has been invaluable. Philip Riley corrected and pinpointed textual errors with his unerring acuity, quietly suggesting that I tighten the style and banish most brackets and semi-colons. This was done with great kindness and verve by Dilys Barré, who spent a weekend treating me as her pupil. The military detail was scrutinised and improved by Major Malcolm Ross retd. at the Gordon Highlanders' Museum in Aberdeen.

The book spent six months with a well-known agent in London, before being rejected with encouraging comments. The decision to 'self-publish' was advanced by my long-suffering husband, Julian Todd, whose kindness and support has been tireless. After another séjour with Philip Riley for fine-tuning, it was placed in the hands of Authorhouse who are responsible for the finished product.

Dramatis Personae

Jean Belliot	– son of a tenant farmer on the Favoret estate
Michel Belliot	– Jean's father
Tom Creighton	– Territorial officer in the Seaforth Highlanders
Robert Cummings	– Scottish wine merchant and territorial officer in the Gordon Highlanders
Hugh Cummings	– Scottish doctor – elder brother of Robert
The Curé	– parish priest
Tadeusz Donska	– Polish cellist
Maître Fauchon	– father of Cécile Favoret
Marcel Favoret	– the name of Rémy Favoret's father, grandfather and great-grandfather
Rémy Favoret	– father of Anne Favoret
Sergeant Fraser	– blacksmith and territorial sergeant in the Gordon Highlanders
Colonel Grey	– officer in British Intelligence

Colonel Jamieson	- officer in the British Army
Private Macrae	- territorial soldier in the Gordon Highlanders
"Marcus"	- paratrooper and British Intelligence officer
Private Menzies	- soldier in the Gordon Highlanders
Hervé Millet	- father of Marie Millet
Stephen Murray	- Scottish doctor
Major Murray	- brother of Stephen
Bernard Piot	- head master of the state primary school in Quinon
Paul Raven	- English violinist
André Roche	- labourer on the Favoret estate
Charles de Valliet	- brother of Edmond de Valliet and joint owner of the Ronval estate
Henri de Valliet	- owner of Ronval estate until 1916 and colonel in the French army
Edmond de Valliet	- joint owner of the Ronval estate.
Francis de Valliet	- son of Edmond de Valliet
Pierre Vanne	- labourer on the Ronval estate
Soeur Antoinette	- Irish nun

Betty Cummings	– wife of Hugh
Emily Cummings	– mother of Robert and Hugh
Elizabeth Creighton	– sister of Tom and cousin of Edmond and Charles
Veronica Creighton	– sister of Elizabeth and Tom
Mlle Crochet	– Francis de Valliet's nurse
Mme Fauchon	– mother of Cécile, grandmother of Anne
Anne Favoret	– daughter of Rémy Favoret, and pianist
Cécile Favoret	– mother of Anne and daughter of Maître Fauchon
Mrs Jamieson	– wife of colonel in the British Army
Marie Millet	– daughter of Hervé Millet and adopted sister of Anne
Mme Millet	– mother of Marie
Reverend Mother	– Mother Superior of the Convent
Alice de Valliet	– mother of Edmond and Charles (née Creighton)

Prologue

1999

Last month I went back to St Valéry and stood on the west side of the harbour wall recalling the events of June 12 1940, when the armies of both the men I married were surrounded by Rommel's tanks. Early in the morning on the west beach I heard the shouts of the French, among them Edmond's decisive voice, the relentless pounding of gunfire from above, the noise of confusion, men penned like sheep between the chalk walls and the tide. I crossed the bridge to the east side listening to the burr of angry Scotsmen. I saw the white flag torn from the church tower and the fury of soldiers – some even defying regulations and wearing kilts – refusing to be driven like cattle, still fighting to hold the narrow streets and the seafront while St Valéry burned. One of them was Robert.

I looked up at the flags which fluttered everywhere, their message of brotherhood and unity in motley colours, the Tricolor and the St Andrew's cross dipping in the wind beside the black, red and gold of Germany. Beneath them scores of masts pointed upwards like spears, an army of pleasure boats in silent order waiting for the tide to turn and the bridge to be raised, so that they could glide freely into the milky water beyond the outer harbour. That morning the tide was low and weed lay strewn across the narrow strip of water marked out by buoys which guide the yachts out to sea.

The Mairie, rebuilt by the Scots, towered above them in bold post-war style, the wide orange brick front facing the yachts, its back turned from the sea, with flowers nurtured into patterns, red and white geraniums spread like a carpet over the sloping banks in front of the building. Another floral display announced the latest attraction at St Valéry, the total eclipse. It would draw thousands to the beaches where defeated soldiers once huddled in the companionship that shuts out despair. Behind the Mairie, shops and cafés sprawled round a wide square, the chairs and tables inviting the tourists to eat and drink slowly, careless of time, enjoying the sea breeze which tempers the heat of a Norman summer. The narrow streets wind upwards but stop before they reach the cliffs; the same chalk cliffs edge the south coast of England, a pilot's vision of home and safety in the late summer of 1940, but here on that June 12 the end of an uneven struggle. At the silent bathing area and children's pool, I gazed at the prosperous resort, twinned with Inverness and Sondheim, and, returning over the bridge, I stood in front of the half-timbered house dating from before the sixteenth century, where Henri IV is reputed to have stayed. In a dark, downstairs room the tourist can watch a worn film, telling the story of the surrender and liberation of St Valéry in disparate clips. The voice-over is barely distinguishable, but the story tells itself. Before I left, I was driven to a lonely spot outside the town where a plaque remembers the brave men and women who weren't soldiers, but gave their lives for the Resistance. Among them is the name of my childhood friend:

Marie de Valliet morte pour la patrie – 1944.

I had seen it many times, but standing there I remembered her as I had always known her, vulnerable, obedient, giving. I knew the truth at last.

But it's my story that you wanted me to write. You, Robert and Gordon, asked me again last Christmas. We were gathered here at Ronval which has been Franco-Scottish as long as I can remember, with its bulky British furniture draped with tartan rugs, incongruous amid the elegance of a French manoir built in the mid fifteenth century when England was our common enemy. How often you boys have come with me to St Valéry, full of questions about your grandfather, and always disappointed not to find his grave among its heroes! But the story is also for my French family, and the last piece of the jigsaw which I fitted only six months ago might have caused distress, if not to them, at least to Francis. You all loved him, and accepted his cassock as part of his kindness. He was the sort of uncle that everyone needs, someone who gives you his undivided attention, who enters into the spirit of every game with unfeigned earnestness, who would never patronise or play a lofty part.

My story begins here in Calvados, where two Norman houses stand on either side of a river, and a child's swing once hung from a great oak that might have been an acorn at the time of the Conqueror. The story took me to North America, it covers the war years which I spent in Britain, and it reaches out to Germany. Robert crossed the Rhine into Germany and died there; Edmond worked in Baden-Baden in the post-war period, and it was in Germany that Charles became a priest. Our lives were ordered by war. Loyalty and manipulation, sacrifice and betrayal were the cross-threads of its fabric.

Part 1 1917 – 1940

Chapter 1 1917 – 1923

I was an awkward child, a tall, long-legged red-head, dreamy and in constant trouble. Who else would play the piano without taking off coat and boots, unconscious of snow dripping on to the floor and forming a puddle under the pedals? It was like the blots on my schoolwork and grazed knees in the playground, impulsiveness that earned frequent scolding from the nuns who told my mother I needed firm handling.

The nuns were much less direct with my father, partly because he was a man and partly because they were (with one exception) a little afraid of him. At the time I thought this was hypocritical. As maire of the commune, and an avowed republican, he should have sent his daughter to the state school for which he was responsible, but my mother and grandmother overruled him. Reverend Mother understood the power of politics and influence, and made the nuns relish their triumph in secret, deferring to the maire with unusual respect. She was small and commanding with a clipped way of speaking, which expected instant obedience as she swept past in black cotton and sandals. As for the bald-headed curé whose high-pitched voice and subservient manner my father despised, calling him a milksop and a drunk, he was terrified of him.

If I did have redeeming features, Papa was one of the few people who could see them. I loved walking with him through the orchard and fields which were really ours, but were rented to Michel Belliot. Papa was a good businessman, who sold Norman cheese as well as cider and calvados to the markets and retailers in Rouen and Paris. One of the outhouses at La Chenaie was used for pressing the apples. I remember the old horse trudging round and round, straining at the straps attached to the grindstone as it crushed the apples which fell through a chute from the loft. Every now and then André Roche would let him stop. He would snort wearily, take some oats from the sacking nose-bag and start again. I could tell that André liked him from the way he put on his harness, patting his back, looking for sores where the leather rubbed his coat. I spent hours there, savouring the homely smell of horse and hay and oats, mingled with the sweetness of the mush which spewed and squelched in the outer groove under the relentless movement of the stone.

It was a happy childhood, in spite of school and the girls who laughed at me because I played the piano and was always in a scrape. Marie was the only one who didn't. She was talented too, but her drawing, like her personality, was quiet and controlled, whereas everything I did, from playing Bach to losing my pencil-box, had an element of exhibition as far as the nuns were concerned. At home my parents took me seriously, and didn't patronise me the way parents usually did in those days. I loved the long evenings in the summer at the top of the steps which led to the main part of the house. It was much more interesting to hear them talking about Paris and business and the labyrinth of French politics than to do my homework. My parents were very insistent that I did my homework, and gradually my school reports improved.

These were the times when my father would tell us the family history, which you have often heard, so I shall try to keep it short and to the point. His great-grandfather, Marcel Favoret, fought at Austerlitz, having risen from the ranks to become a colonel in Napoleon's army. He returned to Normandy with a leg wound and a Légion d'Honneur medal, a hero of France and a favourite of the Emperor. His fighting days were over, but not his ambitions. The property of La Chenaie was empty. The owners had fled to England during the Revolution after the death of Edmond de Valliet, who had owned two adjacent manors and the surrounding land. The other house, more like a small chateau, was called Ronval.

The first Marcel was a soldier rather than a businessman. In 1815 the de Valliet family came back to Ronval and claimed their rights to the house and land of La Chenaie. The Restoration favoured the families of the *Ancien Régime*, and after an expensive law-suit, Marcel and his family were evicted.

But Marcel's son (the second Marcel, my father's grandfather), went into business and made a small fortune. Capitalising on the "Légion d'Honneur" family status, he found the means to buy back La Chenaie and its land. The de Valliet family had lost money on foreign ventures and had suffered from the political changes caused by the revolutions of 1830 and 1848. Having paid an extortionate price, the second Marcel, already in his fifties, settled there, making some improvements to the farm, and raising a family during the reign of Napoleon III.

Then the de Valliets, wanting to recover their property, fabricated a charge of embezzlement against my great-grandfather. It was never proved, but the lawsuit and self-defence proved costly, and it looked as though the Favorets might again have to relinquish their property. But the second Marcel's son, my grandfather, was a soldier like the hero of Austerlitz. Having distinguished himself in the Franco-Prussian war, he returned to La Chenaie, determined to keep it in the hands of the Favorets.

The Franco-Prussian Marcel was neither a businessman nor a farmer, a red-headed and irascible army captain with a bristling red moustache, who defended his estate with the instincts of a commander under siege. The red hair must have been some throwback to our Viking ancestors – wasn't the son of the Conqueror William Rufus, or "Red-head"? He kept dogs and a patrol of farm hands who roamed the property day and night. The de Valliets launched an equally vigorous campaign – both families had learned the financial risks of going to law. In a series of skirmishes, which the Favorets usually won, so I was told, one de Valliet was so badly mauled by a dog that he limped for ever after. Several of the dogs were shot and had to be replaced. The local gendarmerie took very little interest in the squabbles, as long as no one was killed. But the surrounding farmers mainly supported Capitaine Favoret, who had the advantage, moral and military, of being the defender. The chief object of the attacks was the dovecote which was a sign of seigniorial status. It was nearly burnt to the ground, but, on principle, rebuilt when other farm buildings were crumbling.

By the turn of the twentieth century, Capitaine Marcel was living with his wife and three sons at La Chenaie. He kept a gun under his bed, and had just enough to support his family. The three children all went to the new state primary school for boys, attached to the Mairie, but only my father, the second son, took an interest in learning. Having inherited the acuity of the second Marcel, he soon realised that the fighting would have to stop.

Henri de Valliet, the current owner of Ronval, started another lawsuit, this time over a path which led from La Chenaie past the boundary of the Ronval estate to the main road. Realising that if his enemy were to win, my grandfather would have had to cut through an orchard to clear the way, my father decided to seek legal advice. The ageing Capitaine was by now a bed-ridden widower, though he still kept a well-oiled fire-arm at his side. He warned against the expense, and emphasised that he could pay little towards the costs. With much trepidation, my father set out in 1912 to engage the services of a well-known advocate in Caen.

It was while waiting to consult him that my father caught his first glimpse of my mother, the lawyer's daughter who had opened the door in the absence of a maid. She was tall, like my father, with dark brown hair and hazel eyes, which glinted with fun. Her twin brother was a prankster, but my mother's sense of the ridiculous was more measured and tolerant of the grandeur and pretensions of her parents and their côterie. Both brother and sister chafed under the restrictions of their strict upbringing; they longed for adventure, and wrote stories which they read to one another. My uncle, Jean-Luc, played the piano. He could have been a professional, but that was unthinkable to my grandparents. He was to be a lawyer like his father and Cécile, my mother, to marry well. My grandfather owned a beautiful old house in Caen, which was one of the loveliest French cities until the allied landings in 1944. It was a rambling town manor, with offices on part of the ground floor. My father was ushered in, though not by my mother, who had been hastily called away by my grandmother. But by that time my parents had exchanged a few words. It was enough.

My father was a master of self-control, but his heart beat strongly as he sat before the dapper Maître Fauchon, sleek and well-dressed, the middle finger of his left hand touching his gold watch chain, the picture of professional command and concentration. The contrast with the country farmer, explaining the history of an ongoing feud with the aristocracy, in a softened version of our Norman patois, would have made Jean-Luc laugh if he had been there.

My maternal grandfather saw the arguments clearly. My father showed him the deeds which proved that La Chenaie had been bought by Marcel the second. The case of embezzlement had not been proved, and the path hadn't been disputed when the purchase had been made. The existence of a Napoleonic Légion d'Honneur might be a useful back-up. By 1912 the glory of France and the victories of the first Emperor were much valued, even by leading catholic families.

The law-suit passed in our favour, much more quickly and inexpensively than the Favorets could have imagined, but my father now plunged into another contention, this time with Maître Fauchon, over the hand of his daughter. There would have been no hope for either of the lovers without the machinations of Jean-Luc, who quietly took his sister's side. Thanks to Jean-Luc, my mother once ventured out to meet her fiancé dressed in her brother's clothes!

An impasse was reached. When my mother proved obstinate, my grandparents reluctantly allowed her to marry a man whom they regarded as a peasant of property, but withheld her dowry. She reached La Chenaie in the spring of 1914. If she was horrified by the state of the house, she never admitted it, although she later confided to me that she found my father's brothers uncouth and unwelcoming. She never met Le Capitaine, who had died before he knew that his son would bring a daughter of the Caen haute-bourgeoisie into his house. She established order where she could, quickly learning to cook, clean and find people to draw water from the well, mend the ramshackle furniture and sweep out the smoking kitchen chimney.

Nobody could have anticipated the events of 1914-1918. The death-toll made no distinction between de Valliets, Favorets and Fauchons. The first casualty was my father, who came back from the trenches with a wounded leg – not unlike the first Marcel who had fought for Napoleon. He had led a bold sortie in 1916, when the armies had reached a stalemate. During the following months both his brothers were killed, and in 1917, my grandparents were told of the death of Jean-Luc. Henri de Valliet was killed in the same battle.

1917 was the year I was born, 1917, the year when communism sprang to life in Russia, an insidious malaise which spread and poisoned the patriotic spirit in France, and divided the Resistance when the second war came. For my grandparents 1917 was the end of their happiness, although my birth brought healing as well as disappointment to the family. My mother, who wanted a large family, had hoped for a son to replace her brother in her affections. But she had only one child, a girl with the Capitaine's red hair, who looked like a caricature of her handsome brother, with the Favoret blue-green eyes staring at the world above a long nose and freckled cheeks.

But my birth did bridge the gap between my mother and her parents, who admired La Chenaie, and recognised the business acumen of their son-in-law. The dowry was given, and Jean-Luc's upright piano moved into the salon before my baptism, an event which jarred against the instincts of my republican father.

Chapter 2 1925 – 1926/7

My father was a shrewd businessman whose kindness was hidden behind a screen of pragmatism. He refused to buy the surrounding small-holdings where widows and orphans scraped a miserable living, buying their milk at a fair price, and, on the pretext of profit and self-interest, making sure that their herds were well stocked.

To no one was he kinder than to Marie and her family. This kindness had to be kept secret, or at least his gifts had to be given in as quiet a way as possible, because the Millet farmstead was on the Ronval estate. It was run-down, bare of any comforts except an old treadle sewing machine, a smoke-filled hovel, attached to a barn where two cows were daily milked by Marie's mother.

Hervé Millet had been at school with my father, and they set off together for the war in high spirits in 1914. There were few likenesses between them, Hervé small, dark and timid, my father tall and fair with the Favoret strong features, and intelligent blue-green eyes. Within eighteen months my father was promoted and then commissioned as lieutenant. So many young officers were being mown down that there were always vacancies for men of ability, and my father was welcomed as the great-grandson of a Légion d'Honneur hero of Austerlitz. He lost touch with Hervé who eventually came home from the trenches shell-shocked and broken. Day by day he sat by the fire gazing into space while his wife, and later his daughter, tried to run the farm and household.

I say that they lost touch, but I have good reason to believe that my father saved Hervé's life, not from the enemy but from the French. Papa never told this story, whereas he loved to tell us all about the Capitaine and the hero of Austerlitz. He may have remained silent because it portrayed his loyalty in bold outline and he couldn't make excuses for it; or perhaps he had come face to face with his enemy, Henri de Valliet, and had had to acknowledge that enemy's advantage. No, it was from another source, a letter written from the trenches, of which I was told years later, that I learned of this episode. But to tell you who it was would be to jump ahead of myself!

In the First World War there was little sympathy for those whose nerves had been damaged by noise and gun-fire – and later exposure to poisonous gas. The distinctions between the coward and the unhinged were largely ignored. Witless men found wandering from their posts, unaware of time or direction, were shot by their officers for desertion.

Hervé, who was attached to a regiment commanded by Colonel Henri de Valliet, had never been entirely sound in his mind. My father, now a lieutenant, sent with some mission to the headquarters of the brigade in which Henri de Valliet was a colonel, found that Hervé Millet was being tried for desertion. Papa insisted on speaking on his old friend's behalf, and, pushing through a cordon of officers, he found himself face to face with his old enemy.

"This man is innocent," blurted out my father.

"How would you know, and anyway who are you?" blared back Henri de Valliet. He was a tall handsome man with a small moustache, classical features and piercing blue eyes. The two men looked at one another from the same height, traditional enemies, each brave, uncompromising and determined. From what I know of Colonel de Valliet, he was a man of integrity, who balked at the idea of shooting a man who was incapable of defending himself.

"I know this man, sir, and I also know you. My name is Rémy Favoret, and Hervé Millet has been my friend since childhood. He wasn't capable of defending himself then. Now that his nerves are wrecked by shock, how could he have known that he was abandoning his post?"

"I recognise you, Favoret. We have never been friends but I shall bear in mind what you say."

This was the only verbal exchange between your grandfathers, Louis-Rémy and Henri-Bernard. They never saw each other again. My father was wounded shortly afterwards, and during the next offensive the colonel was killed. Hervé was sent home via a sanatorium for the mentally deranged. He never recovered. I hope that he wasn't exposed to electric shock "treatments" which would have aggravated his condition.

It was my father who made sure that the cows calved, that the milk was sold at a fair price, that there were logs to keep the smoky hearth alight during the winter, that they all had warm clothes, food to eat and medical attention for Marie's mother who had developed a sinister cough. Marie's school fees for our "*école libre*", a school outside the state sector, were paid by another source. The fees were small but not inconsiderable for poor farmers who wanted their children to go to catholic schools.

But in spite of regular visits by the local doctor, Marie's mother's cough, exacerbated by hard toil and insanitary conditions, worsened. The only medical cure in those days was to be found in expensive mountain clinics in places like Switzerland, where recovery was never guaranteed, especially if the disease were far advanced.

By the time we were eight, Marie was driven to school with me, first in the horse-drawn wagon, and later in my father's car, the first ever to appear in the Quinon area. It looked prestigious but, as the roads were little more than dirt tracks, it was slower and less effective than the wagon. Marie and her mother would walk towards the end of the path which wound round the boundaries of the two estates, the path which had been disputed in 1912. We would stop and my father would help the little girl to clamber up the steep steps into the wagon, and later open the car door with his customary gallantry, saying "Bonjour, Mademoiselle Marie!"

One morning there was no sign of them. A farm hand came scurrying down the path to say that Marie would not be coming to school, but gave no reason why. If my father was prepared to accept such vague excuses, the nuns were not. Where was Marie Millet? Absence without apology was a serious offence. Inquiries were made, the nuns even asking the maire to make further use of his car!

But they had not anticipated the more practical, foreseeing and less judgemental assistance of my mother. She had already had the horses harnessed to the wagon, and, unafraid of any political considerations, set out for the Millet home as soon as she had heard from the servants and farm hands that something was amiss. She sent for the doctor, who arrived on horseback.

Nothing could have been more pathetic than the sight of the dark kitchen, with the ashes of a long extinguished fire spilling on to the stone floor and pervading the atmosphere with an unhealthy dust. In a corner sat the shell-shocked Hervé crossing his arms and clapping his shoulders in an effort to keep warm, while the small child tried to put more clothes on the bed where her mother lay coughing and helpless. My mother was making arrangements before anyone else arrived. Mme Millet would be taken to hospital, her husband to an "*asile*" for "*mutilés de guerre*", and Marie would come home with us. There was no point in arguing. The cows would be the responsibility of the owners of the estate. The nuns would have to wait until lunch-time for explanations of absence.

Marie hardly cried at all. Maman promised that she would see her mother at least once a week.

"Will it be warm in the hospital?" she asked.

"It will be warm and your mother will have the medicines she needs."

"What will happen to Papa?"

"He too will be warm – and safe."

Marie never saw her father again. She hadn't known him except as a helpless halfwit, and her mind could only cope with her mother and her illness. For a while she fretted about the cows, and her pet cat which came to La Chenaie, treating us with great disdain and eventually returning to its old home to live on mice in the barn, as it had always done.

My father continued to visit his old friend from time to time until Hervé died in 1936. But Mme Millet only lingered until the early summer of 1927. After the funeral we all went to St Valéry-en-Caux for three weeks in the villa which had become our holiday home. It was spacious and comfortable, overlooking the harbour on the west side of the town.

My father's kindness to Marie – and my mother's too of course – was unstinting, and always cloaked behind a veil of imagined self-interest. It was good for me to have a companion, for his wife to have another child to care for, and one whom we knew to have such an obliging nature. If you adopted, how could you be so sure of welcoming into the family a child so talented and adaptable?

Yes, she was all of those things, but was I?

"Anne, we must put another bed in your room, for Marie," said my mother the day Marie arrived.

"Why? Why can't she have the room at the top of the stairs? It's nearly as big as mine."

"If you had younger brothers and sisters, you would have to share with them." It was sad for her that she didn't have more children. She would have been the ideal mother of six.

"But I don't have younger brothers and sisters. My room has always been mine."

My mother called me selfish, finally insisting that we share a larger room which had always been kept for guests. It had dormer windows which looked down on the land of La Chenaie on one side and over the river to Ronval on the other. Immediately below us, on the half-floor which you reached by steps from the salon, was my parents' room. On the other side of the landing was the room which had always been mine. Above it was another room, almost the same size, and two smaller attic rooms each with a dormer window, where our maids slept.

But it was not without some struggle that I gave in, aware for the first time of "space", of wanting my own territory, not just physically, but an interior space where creative impulses grow, a fortress from which I could view the outside world. Fortunately such independence, recoiling from being locked into interdependence, was in some way a trait of Marie's too. She loved to draw, often from memory with astonishing attention to detail. Her pencils and crayons, and later her paints and brushes, were always neatly stacked at a table in a small room adjoining the salon. It was filled with light which poured through the broad windows.

My inner world was one of sound, not just music, but also of words. It was personal and much more valuable than my possessions, which I was always losing. That world found expression at the piano, but also in writing poems, and, to the exasperation of the adult world, in daydreams and solitary walks, which I needed when I was tired or hurt.

Marie understood – more than understood. If I wandered off on my own, I would come back to find my mother furious and Marie at her table drawing. I sometimes wondered whether my mother longed to hear her say, "Anne, wherever have you been?" But she never did.

Marie had her own escape route, from a much harsher world, a world which, although behind her, she could never completely shake off. It was more of a denial, a cut-off, than a retreat. Only rarely did I see her face empty, its features rendered commonplace and plain, a face which I sometimes envied for its grace and beauty. But if I felt jealous – and sometimes she did make me feel like a cart-horse beside an Arab filly – it was a minor threat. I needed to be alone, and, provided I could be free of the constant need to adapt to others, Marie would always be my friend.

My parents had more practical ideas for two eight-year-olds. Walking alone for me was a safety valve, for them a danger. They wanted us to "play together", and it was only when my father attached a swing to an old spreading oak with a trunk split by lightning many years before, that we found something we wanted to share. We walked there together before and after school that first summer, sometimes talking, but usually in silence. It was in the middle of the wood and to reach it we had to take the path leading down to the river which was forbidden territory. It was always exhilarating. We took turns to rock higher and higher, feeling the wind on our faces, looking down on the woods and fields, the river sparkling in the sunlight, and on either side, the manoirs and gardens of La Chenaie and Ronval. We could just see the hexagonal tower in the distance.

My parents had their reasons for wanting us to be together, because in the wood we were not alone.

Chapter 3 1926 – Spring 1929

If La Chenaie was my home, Ronval was a dream. La Chenaie was half-timbered and heterogeneous, as it had been changed and added to from one generation to the next. Ronval was built of stone, its outline misty because we always saw it in the distance. Sometimes the tower would shine in the evening sun; radiating light like sparks from a smithy's hammer, making us shade our eyes when we caught sight of it. Inspired by stories of princesses and castles, we called it the château, but we had to be careful not to say so in front of my father, who reckoned it was as much a Norman manor as any other. It dated from the middle of the fifteenth century, when the English were driven from France at the end of the Hundred Years War.

Each property had an orchard which sloped down to the river and beyond it, a grassy bank about ten yards from the water's edge. There was one wooden bridge over the river, but I still don't know who was responsible for its upkeep. My father said it was dangerous, and we thought of it as some sort of mirage that would vanish if we tried to walk over it. We could just make it out from the wood behind our house.

The wood was a place of fantasy, full of dryads and other tree spirits which were mainly benign, but which we felt we mustn't disturb by breaking branches or scouring bark. There were oaks and beeches, spindly birches, alder and tall poplars. The oak with our swing was by far the widest, if not the tallest, the hollow part of its split trunk crawling with snails, slugs, and woodlice. The slugs oozed with complacency and the snails marched solemnly like serious officials on state occasions, but the woodlice and beetles were always busy. One side was wider and stronger than the other and it was here that we had our swing. I realise now how lucky we were, not penned in like sheep in a garden and forbidden to go beyond the gate. It was a place where time stood still. Usually we were alone, but sometimes we were aware of intruders – we would listen for the rustle of leaves or the snap of a twig, and somehow know that it wasn't a fox or a rabbit.

The most frequent spy was Jean Belliot, who was four years older and at a school run by Jesuits in a nearby town. He had been a leader at the boys' primary school which was divided from ours by a wooden fence. The boys often clambered up to laugh at the girls on the other side; and on my first day at school, when I fell and grazed my knee he was the leader of the group that jeered and shouted "Sorcière, Fille du Maire," laughing at my red hair and calling me a witch. He had a crooked smile and a practical intelligence which my father admired. Papa bought and sold the cheese made in Michel Belliot's – Jean's father's dairy – to the Rouen and Paris markets; and in his spare time Jean helped Michel look after the growing herd. Papa was satisfied that the business would thrive in the hands of Michel's son.

But I didn't like him. I always felt that he was mocking me, and he had dismissive ways of talking about people. He would come up to us when we were on our swing and shove me hard, but if it were Marie, he would push her gently and lightly.

"Do girls climb trees?" he asked one day.

"Of course they do," I replied.

He clambered up our tree with the speed of a monkey, and we felt that we had to follow, taking care not to tear our skirts, although we scratched our arms and knees which weren't protected like his.

"Not bad," he said patronisingly. "Can you set traps for rabbits?"

"I don't think we should trap the rabbits," said Marie.

"Why not?" I said. "The cows are slaughtered – and the pigs – and André Roche wrings the chickens' necks when we want one for supper. We had rabbit last night."

Marie looked uncomfortable. "Don't worry about that, Marie," said Jean. "You think about your pictures. At least they're about real life; better than thumping a piano!"

"I don't thump, Jean Belliot. Get back to your cows and leave us alone!"

"I've finished for today!" he said and gave a little mocking bow as he left.

By the time we were twelve we had outgrown the swing, but out of habit walked to the tree to chat, one sitting on the swing idly swaying, the other perched on another tree stump which made a comfortable seat in dry weather. It was a place where Marie would sketch while I thought through my pieces, read, or jotted down poems. In the summer it was dry enough to leave pencils and pads in a bag inside the huge trunk. We had often crouched there when we were younger, pretending that we were on a ship or in a railway compartment.

One morning we had been given permission to walk down to the river. We sat looking up towards Ronval and its tower which Marie was always sketching. I had a book with me. It began to look as though it would rain, and we decided to go back. Half way up the path past the orchard, Marie clutched my arm.

"We're being followed," she whispered. She stuffed her pad and pencils into a bag, I closed my book, and we started to run. We heard footsteps behind us. Marie was ahead of me. I stopped, out of breath with an aching stitch. I bent over to ease it. The footsteps stopped.

"Quick, Anne!" We ran as fast as we could but I couldn't go any further. We had reached the tree. "Let's get inside the trunk," said Marie.

"I'm too big," I panted.

"Come on!" She climbed into the huge trunk which was quite hollow and dry, and covered by low branches. I clambered after her and slid heavily to the earth inside, disturbing the woodlice and beetles, which ran up my legs. I was too cramped and breathless to notice. My book fell beside me, the open pages covered in dry dust and tree mould. We waited as I caught my breath and tried to breathe quietly and evenly. The footsteps grew louder and nearer. Marie held on to my arm.

"I saw them a minute ago," whispered someone I didn't know. It was said slowly and deliberately, in a voice quite unlike my father's – much more like my grandfather's. "The swing is over there. Perhaps they're hiding in the tree."

We held our breath. "They're only girls. Girls hate creepy-crawlies. They've probably run away." It was another voice, with the same sort of accent but more disdainful.

"We can't shoot rabbits with children around. There might be an accident."

"We could come back at six tomorrow morning before they're awake. Belliot will be busy milking cows and we can kill some of Favoret's rabbits! Come on!"

"We'd better bring one of the dogs."

We heard their voices trail into the distance. I was furious. I wanted to jump out and tell them that they were trespassing – and that they couldn't shoot rabbits on our land – and I was curious to see what they looked like. Marie held me back. We were both cramped and itching; we climbed out and ran back bending over, and trying not to be seen. I felt like a retreating army, covered in mould and livestock. Worst of all, we ran into Jean! We must have looked a terrible sight. He burst into laughter. It was too much!

"You've been spying on us, Jean Belliot!" I shouted.

"Not on you, Anne, but on two poachers from Ronval. It won't be the first time they will have come here to shoot rabbits – nor the last!"

"Why haven't you told my father?"

"Well, Anne, that's for you to decide. Why don't you tell him yourself – when you've cleaned yourself up?"

I stamped my foot with rage. Jean gave a malicious chuckle and then walked away.

After supper I spoke to Marie.

"We're getting up early tomorrow morning to stop those boys coming over the bridge. It's our land and they've no right to shoot our rabbits. They'll soon see that we're not 'just girls'!"

Marie gasped. "But we're not even allowed to go down to the bridge without letting someone know. Why don't you tell your parents? It's up to them to stop trespassers. And the boys will have guns!"

"There's no point in talking to my parents. Maman wants us to know the de Valliets because they're what Mamie calls *Vieille France* – rather like some of her friends in Caen. I can't think why – they've always been our enemies, and they don't seem to want to be friendly now! As for the guns – even the de Valliets of the last century didn't dare to shoot people – that would be murder. Anyway they weren't too keen on shooting while we were around yesterday!"

"And what about Papa?" asked Marie timidly. (She called my father Papa because he was her first real father. Maman she called 'Tante Cécile'.)

"He'd have to agree with Maman. He had to give in over my

school. I didn't understand at the time, but Maman had her parents to back her; and Papa was the first owner of La Chenaie to want to live in peace with the Ronval people."

"Then why do you want to start quarrelling with them again?"

"They are the ones that are quarrelling! It's as bad as when they came over to burn down the dovecote in my grandfather's time!"

"But they only want to shoot rabbits!"

"I didn't think you liked the idea of shooting rabbits! Anyway it's about much more than that. They want to behave as though La Chenaie still belonged to them, and they had the right to come here and do what they like. It means that they are just as horrible as the old aristocrats who trod on everyone who wasn't one of them! No one is going to walk over the bridge and tread on our land without being invited!"

"Oh Anne, we will be disobeying your parents!"

"I know, but secretly I think that's what Papa would want. Can't you see that we are Favorets, the descendants of soldiers and businessmen who aren't afraid of fighting whether for profits or justice – or just glory? I'm a Favoret. I even have Grandfather Marcel's red hair!"

It may sound a little far-fetched that a child of twelve should put forward arguments like this, but I had heard them over and over again when my father told us the family stories.

"I still think we should tell your parents. Papa could come with us!"

"No! If you're so frightened I shall go alone!" (I very much hoped that she would come with me and that I wouldn't be on my own!)

Marie tried another reason. "The de Valliets are much kinder than you imagine, Anne."

"How do you know?"

"Our farm was on their estate. One day the steward came to ask Maman for money and she hadn't any to give him. He started to shout and Maman was crying. It was terrible because we thought we would have nowhere to live. The next day Mme de Valliet came to see us on foot and talked to Maman. We never saw the steward again, but every morning Pierre Vanne came over to collect the milk that we didn't need for ourselves. You see she let us have the farm free!"

"Papa has done the same things here, but he's clever – he makes sure that the milk is made into cheese that's sold to make a profit for us and the farmers!"

"But that's not what I'm saying! What I mean is that Mme de Valliet is kind, so I think you should forgive her sons for poaching."

"No! Soeur Antoinette is always talking about moral courage and this is the time to show it!"

"Soeur Antoinette is always quarrelling with the other nuns – especially Reverend Mother!"

"That's because she's Irish!" I laughed. "You won't believe this but she told me that she had red hair just like mine. I couldn't imagine that nuns had hair or even ears under all those layers of black and white. All you can see are the unfriendly faces with unkind tongues. But Soeur Antoinette is at least human. She laughs as well as scolding!"

"I would be afraid to have piano lessons with Soeur Antoinette. She can be very fierce!"

"That's because she shouldn't have become a nun. She's wicked as well as funny." (Secretly I thought that Soeur Antoinette could be terrifying – especially if I hadn't practised enough.)

"But no one should quarrel! Haven't there been enough wars and quarrels without picking one just because you feel insulted?"

"If that's how you feel I shall go alone."

Finally Marie agreed to come. It was typical that once she had accepted an idea she should think of practical ways of carrying it out. She asked one of our maids to give us bread and milk to keep overnight in our rooms so that we would have something to eat before venturing out, and suggested that we crept along in bare feet until we were well away from the house. It was also typical that when we did find ourselves on the path she seemed much less afraid than I was. It was as though, once I had overcome her fears, she felt confident because she believed me, whereas her misgivings had transmitted themselves to me.

"Come on, Anne! It's ten to six," she whispered.

I tried to think of the most frightening thing possible – of Reverend Mother at her most spiteful, or of Soeur Antoinette in a rage, which was worse. Then I remembered her telling me to have "moral courage", and somehow I felt I had a fellow conspirator who gave me confidence. It made me realise how peaceful the wood was at that time of the morning. There were rabbits everywhere, not scurrying away but sitting at the side of the path. There were squirrels in the trees staring at us, and birds singing more clearly than I could remember. Shafts of sunlight beamed through the branches of the trees, veiling the green and brown with rays of gold and silver. There were blue patches above the leaves, and glistening threads of dew and cobweb on the grass. The smell of fresh earth made us breathe deeply. "This magical place is mine," I murmured.

Our feet felt wet and we had difficulty putting on our socks and shoes, but somehow the pull of adventure was on us. There was no turning back. We ran past the swing tree and down the path to the forbidden place between the orchard and the river. We could see two figures and a dog in the distance coming down the side of the Ronval orchard. We crouched and waited. We heard voices, then the sound of feet climbing the stone steps that led to the wooden arch across the water, and the panting of a dog being restrained on a leash. I breathed so hard that I felt faint, and had to take a shorter breath to steady myself. I stood up, Marie beside me.

"Stop!" I shouted. "You are poachers. You can't shoot rabbits here. This is our land!"

Then several things happened at once. The dog recognised Marie. It had known her since the time when it ran beside Pierre Vanne, who looked after the Ronval dogs and horses, on daily visits to the Millet farmstead. Full of excitement it pulled away from its lead and collar, bounding towards her and jumping up in its eagerness. Marie kept her balance, but I fell over. There were feet running across the bridge.

The next thing I knew, someone was helping me to my feet.

"*Vous en avez du courage, Mademoiselle!*" It was the first time anyone had called me "*vous*".

He turned to his brother. "Take Hero and go back to the house with the guns. I'll walk with the girls up the hill."

The other boy whistled; the dog gave Marie a last lick and ran back over the bridge. I didn't argue. We retraced our tracks up through the orchard where the apples were ripening, the sun now warming our backs and the trees in dark green without the pale shadows of dawn; it was as though they were dressed in ordinary clothes for another day. Hearing the shouts from the bridge the rabbits had scattered. We reached the swing tree.

"I shall say goodbye here," said Edmond de Valliet. "I promise we shall not come back to poach your rabbits." He shook our hands, smiled, made a slight bow and left.

Chapter 4 Spring 1929

It was not the last drama of the day. No one seemed to have noticed our absence. The household was just stirring, and there was a smell of bread in the oven and the clatter of crockery and knives and spoons being laid on the breakfast table. I sat at the piano to practise, knowing that I had a lesson that day, but my thoughts were miles away. The Two-part Invention which I should have learned (separate hands – Soeur Antoinette was very thorough) was inadequately memorised, and the written work forgotten. I knew that there would be a storm, possibly a letter to my parents and a summons from the convent to the maire, which would give Soeur Antoinette the power she craved, and embarrass my father, as she thought an atheist deserved.

The situation between us and Soeur Antoinette at that time had become complicated. My parents and grandparents wanted me to go to the Conservatoire in Paris, and, although they all thought highly of Soeur Antoinette and her teaching, there was one serious drawback. As Soeur Antoinette also played an important part in the story of the swing, and indeed would prove how very brave she was, an explanation is needed.

I shall always be grateful that I had her as my first piano teacher (in spite of the rows and demanding assignments). She often spoke in Irish-English, particularly when she was annoyed, and even when she spoke in French, it was so heavily accented and the idiom so Irish-English that I found, even then, that I was learning the underlying thought behind English syntax.

She taught the British (she wouldn't have liked that!) system of notation, using the alphabet from A to G. The French have a different method about which they are just as intransigent as Soeur Antoinette was, a method called "solfège", calling C "do". (For details there are notes at the back of this book. It's not tonic sol-fa, anything but!) If I had had a French piano teacher to start with, it is likely that the solfège would have made me give up out of boredom, but Soeur Antoinette, for all the discomfort that she caused me, was never boring. She made music live in a way that many professionals don't, and when I was in my twenties and giving concerts, it was often enough to think of her quaint Irish-French expressions to wrest me out of being just correct into a sphere where music expresses the whole gamut of human experience.

I shall never forget learning the C major prelude from the first book of the "Forty-eight", at the end of my first year of lessons. It wasn't difficult to read or learn. The piece came immediately to life, the harmonies rising and falling as Antoinette explained, sang in her lovely voice, conducted, cajoled and insisted on the correct hearing of a chord in the middle, which is easily thought of as a "diminished seventh"! As I was eight at the time the refinement passed me by, just like most of her enthusiasms and missions which were far above my head, but the message was plain. Always study in depth and make it live!

Difficult lessons were usually followed by a letter to the maire, which my father always dreaded. But this time Soeur Antoinette (who enjoyed being unpredictable) wanted to show me off to Papa, who was impressed, shook Soeur Antoinette's hand with tears in his eyes, and thanked her for what she was doing for his daughter. Soeur Antoinette had achieved what she wanted, satisfaction in her teaching, and another minor triumph over the anticlerical maire.

One of her missions was to fight tooth and nail against solfège, which had been her undoing since she came to France. Soeur Antoinette had had her wars too. During the "Troubles" in Ireland her convent on the border between Northern and Southern Ireland had been burnt down, and the Mother House had to find new homes for the nuns. Most of them went to Scotland, but Soeur Antoinette, whose brother had been killed by British soldiers, came to Normandy. She hated the British and the Protestants (she pronounced the word Protèstants, all the letters spat out with Irish venom) and was glad to come to a catholic country, albeit infested with anticlericalism. But she was doomed to frustration. Her first piano pupil had had lessons with a French teacher. She called C "do(h)". Antoinette tossed her head, shouted "stuff and nonsense!", which the poor child only partly understood, and explained, prodding random notes and spluttering in her Irish-French, that every note on the piano was "doh"! The confusion reduced the child to tears, and was followed by a painful scene with Reverend Mother, who had had French piano lessons too. With spiteful glee she told Soeur Antoinette that either she taught the French way or not at all. Soeur Antoinette refused. Later, when I had justified her methods, Reverend Mother gave way, and, although most of the piano pupils were less than promising, Soeur Antoinette would always have a good girls' choir.

But before then, it seemed that a fine musician and teacher would waste away unnoticed, except for Sunday mornings when she played Bach on the organ, sometimes from memory. Few people realised just how talented she was! But Soeur Antoinette had a secret ally, and it was that ally who recommended that she should teach me. It was all kept very quiet, but the source was one of great satisfaction to my mother and grandparents, who applied to Reverend Mother for permission for Soeur Antoinette to teach me. Reverend Mother could only comply. There were financial as well as political considerations…

But by the time I was twelve I was proving to be as talented as my uncle. As the Paris Conservatoire would only accept me if I understood, and had practice in solfège, a teacher in Caen was approached. To Soeur Antoinette this was betrayal. She stormed at my parents, told me that we were all ungrateful, and refused to speak to my mother for six months. A compromise was reached. We were to go to school in Caen during the week. Lessons in solfège would be part of the programme, and I would have piano lessons with La Soeur on Saturday afternoons. Soeur Antoinette was sure that my playing would be tainted by such unmusical influence, but she had made her point. She became more demanding than ever. Usually I was up to her ploys, which would only stand me in good stead in the future.

But not that day! My head had been turned, my harmony neglected and my memory unclear. Lack of clarity was lack of integrity. A penance was required, and we went through the litany of my being a spoilt child indulged by rich parents, one of which had no faith, the other liberal-minded and underhand enough to look for a solfège teacher. I dared to look at the clock during the harangue, and the temperature rose accordingly.

"And when are you starting these lessons in un-music with that poor M. Gabon *(les cours d'anti-musique de ce pauvre M. Gabon)*, Mademoiselle?" She always called me that when she was in a bad mood. I wondered whether this sudden sympathy for M. Gabon sprang from his having to teach me, or his benighted system.

"In September, *ma Soeur*." She already knew the answer.

"I don't see why you have to go to Paris to study. Not long ago Gounod taught there!" Antoinette never forgave Gounod for writing a melody sung to the words of *Ave Maria* over the first Bach Prelude – the one I have just described. It had caused further friction with Reverend Mother, who asked Antoinette to play it after Mass. This time she had to give in, but with what she would have called "a bad grace"! It was always amusing to see them together, one petite, almost elfin, thin-lipped, controlled, precise and essentially French, the other like an apple, round and rosy-cheeked, with a selective memory and a furious temper.

"But it's where all French people study. Debussy was there!"

"The French don't deserve to have a composer like Debussy. Anyway, they say he was a rebel!" Her eyes glinted with mischief. She changed tack. "Mind you, don't think you'll even get there if you carry on with your lazy, disobedient ways. You'd never get anywhere without me. I make you work. I daresay you'll twist poor M. Gabon round your little finger!" She looked down at my hands which were growing, like my legs and feet. "Time for you to start the Chopin Studies, Mademoiselle – and for some sight-reading!"

I sighed. The difficulty of the sight-reading always depended on her mood, and I knew what was coming. I looked furtively at the clock while the test piece was being chosen. There were still ten minutes to go. I struggled with another Bach Invention, hands together, and longed for the bell. At the end of it, Soeur Antoinette crowed with satisfaction. "Playing like that would never get you *near* the Conservatoire!"

I waited for a letter to be sent to the maire. But she had proved her point and let me go.

Chapter 5 Spring – Summer 1929

Marie and I walked towards the Mairie, deep in conversation. She commiserated with me, reiterating that she would never have the courage for private lessons with Soeur Antoinette, while I enjoyed the relief of talking to someone who understood my feelings. We nearly bumped into another conversation as the road veered round towards the centre of the town. Jean Belliot was talking to Bernard Piot. It was interesting to catch Jean unawares, deferring to someone older, his face young, fresh and enthusiastic. The crooked smile that had often made it so unpleasant was gone. He looked almost handsome, but less handsome than his companion. Bernard Piot was the head of the state primary school. My father had the highest opinion of M. Piot, a natural teacher with a fine-tuned understanding, which was quick to detect ability even in mediocre pupils.

He was of middle height, fair and bronzed, the picture of health and well-being, with rimless spectacles, which gave his face a look of authority and increased rather than diminished his powers of communication. I had seen him before, but the eyes of a twelve-year-old, who has been formally addressed as "*vous*" and has won her point in an encounter with boys four or five years older, are more open and impressionable. I wondered whether he was more attractive than Edmond de Valliet, only to disappoint myself by realising that we had had hardly any eye contact. The vision of the boys coming over the bridge was a blur. Falling, gasping for breath, being escorted back to our tree, and the satisfying promise made under it, all coalesced. I had won. I had felt his presence with an intensity which I would never forget. But I had no clear picture of him.

It seemed as though Jean and Bernard stopped in mid-sentence. Turning sharply to greet us, they had to rearrange their thoughts, putting themselves at a disadvantage, and giving the meeting an air of equality which took me by surprise. I was twelve, Bernard at least twenty-six, but we were the same height. Marie was four inches shorter, but there was less sense of contact between adults and children than I expected; we were one side of the convergence, the others, if I remember correctly, slightly unbalanced, if not embarrassed. I detected a flush across Jean's face wiping away any possibility of taunting us.

"Bonjour, Mesdemoiselles," said Bernard shaking us both by the hand. We said "Bonjour" in turn and then shook Jean's rough hand, something which had never happened before.

"We were on our way to the Mairie to see your father, Mademoiselle Favoret." Once again the formal address. I saw Jean squirm out of the corner of my eye. Would he also call us "*vous*"?

"That's where we're going. My father will drive us home in the car."

"May we accompany you?" asked Bernard. "The holidays are approaching and I am making plans for the summer. Where will your family go?"

"We have a summer house in St Valéry-en-Caux. My mother takes us there for a month and my father joins us when he can. The sea bathing is only possible on the east beach, beyond the shingle at low tide, and we are sometimes fortunate enough to go out to sea in one of the yachts, when the sea is calm." Had I said too much, or spoken too quickly?

"I am organising a youth camp in Brittany. Jean is going to help. He tells me he will have to find someone to help with the cows and the milking in his absence. He wants to discuss this with his father and yours, but I'm sure that we can come to some arrangement."

"Where will you go in Brittany?" I asked.

"To Morbihan, not far from the estuary of the Vilaine. It is further south than Calvados, or Seine-Maritime of course, but we'll also be able to bathe in the sea."

We reached the Mairie and climbed into the car which always stood outside, and was left unlocked. Once again we shook hands. Jean said "Au revoir," avoiding any distinction between formal politeness and the familiar mocking superiority.

We waited longer than usual for Papa. By the time he arrived we had both found books to pass the time and were surprised by his briskness. Usually he would ask us about our day at school. While I was relieved that he didn't, I sensed that something was disturbing him, and hoped that he hadn't heard about our morning escapade. I looked at Marie, both our faces primed with questioning.

"We saw Jean Belliot and Bernard Piot," I said, struggling for a safe topic.

"I know," was the gruff reply.

"They are going to a youth camp," I blundered on.

"So they tell me! And who is to help look after Michel's herd when Jean is away? That young man is getting mixed up in politics, and I'm sorry to say that M. Piot is too!" He paused. "Well, it'll soon be time for military service. That'll knock some sense into his head!"

"Whose head?" I asked.

"Jean's, of course! Bernard Piot is too old now, but he can't have forgotten what it's like to be in the army. He's honour bound not to spread ideas in the classroom… Perhaps I'm imagining things, but I don't like it!"

"What's military service? – and what ideas?"

"Military service is obligatory for all boys after school – for three years. They learn the disciplines of being a member of the armed forces. It's to prepare the country to defend itself in case of war."

"And what about the ideas?"

"Oh, there are so many crack-pot ideas about. There are fascists and communists and there are anarchists who disagree with everyone and everything. The most dangerous are the communists. They threaten business, which is the mainstay of the country. You can't have food if you can't pay for it and you need a strong economy to make sure that people can. And, before you ask, the economy is the way money works."

"Why should the communists want to threaten it?"

"Because they have unpractical ideas about giving everyone their fair share, which means that nobody gets anything. They would destroy all that the intelligent people in France have achieved, and redistribute land so that no one had a real interest in maintaining it. Nothing would be properly looked after and everyone would starve. It's what's happened in Russia. A few idealists and idle malcontents think it's working, but it stands to reason that if the share-all philosophy didn't work in France after the revolution, and we needed a strong leader like Napoleon to sort out the mess, it's not going to work anywhere!"

"So are Jean and M. Piot communists? Does that mean that they don't want us to own La Chenaie – that they would share it out with everyone and we would lose our land?"

"I hope not! Bernard Piot is the best teacher we could have running the school, and Jean could be a wealthy farmer, if he keeps at it. France needs them both, but not if they get caught up in all this woolly nonsense!"

Papa groaned and then smiled. "Don't you worry! There are plenty of soldiers and businessmen around, like us Favorets! By the way, how was your lesson with the fat Penguin?"

It was my turn to groan. "What was it this time, Anne?" His eyes lit up. "She's jealous. Don't take too much notice. Your grandparents are coming for a week before the end of the term and your mother wants to ask *La Soeur* for lunch. That should sort her out!"

We drove up in front of the house and found Maman smiling at the front door.

"I've had a visitor today. I am sure you can't imagine who it was!"

I gasped. We had been found out. Now there would be trouble.

"Mme de Valliet called this afternoon."

"What a nerve!" exclaimed my father. "Her sons slip into the wood to shoot rabbits, while their mother calls at the front door!"

"They won't shoot our rabbits any more," I said. It was Marie's turn to gasp.

"And why should these young de Valliets behave any better than their fathers and grandfathers?"

"Because…"

"Because?"

"I told them not to!"

"Yes," said Maman, gently. "Perhaps Anne could tell us the whole story over dinner."

How my father laughed! Maman found it less funny (and she

did remind us that we had disobeyed her by going down to the bridge without telling her – I suppose her tolerance is what Soeur Antoinette would have called being 'liberal'). But she was pleased that Mme de Valliet had called. It might be the beginning of friendship between us.

That night my mind raced from one adventure to the next, and then criss-crossed in a grid of excitement and uncertainty. There were communists being overturned by French republicans and Irish republicans overturning French solfège (I wasn't sure what it really was, but in my dream it looked like a great black barrier); there were dogs running from de Valliets while I pushed Jean off the swing. A penguin stood at the bridge and told me I would never get into the Conservatoire; then it changed into two gun-carrying seigneurs who wanted to shoot rabbits. The communists wanted to share out our land and the de Valliets wanted to poach on it. The boys at the bridge became Jean and Bernard Piot; they both accompanied us to the swing-tree and started to chop it down; they went on chopping at the trees and I screamed "Stop! You can't do that. You're poachers," but they paid me no attention. And then I heard someone promise not to poach any more, someone who called me *"vous"*.

But I couldn't see his face.

Chapter 6 Summer 1929

Soeur Antoinette could be charming, but she had to be in the right mood. She loved being invited out to lunch, ate two helpings of anything sweet and would keep us all laughing as she told her Irish jokes, some overstepping the strict propriety of my grandparents, but relished by my father. She would hold her glass of wine, so that it could be refilled, and behave like a grande-dame or dowager duchess surrounded by admirers and minions.

Where my grandparents were concerned she had a sixth sense, holding them to be in the same social bracket as the family and friends whom she had known as a girl. She looked upon them as the genuine article, whereas my parents were arrivistes; my mother had diminished herself by marrying my father, and had lost ground to catch up. The lapse was paid for in the insults about my upbringing which she brandished like a poker.

The invitation to lunch was eagerly accepted and Reverend Mother's permission grudgingly given. But Maman had other plans too, plans which would give her, and my grandparents, satisfaction – and put Soeur Antoinette in her place. Mme de Valliet was also invited. Papa wasn't sure about it, but experience had taught him that in such matters it was better to leave the decisions to my mother.

"What does Mme de Valliet look like?" I asked Marie when we were alone. "Is she tall like the boy who went back with the dog and the guns?"

"No, she isn't as tall, for instance, as Tante Cécile. The younger son, Charles de Valliet, is the tallest in the family. Edmond is more like his mother."

"How do you know?"

"I didn't see much of the boys when we were living in the farmhouse, but Mme de Valliet came to visit us from time to time. She's not French. She's Scottish. She speaks French with an accent – a little like Soeur Antoinette – slowly and deliberately. She's very slim, almost thin, with dark hair and she walks gracefully like a dancer even in snow-boots." Marie paused. "I am sure she's lonely up there at Ronval. The boys go to school in England."

"But why? What's wrong with French schools?"

"There are Catholic schools in England. The boys are bi-lingual – that's an advantage."

"But I thought that all the British were 'Protèstants'! That's why Soeur Antoinette came to Normandy! Anyway it's the English who burned Jeanne d'Arc, as we are always hearing at school. It must be difficult to be French if you live among the English."

"I remember Mme de Valliet saying something about the Scots and the French being traditional allies against the English, and how they fought together against the Germans in the last war."

"Then it's still illogical that the boys are at school in England."

"Anne, we all fought together against the Germans. Isn't that enough? Let's hope it never happens again."

A twelve-year-old is capable of strong feelings, but not adept at analysing them. Logic and fairness were part of my creed; Marie had suffered from the broad injustice of life and realised that the world was much more complicated than I imagined. On the other hand a privileged child, whose life has been untrammelled by suffering, sometimes sees more clearly than one who is trying to forget it.

"There will always be wars. Look at my ancestors. They fought for what they believed in, and I think it's better to stand up for what you think than to give in. If you do, you stop living!"

Marie had the last word, one that I wouldn't forget.

"If there is another war, there won't be anyone left to stand up for what they believe."

The lunch party took place on a Sunday early in June. It was a beautiful day; the hydrangeas which flock round the outside of Norman houses were in bloom, and already needed watering. Marie was up before breakfast with her can, pouring water liberally under the pink and blue heads that looked like floral bathing caps, and then spraying the red geraniums in their pots and hanging baskets. There was little formal garden at La Chenaie, where the well-kept grass edging the drive gave way to copse and field, with old but well-kept outhouses, scattered at random, each with its purpose; one for farm machinery, another a cheese dairy, and of course the cider press, the first calvados still (both now too small to satisfy market demand) and the dovecote. In the distance there were more modern buildings, some rented by Michel Belliot, byres for milking cows, a task that was done elsewhere by hand; my father had introduced the earliest form of machinery, improving the lives of the workers and increasing the size of the herds without having to employ more hands.

We had breakfast and then got ready for Mass. My father drove us as far as the Mairie, from where we walked to the church, ignoring his remarks about the curé who stumbled over his sermons, and often started to sing his parts of the Mass before Soeur Antoinette gave him the note. Fortunately she had perfect pitch – she enjoyed the challenge of catching him after he had launched into the *Sursum Corda* or consecration prayer, unaware that only a good musician could cope. Antoinette would shake her head, give him a mischievous grin and transpose the music into whatever key he had blundered.

Afterwards Papa drove us back, with Soeur Antoinette in the front seat and Maman in the back with us.

"You drive well, M. Favoret," said Soeur Antoinette.

I'm sure my father had to resist the temptation to ask her what she knew about driving cars. He disliked not having his wife beside him, but it would have been a terrible squash in the back if Soeur Antoinette had climbed in with us.

"Did you know that Mme de Valliet is having lunch with us too?" I asked.

"Mm…" said Antoinette. "I shall be honoured to meet her." (She didn't sound it. I wondered whether she disliked her because she was British, or whether she quite rightly surmised that the presence of such an august person would limit her fun.)

"She very kindly called a month ago," said Maman with a twinkle, looking at me, and implying that if I had taken the lead in the conversation I should be prepared for the consequences. "My parents are looking forward to meeting her."

"Did you know that she was a concert pianist before the war?" threw out Antoinette airily. I was astonished.

"Yes," said my mother, smiling. "Her name was Alice Creighton. It was she who advised us to ask you to teach Anne."

This was news. I was dumbfounded. My mother knew exactly how to silence me; showing me how little I knew was one way. She also gained a short-lived victory over Soeur Antoinette.

"Oh well, she would have known that I would insist on proper notation." Soeur Antoinette scored.

Maman continued to smile. She had far too balanced a view of life to be distressed by a thwarted nun, and she put a high value on what Soeur Antoinette had done for me. Her thoughts were on the lunch, which she had prepared, and our cook and maids were getting ready.

When we turned into the drive we saw my grandparents' car parked beside the house. They were sitting in the porch outside the front door. They stood up to greet us. Did I imagine it, or did our car lean over, as the front passenger lumbered out like a baby elephant? We kissed Mamie and Papy as French people do, and Maman went inside with Marie and me to see that everything was in order. I was longing to ask her questions about Mme de Valliet, but realised that I would have to wait. There was the sound of a wagon and horses drawing up in front of the house.

We were given instructions to help the maids (with a warning look not to put myself forward) while Maman hurried to the door to welcome her guest.

When we walked into the salon and were introduced to Mme de Valliet, we gave little nick-like curtsies (me reluctantly and Marie with a natural grace which made my clumsiness all the more obvious). We were invited to sit, and a look from Maman implied that we were to say nothing until asked.

"I have been hearing about your piano-playing, Anne," said Mme de Valliet. "Do you think I could hear you after lunch?"

I was slow to respond, not because I didn't want to play, but because I was entranced by her speaking voice. It was like music, not the busy brisk French which I heard all around me, nor just cultured and well-tuned like Maman and her parents, and certainly not like Antoinette, who, when she was rattled translated everything directly from Irish-English straight into French with some very funny results, but slow and dignified with certain vowels turned into diphthongs, like the "è" of "j'espère".

For a moment Maman thought that I had lost my voice, and Soeur Antoinette that I was being cowardly.

"I'm sure that Anne would love to play," said Maman truthfully.

"Yes," added Soeur Antoinette quickly. "A Bach Invention and two Debussy Arabesques." She gave me a stern look.

"I am glad that you play Bach and Debussy," replied Mme de Valliet. "Of course Debussy is a recent composer. When I was a student his works were hardly known, some of them not yet composed. He wrote the twelve studies during the war."

"Soeur Antoinette wants me to play the Chopin Studies," I said. "They look very difficult."

"They are. Not all, but for most you need long fingers with wide stretches between them – and stamina."

"Jean-Luc used to play Chopin beautifully," said my grandmother sadly.

Mme de Valliet looked at Mamie, with questioning eyes, and then down at her hands. I thought I saw them quiver, tighten into a fist and then relax.

As we stood behind our chairs with Papa trying not to fidget, my grandfather said quietly "In nomine Patris et Filii et Spiritus Sancti." Mamie, Antoinette and Marie made the sign of the cross. Maman kept her hands by her side.

I was shocked. It had never happened before. In Caen Papy always said grace, but at La Chenaie we respected my father's independence. The spirit of the red-headed capitaine surfaced. "We're only saying grace because you're here," I said to Soeur Antoinette.

She gave me one of her mischievous grins. My parents tried not to smile, but my grandmother frowned as she took her seat opposite Mme de Valliet on either side of Papa at the top of the table. Mamie wore old-fashioned clothes, with a long silk scarf draped over her white blouse; her thick grey hair was always neatly piled into a chignon, and her face, though young in its complexion, had been scarred with lines of sorrow since the death of Jean-Luc. She pursed her lips with anger at my boldness, and asked Mme de Valliet which part of Scotland she came from.

"From Ross and Cromarty, north of Inverness. We are real Highlanders. The house isn't far from the west coast. There are lochs where the trout fishing attracts visitors from all over the country – and even Europe and America."

"They say that the west coast of Scotland is like the west coast of Ireland," added Soeur Antoinette. "There are islands hidden in the mist which appear and reappear as if like magic. But in Ireland there are longer sandy beaches, like the stretch of sand at Renvyle in Galway."

Mme de Valliet was not prepared to argue. "France too has its beauty spots. Calvados is very different from the Highlands of Scotland. The land here reminds me of the less rugged parts, low lying fertile ground like Moray which lies to the east of Inverness-shire."

My grandfather had visited Moray. "I have fished on the river Spey in my youth," said Papy. "That's where they distil whisky. Ah – the quality varies, they say, according to where the river is: high in the mountains or farther down near the coast."

"There are people in Moray and Aberdeenshire who sell whisky and have shown an interest in our Norman Calvados, a company called Cummings and Hay," remarked my father as he poured out the wine. I watched him. He had learned how to do it from observing Papy. I have no doubt that they went down to the cellar together to choose it. Marie and I drank it diluted. Papa poured out my small dose, under Soeur Antoinette's disapproving eyes. Her face relaxed when she saw me add the water.

Mme de Valliet had noticed. She came to our rescue. "All Scotsmen drink whisky, but they usually add water to it. There is a saying about Scotsmen never drinking one without the other. It's not quite true but it shows how much they value it."

Turning to my father who had sat down and nodded to my mother to start, Mme de Valliet continued, "I have heard of Cummings and

Hay. They are retailers as well as wine and spirit merchants. They had a very good reputation. I hope the venture goes well. It would be another link between Scotland and Normandy." There was a pause as she looked down the table towards Maman. "I believe the children are going to school in Caen in the autumn. It would be good for Anne to meet other musical young people. Does Marie play an instrument?"

"Non, Madame," said Marie.

"She's told us she would like to play the cello," said Maman. "My parents are looking for a good teacher in Caen."

"We've already found one," put in Mamie. "There is a fine cellist in Caen who gives private lessons. She agreed last week to take on Marie. She has just the right personality, and a good reputation as a teacher."

If Soeur Antoinette wondered what sort of personality suited the wayward Anne Favoret, she would have no difficulty in giving herself the job-description. She merely observed with a sour expression, "Marie will have to learn solfège."

Mme de Valliet was quick to gloss over negatives. "Yes, but there are some wonderful French string players! Have you ever heard of the violinist Thibaud? He plays trios with Cortot and the cellist Casals who is a Spaniard, or rather a Catalan. If you ever have the chance to hear Casals, Marie, you must take it. He is one of the greatest musicians alive."

Marie nodded dutifully. She had heard the cello played in a concert which had been organised by friends of my grandparents. Hearing a great artiste seldom inspires the young to learn an instrument, because they feel that they could never aspire to such heights. It is the good performance by an older child that stirs ambition, lays open the possibility that he or she too might achieve something like it.

After lunch, I played the Invention and Arabesques, while

everyone else had coffee. Soeur Antoinette simpered as Mme. de Valliet commended my memory and energy. She liked the lightness of the Arabesques, commenting on the pedalling and sense of space, an endorsement of good teaching.

This was Soeur Antoinette's moment of triumph. She had been denied her stories, which would have been out of place, but she looked at my grandfather and, as if on cue, he asked for some duets.

My heart sank. Soeur Antoinette took the wide volume of Mozart from the top of the piano and sat down on the stool. Playing duets with her was purgatory, one of the most uncomfortable ways of playing the piano imaginable. One didn't play duets *with* Soeur Antoinette, one played them *round* her. She sat almost centre to the piano and hogged the primo part, while I groped sideways for harmonies – and scale passages – in front of the black wimple which concealed her face, covered her arms and made her seem wider than she was. My right arm used to ache afterwards. It was already tingling when Maman found me a chair, on which she placed a cushion.

The French call duets *pieces for four hands*, but with Antoinette it always felt like three and a half because my right arm felt so constricted. The Mozart duo in D major caused me such tortures that I could never hear it afterwards without wincing. There are three movements, and by the end I wished that Mozart had never written it.

Everyone clapped. I saw Mme. de Valliet smile – or did she wink? She understood.

Chapter 7 Autumn 1929

For five years we lived in Caen, its streets busy with the clip-clop of horse-drawn carriages and wagons, among them a few cars which moved at the pace of people shopping on foot. The half-timbered houses and much of the surrounding area were destroyed in 1944, but the Abbeys survived the bombing and gunfire. The handsome Mairie, always the centre of a French town, was rebuilt after the Second World War, a symbol of continuity, the face of the republic with its tricolour and nineteenth-century exterior.

We lived in my grandparents' house, which was more like a Norman manor than La Chenaie, more dignified and imposing, but with grounds that were little more than a town garden. The rooms were spacious; there were bathrooms with running water and electricity, and a telephone which connected, after much waiting and frustration, to the Mairie at Quinon. I was given my uncle's room and Marie, my mother's. Looking back on it, I think that it was a time of healing for my grandmother, who had kept Jean-Luc's room as a sort of closed mausoleum for over ten years. It was aired and redecorated for my arrival. I was only partially aware of how much planning had gone into our coming, but I was delighted to find all his scores stacked in a cabinet in the corner. Above all I was given free access to his Bechstein grand piano, which stood in the corner of the larger drawing-room, which was only used for entertaining. My grandmother insisted that the maids make up the fire when it was cold.

My mother's bedroom had also been prepared for Marie, but it was Maman who made all the changes – after all, it had always been hers. An airy attic room was turned out and made into a studio, with a fireplace and access to running water. Here Marie painted from memory the streets and the buildings, the abbeys and the parks, and on fine days she would take her sketch pad into the garden with its clipped shrubs and manicured lawn.

My grandparents were as welcoming to Marie as if she were their own grandchild. She could not have been more grateful. I suspect that they hoped that her careful ways and precise thinking would rub off on me. There were times when I felt like raging against nature which turned her from a graceful child into a beautiful woman, while I burst out in all directions and was constantly scolded by my grandmother for eating too much. Didn't she realise I was hungry? But if life seemed unfair to a podgy fourteen-year-old it redressed the balance when I reached sixteen. I stopped growing and slimmed into an attractive girl with fashionably bobbed hair, a straight nose, long legs, and freckles that had almost faded into an olive complexion.

The nuns at our new school seemed colourless beside the warring Soeur Antoinette and Reverend Mother in Quinon, but the lessons were mostly enjoyable; there was a lay teacher who gave us an objective approach to recent history which filled out the stories of the nineteenth-century Favorets. The solfège turned out to be innocuous, the written exercises much less demanding than the harmony tests in which I had been drilled, and the knack of saying the notes as well as thinking them helpful for memory and accuracy. But I shall always maintain that Soeur Antoinette was right. It didn't enhance the music or deepen a sense of harmony and analysis. It was a tool but not a well of musical thought.

On the other hand there was the embarrassment of finding that "poor" M. Gabon also wanted to give me piano lessons. He was a good teacher and I tried to steer a path between his French approach to technique, and the Celtic spirit, the whole-hearted grasp of understanding and interpreting music, that had been instilled since the first Bach Prelude. By that time I had long discovered what a diminished seventh was. When I was eight, Soeur Antoinette had made it sound like some sort of poacher or intruder.

The ties which bound me to her gradually loosened, and a different friendship developed. It started in October 1929. The stock market crash in Wall Street made little impact on the life of nuns who tried to subdue nature to prayer through self-denial, only to find that the self which they wanted to flatten popped up again like a jack-in-the-box. Reverend Mother administered the convent finances, and even she looked upon faith as the best method of accountancy. But not my father, nor my grandfather! There were huge issues at stake and weekend after weekend they were closeted together in my grandfather's study, working out the knock-on effects of a possible world economic disaster.

It was only then that I began to be aware of Germany. I was told of the terrible inflation in the early 1920s, of the importance of financial stability, which had broken down in France in the early years of the revolution. Papa and Papy argued back and forth about the best way of investing the family money, finally deciding to put a certain amount into gold reserves and to wait for property to fall in price in the south of France, which had become a fashionable resort for the wealthy. With foresight which still amazes me, they avoided the north of France, in spite of the nearness of places like Deauville. After the scenes of desolation in the First World War, even our safe corner of Normandy appeared too near our enemies of 1870 and 1914.

The weekend conferences went on well into December, during which time we stayed in Caen, missing our weekend visits to La Chenaie. In the meantime, I began to accustom myself to more organised, if less inspirational, piano lessons, with the introduction of Liszt, as well as Chopin and a number of lesser composers whose music excited me at the time, and which the techniques taught by M. Gabon helped me to play. When I returned to Quinon after several weeks' absence, I knew that storms would be brewing.

It was with trepidation that I set out for the convent one Saturday afternoon in December 1929. But the storm I met was not in the convent.

Bernard Piot was talking to Jean Belliot and another man; he was making no effort to lower his voice.

"There have been hunger marches in Britain, and suicides among the capitalists in America. The world is changing. There is going to be hardship even here in Normandy. Order is needed, like in Russia where they have introduced careful rationing."

I walked up to them. This time I wasn't interrupting a private conversation. "But we all have food in Normandy, so why worry?"

"Ah, bonjour, Mademoiselle Favoret," said Bernard. "France will soon feel the after-effects of the financial collapse in New York."

"That may be so," said someone who had come up from behind me. It was a voice I recognised, high-toned and dismissive. "But it is arrogant to try to change a world which may be imperfect but is still stable. The nation needs a deeper respect for the past, not upheaval which always leads to violence."

"Change need not be violent."

"The revolution in Russia overturned everything, as it did in France. There was war and terrible suffering at all levels of society. You cannot change life. Change happens but it is the worst kind of pride to think that *you* can change anything."

"No! That is backward looking. We must go forward and make a new society in France…."

"Who are you to dare to speak to people in this way? You are a communist. You should be arrested. People like you are a danger to society!" I realised who it was now. Charles de Valliet must have been seventeen, but his voice had the authority of someone much older.

He went up to Bernard and took him by the collar. Bernard shook him off. There was a scuffle. Jean drew back. I saw our gendarme coming down the street.

"What's all this about?"

Bernard turned to the policeman. "We were having a political discussion. There is no trouble."

"Well, off you go, back to your homes. Quinon is a peaceful town and that's how it's going to stay." He turned to me. "Ah, bonjour, Mademoiselle Favoret!" There was a slight note of admonition in his tone.

"I am on my way to the convent," I said hurriedly. Charles de Valliet raised an eyebrow, Bernard gave me a bow and Jean stalked off. I didn't see the other man go.

I walked to the convent deep in thought. Would the stock market crash bring hardship to France? Surely not here in Normandy, the land of plenty I had known all my life. I reached the door of the house where I had always had my lessons and rang the bell, deep in thought. I waited for five minutes, glad to have the time to think of what to say.

"Ah, Anne Favoret," said Soeur Antoinette as she opened the door. "What brings you here?"

I sat down on the fauteuil near the grand piano which had been donated to the convent years before. It still had the power to fill me with foreboding.

"I haven't been able to come to see you since the end of October. There have been long discussions about the stock market which have prevented my father from bringing me back to Quinon."

"Thank you for being honest, but I can't give you lessons unless you come regularly." It was said with very little bitterness, not even out of contrary desire to be unpredictable.

"May I come to play to you from time to time, then?" It was difficult at thirteen to latch on to catch-phrases like "Of course I really value your judgement."

"Yes. What are you playing, now?" she asked.

"Soeur Antoinette," I said, "I have just seen a confrontation in the street. There was a scuffle. Fortunately no one was arrested, but Bernard Piot was challenged by Charles de Valliet. A policeman came and told us all to go home. I think he was surprised to see me there!"

"Piot is a communist, Anne. He shouldn't go spreading his ideas around. They are dangerous."

I was amazed. What would a nun know about communists? "But didn't Voltaire say something about …?"

"I hate what you say, but I am prepared to die for your right to say it." She paused. "Voltaire was a very clever man, but he denied the existence of God. I am afraid that atheism goes further back in history than you think."

At thirteen I swung between the extremes of thinking that I knew a lot and the more realistic feeling of total ignorance. "But the French all admire Voltaire." I paused. "You always talked about moral courage. Isn't that what Bernard Piot has, standing up for what he thinks?" Bernard Piot would prove to be the most courageous person I ever met.

"Yes, Anne, but communism is a dangerous theory to preach. Your father and I would agree about that!"

I played to Soeur Antoinette, but life had changed. She was in agreement with my father over the communists; she had lost the hold over me she once had had. I was growing up.

Chapter 8 February 1933

I have already said that Marie grew into a beautiful woman; she had slender limbs, long dark hair lit with reddish tints that glinted in sunlight, a fair clear skin and blue eyes which were almond shaped with long black lashes. Untalkative by nature, she grew more confident in Caen, but she only spoke when necessary; she wasn't afraid of gaps in conversation as I was; she would never blurt out the obvious or the banal in an effort to attract attention. She had the assurance of a woman whose presence is always felt, even when she is silent. It seemed strange that she was the child of Hervé Millet, still hanging on to life by a thread in his *"asile pour les mutilés de guerre"*, where he was well treated. I could only presume that she had de Valliet blood in her veins, from many generations before, when the seigneur expected favours from the daughters of his tenants. She was admired wherever we went, and, to my credit, I was seldom jealous. Perhaps it was because I had my own talent, which projected and impressed when I wanted.

She worked hard at school, had an exhibition of her paintings, some of which were sold, to her great surprise – I don't think she wanted to part with them – and the cello lessons were a success. By the end of the first year I found myself accompanying Fauré's *Après un Rêve*, and Baroque sonatas by Bréval and Marcello, and, although she never made a big sound her tone was sweet, her phrasing artistic and her intonation as precise as everything else she did.

But in spite of her success in Caen, she was happiest at home with me and my parents. At La Chenaie she loved to be busy in the kitchen, especially when our cook had a day off. Even *she* made no objection to Marie's presence in her domain, while Maman had to exercise a great deal of tact and tolerance. (Our cook was temperamental.) But Marie would smile, glide noiselessly with a saucepan or a dishcloth, keeping out of everyone's way and make such good food that my father would ask (quietly) when cook would next be away.

I took it for granted that she had admirers in Caen, but I was too naïve to imagine that there were any in Quinon. After the debacle I described in the last chapter I saw little of Bernard Piot, who continued to run the primary school, and restricted his proselytising to bigger cities with established communist cells. His predictions came to pass. The stock market crash was followed by the depression and there was hunger in the towns, if not in rural Calvados. The Parti Communiste grew during the 1930s and attracted many, the under-privileged, the unemployed, idealists like Bernard himself, and the ambitious, who would latch on to any "ism" that was likely to give them political opportunities.

I don't think that Jean fitted into any of these categories, or perhaps he was a mixture of them all. He was too cynical to be an idealist, and, as Michel Belliot's son he was hardly downtrodden; but he was ambitious, and he had a young man's yen for adventure, a challenge, something new. He also had an eye for a pretty girl. I was slow to realise how he felt about Marie.

We seldom saw him together, and, when we did, he called us "Mesdemoiselles" and addressed us as "*vous*" like Bernard. With me I detected a degree of reluctance, but I was his landlord's daughter, and some deference was perhaps expected. I had no doubt that his respect for Marie was genuine. After all, he had been much kinder to her when we were children, teasing her as if he were an older brother. I discovered later that she saw quite a lot of him. While I was practising in the house she often walked out with sketch pad and pencils, either to the swing-tree or down by the river where there was now a wooden bench for us to sit. He would wait and follow her.

The first I heard about it was from Maman who told me that Jean had asked Papa if he could marry her. I was dumbfounded! Marie was only sixteen. She had her whole life in front of her. I had always presumed that she would come to Paris with me when we were eighteen. We had talked about Art Schools, or rather I had talked and she had listened.

"She can't marry Jean. She doesn't even like him," I said.

"You don't like Jean, but have you ever asked Marie what she thinks?"

"She thinks well of everyone, but she never told me that she liked……ugh! Anyway, he's a communist. Papa would never let her marry him."

"Jean likes Bernard Piot and he listens to him, but he's far too shrewd to commit himself to something that would prejudice him in Papa's eyes. You're right about Bernard. But he respects Papa also – too much to spread his ideas here in Quinon, especially after that confrontation you witnessed a few years ago! Your father was furious.

"Anne," she added kindly, "I don't want Jean to marry her either. But the most important thing is that she marries someone who will give her security. She will always remember the unhappiness of her early life."

There was no more to be said. From that day I watched Marie, hoping that she would open her heart to me. An opportunity soon arose. We had been walking down to the river, pausing as we always did at the swing tree, when Jean came up to us and greeted us, shaking our hands and trying to engage us in conversation.

"Have you seen the poachers again?" he asked me.

"No. I think that they know better than to trespass on our land." I wanted him to go away. "Have you seen them? The last time I saw M. Charles he was arguing with M. Piot."

He was wrong-footed. "Ah, M. Piot! He doesn't have meetings in Quinon any more. But I don't think that it's Charles de Valliet who stops him, but *le patron*." This is how he always referred to my father.

"And do you go to his meetings elsewhere?" I probed.

"Sometimes," he said sheepishly. "M. Piot is a good sort – *un bon gars*."

"I don't think that my father would like that," I said pompously. Jean smirked at Marie, scowled at me and left.

"I know what you think of him," said Marie when he was out of earshot.

"Well?" I exclaimed.

"I don't dislike him as you do. His parents were kind to mine where we were so poor. Michel and his wife used to visit us and bring presents of food – a bit like Tante Cécile and Papa."

"But you can't marry someone just because you feel grateful to his family!"

"It's not just that. I like being here in the country, and though it's been lovely living in Caen, and doing all the things that we do – like playing the cello and going to concerts I feel that my life is here. It's where I belong."

"So you don't want to come to Paris with me?" She had already visited Paris and enjoyed the Art Galleries, particularly the Louvre. My parents had a flat in the rue de la Motte Piquet, where Papa stayed when he was on business.

"You know I like Paris, but it's too big, and I don't think that I would profit from going to Art School. I love to draw, but I'm not ambitious like you. I want to live in Calvados and make myself useful to your parents – have you ever thought how much they would miss us? – and just as useful, some day, to a husband and family, not far away." She paused. "You don't know what it's like when I pass the farm where we used to live, with Maman coughing and my father sitting staring into space. I still feel guilty because I couldn't love him. I just wished he'd go away. If I married Jean I would find someone not so unlike my father and perhaps one day I would stop feeling like that."

"But Marie, you can't marry him if you don't love him! You don't, do you?" I held my breath.

"No, Anne, I don't love him. I wonder what love is, except that your family has given me so much. So would Jean – and perhaps I would learn to love him too!"

"But he's not like us!"

"No, Anne. He's like my parents." She paused. "I promise you that I shall wait. I don't want to marry anyone yet, and I don't want to argue with you."

I was disappointed especially about her not coming to Paris. I had made plans for us to live together in the flat. It looked as though I would have to go there alone.

Chapter 9 Spring 1933

We had often gazed at the wood and orchard on the other side of the river, but, unlike Charles and Edmond, had never crossed the bridge, partly because we had been told that it was dangerous (only when the river was swollen in February after the January snow); and we didn't want to trespass on the de Valliet land after having made so strong a point about poaching when we were twelve. But we were curious, as all young people are. My parents had had several invitations to Ronval after the lunch when I had to play a duet with Soeur Antoinette, but we hadn't been included. I longed to meet Edmond again, although I could hardly remember anything about him except his voice, the slow gentleness of its inflexion and the formal kindly address. But we had to wait. It wasn't until we were sixteen that we received a message asking us to have tea with them one Saturday afternoon.

On a warm day at the end of March we walked up the path through the trees, which were like a picture that had come to life. The mimosa and crocuses which brighten February were over and daffodils were scattered in clumps of white and yellow. There were pines whose bark and needles had the scent of resin, and there was an oak almost as gnarled as the one which had hidden us from the poachers. We were met at the door by Mme de Valliet who welcomed us kindly. She seemed less strained than I remembered, dressed in a mid-calf tartan skirt and strong shoes in which she moved with ease, a slender figure with a lined face, lit up by the twinkling humour of her eyes that I had noticed after the Mozart duet.

As we approached the salon I heard the sound of a Chopin Nocturne, and I stopped to listen. We all stood still, suspending questions and answers. It had reached the rolling section in the middle. I was transfixed. Slowly Mme de Valliet opened the door into a room unlike any that I had ever seen before. The bulky British furniture was draped with tartan rugs which smelled of dogs, and the faded Louis Quinze chairs were pushed against oak-panelled walls hung with portraits. The tables were littered with books and papers. The room was smaller than the salon at La Chenaie, and in each corner, near the windows, but shaded from the sun, was a grand piano covered with photographs. Edmond sat at one, his posture still, and intent upon the music. He was playing from memory; even at that age I realised that he was interpreting the music with a mastery which is denied to many professionals, communicating with Chopin, not an audience – yet his audience stood spell-bound. I looked at Mme de Valliet's face, and then at Edmond's. They both had the same fine bone structure. I could see from the way that she looked at him that she loved him. It brought the ways of the two families together, because I knew that that was how Papa looked at me when I played.

"Welcome to Ronval," he said. "Please sit down." The mellowness still held its magic. It made me think of a French horn.

"That was beautiful," I said.

"You must ask Anne to play," said Mme de Valliet in clear English, with a strange diphthong on "play" which sounded like a cadence. We Favorets speak fast, challenging the world around us, and holding our own with tenacity; but the old established families savour their words and subdue time to their own measured pace.

"You must try both the pianos. Edmond likes the Blüthner, but I used to prefer the Steinway."

"May I try the Blüthner? My teacher has one." I adjusted the stool.

For an hour we played to one another, with Marie listening quietly, and Mme de Valliet gliding in and out of the room with the grace of a ballet dancer. She arrived with a tray of things for tea – English tea – with wafer-thin sandwiches and cakes – which you must eat sparingly. I had heard all about it from Maman and Mamie, both of whom had visited English families when they were about our age. I asked for lemon, not milk, and looked longingly at the cake. Edmond offered us cucumber sandwiches and drank weak tea like us. Mme de Valliet's cup looked as brown as beech leaves in autumn.

As I got up to take my cup and saucer, I caught sight of a photograph on the other piano. There was the youthful Alice Creighton beside a young man, with the same deep-set eyes. There was laughter on both their faces.

"Is that you, in the photograph?" I asked, curious to know more.

"Yes," she sighed, "with my brother, Ben. He was a very fine violinist. We gave many concerts before the war playing all the twelve Beethoven sonatas – the *'Kreutzer'* was my favourite – its ruggedness reminds me of Scottish mountains - but he loved the *'Spring'*. He had a wonderful sense of humour. There is a moment in the scherzo when it seems that the violin and piano are a chord out with one another. Someone even commiserated with us on our shaky moment after a concert! But it's deliberate! Ben loved it – as he loved the lyrical Adagio, and the broad tune at the beginning of the last movement.

"Ben was also a soldier. In Scotland we have a voluntary as well as a professional or regular army. We call them 'territorials'. He was a captain in the Seaforth Highlanders at the beginning of the war. Even before the war it was difficult for us to plan concerts because he wanted to be in Scotland for weekend territorial training and expeditions. His men admired his courage, and he took trouble to learn Gaelic, which many of them spoke – and he also played the pipes! When the war broke out, his regiment joined the 51st Highland Division and came with the British expeditionary force to France.

They are a famous division, one with a strong bond of comradeship and loyalty, to each other and their French allies. Highlanders are courteous off the battlefield but such ferocious fighters that the Germans were frightened of them in their kilts, and called them 'Ladies from Hell'. Ben won a medal leading his men into battle at a place called Beaumont-Hamel. There is a monument there to the 51st, which I saw Maréchal Foch unveil in 1924. The inscription is:

Là a' Bhlàir s'math na Càirdean

It means 'Friends are good on the day of battle'. I don't think I have ever felt the bond between my country and my adopted country as strongly as on that day."

"I hope there won't be any more wars," said Marie.

"There has always been a bond between the French and the Scots," said Edmond. "It was called the Auld Alliance.

"And we still need an army to defend France," he continued. "On the French side of our family there have always been professional soldiers. Not territorials like so many of the Scots. I shall be leaving for St Cyr in a few months time."

"Is your brother going to be a soldier too?" I asked.

At that moment the door opened and Charles walked into the room. He shook our hands and gave a slight bow, his movements more stilted than his brother's. He was taller than I remembered, fair, with eyes that were blue, but pale and strained. He seemed tense while willing to be correct.

After his greetings which were a little stiff and protracted, he continued, "Forgive me, I couldn't avoid overhearing what you said. The answer is no. I am going to be a priest, or rather a monk who is also ordained. I shall live in a community where I shall eventually administer the sacraments – in Bavaria. The Abbot is an old friend of my father's."

"They are both going away, and I shall be alone," said Mme de Valliet.

"But you were alone when we were at Ampleforth, Mother," said Edmond.

"You came back for the holidays. I always had that to look forward to. Now I shall have to wait for permission from colonels and abbots to see either of my sons." She sighed.

Changing the subject, Edmond turned to Marie and asked, "Have you enjoyed living in Caen? I miss Normandy, the fields and the hedgerows – and of course, Ronval – when I am away."

"Yes," she replied, "but it's good to come back to La Chenaie. I too miss the country, the woods and the river." She looked at Mme de Valliet.

"I have so often drawn the tower that I would love to see it. There must be a good view of the river and the woods at La Chenaie."

"But yes, of course," said Edmond. "It's my studio. Come and see the view. I spend hours there drawing. It's another thing I shall miss when I join the army."

I saw Charles glance at his mother. There was anxiety in both their faces, reluctance for us to see the tower, which Marie, despite her usual sense of what was happening, had missed.

We climbed up the winding staircase in semi-darkness, with only narrow slits in the thick stone walls to guide us. The steps were worn and uneven and I held on to the rope rail to steady myself. When we reached the top, we blinked in the light which flooded the hexagonal room and gasped with surprise. There were paintings stacked against the wall, with one piece of unfinished work on an easel – the river with our orchard and wood in the background. Two small figures were sitting on the bank, and you could just make out La Chenaie in the left corner.

"You have been painting us!" said Marie.

There was the same ease and clarity in the water-colours that there was in his playing. I wondered what else he could do with such confidence, careless whether his gifts were noticed or not. Everything seemed to flow naturally from his hands, which were long and still like his mother's. It was only the memory or association of war and bereavement that had made them tight. When he moved, it was with a sense of grace and repose, and when he sat and talked there was an economy of words and choice of phrase that communicated exactly what he meant. Marie was entranced. She crouched down to look at the pictures propped up against the five sides of the wall as the doorway took up the sixth.

Suddenly she smiled and said, "Were you poaching when you did this one?"

"I painted it from memory, but I had to examine the tree first."

There was our swing! We all laughed.

"It's so clear that you can see your tree from here." Marie followed Edmond to the window, which looked straight ahead.

I watched them stand together and for the first time I felt excluded from Marie's company. I looked round to relieve my feelings and caught sight of a pen and ink drawing. It was a figure bending over an easel – it was Marie, her long hair falling down her back and her eyes intent on her work. I looked up. Mme de Valliet was also gazing at the picture; we both felt pain – hers deep, mine complicated.

"It looks as though it might rain," said Charles, falling back on his English manners which use the weather as a punctuation mark, or an emotional screen. Our Norman weather is nearly as changeable as the British, but is less relied upon as a prop. "I shall go and find umbrellas."

It was more difficult to keep our balance going down the stairs than going up, and I had to hold tightly on to the rope rail. Mme de Valliet led the way, followed by Charles and then me. We had reached the bottom, and were lingering in the flagstone passage which led to the salon, before Edmond and Marie appeared.

The boys accompanied us down to the river, Charles walking with me, followed by Edmond and Marie. Large drops of rain were already falling when we reached the bridge. We walked up the hill by the orchard and past the swing tree towards La Chenaie, as thunder clapped and the shower hissed down on the black canopy above me.

Chapter 10 1933 – 1935

Although we would often see Charles, we only met Edmond once more that year, in late August, when he came back for a short visit to his mother. Secretly we both longed for another invitation to Ronval, and, in the idleness at the end of the long holidays we spent lazy afternoons gazing up at the hexagonal tower veiled in the mist and fantasy of Norman summer light.

We had had a bathe in the cool water, and Marie had set up her easel, to paint my portrait, using greens and reds to capture the colour of my short auburn hair. I was reading, or rather reciting, poems by Baudelaire, their meanings as elusive as the tower or the reflections in the water, the sounds and images that crept into our minds seeming in tune with the lethargy of the afternoon and the restive longing of our thoughts. I remember admiring Marie's long dark hair and slender arms, her wide eyes fixed in an intense concentration which embraced everything she painted.

We both looked and saw a figure walking towards the river. I told myself not to be disappointed, that it must be Charles, but the supple movements and easy gait were unmistakable. Edmond waved and we walked slowly to our side of the bridge.

"Bonjour, Mesdemoiselles," he said.

"Bonjour, come and join us," I said.

He crossed the bridge and sat down on the grass, as my mind raced in half-sentences, and I tried to assemble something coherent.

"My mother sends her best wishes and asks you to join her for tea. She's been away, but she would love to hear you play again, Mademoiselle Favoret."

"I haven't practised for a week," I said limply.

He smiled. He had a knack of filling time without fear of silence, even with those he hardly knew. He looked at Marie's easel.

"I don't think that Mlle Millet is out of practice," he said, and turning towards me added. "May we expect you at four?"

He smiled, inclining his head slightly, and walked back to Ronval.

It was Edmond who met us at the door and led us to the dusty salon, its tables strewn with papers, and windows filtering light through the smudges left by rain and wind. Once again we both played, with Mme de Valliet reclining on one of the bulky sofas. (British furniture is made for comfort not elegance.) When we had finished she asked Edmond to fetch the tea things.

"It's a British custom – we don't seem to be able to get through the afternoon without it," she said languidly. "Now tell me, Anne, when are you sitting the entrance exam for the Conservatoire, and what are you going to play? I well remember my own audition in Vienna."

I told her about my plans for the year, of M. Gabon's insistence on Bach, Beethoven and Chopin, but of my own preference for Ravel's "Ondine". "It feels less dangerous than the Chopin Studies."

"We had to play studies by Liszt too in Vienna. Fortunately there was a strong accent on the classical composers, and I played a lot of sonatas by Mozart and Beethoven. Have you ever played a concerto with an orchestra?"

"It's a dream – no, not yet."

I noticed that Marie had slipped out with Edmond to help with the tea, while I stumbled on, it seemed for ages, answering questions which showed me how much there was to learn. Edmond and Marie eventually appeared, one carrying a tray of food, and the other a large silver teapot and matching pot for hot water with a sugar bowl and milk jug. Good behaviour was required from everyone. We drank our tea and ate sandwiches and thin slices of cake exactly as we had done before, talking politely of music and the weather, while my mind seethed with envy. There was no question of going up to the tower, and I wondered whether Marie and Edmond hadn't already been there, while I was answering questions about repertoire. Mme de Valliet asked us to call more often, and we readily agreed.

After that, it was Charles who came down to the river bank on fine Sunday afternoons, to invite us to join his mother for tea. He was less talented than his elder brother, less charming, less at ease with himself, his limbs and gait tense and uncertain. His face was narrow and his pale blue eyes, above a long and slightly hooked nose, looked down on us, not so much as interlopers but as acquaintances rather than friends. But he was intelligent, well informed and devoted to his mother, putting off the date when he would travel to Germany so as to stay with her. He took pains to get to know both of us, and, although there was a gap between us, which we attributed to conceit, or rather a feeling of superiority, we enjoyed his company and learned a great deal from him.

We would see him fishing in the river, catching trout or perch with a natural enthusiasm which was usually hidden behind a self-conscious mask. But it wasn't just politeness which drew him across the bridge to talk to us; he was lonely, having left behind the British world of his education, hovering between two lives, both ordered by the call of bells to prayer, work and recreation.

It was strange to us that he should have chosen a monastery in Bavaria, in Germany rather than Britain or France.

"Monks are flawed individuals, just like lay people, but every now and then you meet someone whose life you wish to emulate

– just like the concert pianists that you admire, Mlle. Favoret. And Bavaria is like Ireland or Austria, a deeply Catholic part of Germany, unlike Britain which seceded from Rome in the sixteenth century, or France which is riddled with anticlericalism."

"And who is the person whose life has so impressed you that you want to live like him?" I asked, ignoring criticism which stung, but which I had learned to accept. Part of growing up was recognising that life evolves in lines which often follow separate courses, sometimes crossing in peaceful ways, sometimes colliding with one another and causing friction, rather than the childish notion that it is graded on a ladder of merit, like marks given for work at school. Perhaps Charles was guilty of such naivety. It is one of the problems of thinking that you are right and everyone else wrong.

"The abbot at the monastery in Bavaria, Father Anselm. He has a quality that can only be described as saintliness. He carries serenity within himself, and looks after the novices in his charge with such wisdom, that no one who meets him can leave his presence without being slightly changed. Of course the change is mostly unnoticed, but I have seen people, even outsiders, come into contact with him and lose their anger, or find answers to practical questions that seem obvious afterwards.

"The time before last when I was in Bavaria – 1929, I think – there was so much unrest and uncertainty under the Weimar Republic that people would come to him, just for reassurance. Their lives had been overturned by hyperinflation in the early twenties, and those who knew were terrified it would happen again after the Stock Market crash. Many were as much afraid of living as of dying, and a man of Father Anselm's stature somehow restored their dignity and self-respect." He looked thoughtful. "German people like order. It's what the new régime is giving them."

"What new régime?" asked Marie.

Charles sighed. "There is a man called Hitler who runs the country now. How long he will be in power I don't know, but there are jobs for people and the currency is stable. Ordinary German people are content. They were like chickens without a mother hen when there was democracy – they don't want to choose, they want to be told what to do. Anyway many of the choices were either unrealistic or downright evil – like the Bolsheviks." He frowned.

"I don't think that the French would like to have a government that denied them choice," I said, still hurt by his jibe at French secularism. I didn't remind him that December 1929 was the month of the incident in the centre of Quinon, when his behaviour had been so far from saintly, that he had grabbed Bernard Piot by the collar, and hardly acknowledged me although he knew who I was.

"No, nor would the British. They have a democracy which has evolved in stages. It means that sometimes they make silly decisions because the leaders are trying to please, rather than do what they think best, but on the whole it works well. But you can't impose democracy without allowing it to grow step by step. It's one of the mistakes that the allies made after the war."

"I think that choice is good," said Marie, "but I can understand how frightened people are of disorder – or poverty." She shuddered.

Charles looked at her thoughtfully. Rousing himself, he went back over the bridge and returned with a netful of trout, to ask if my mother would like to have four of them. Delving into her bag for one of the old cloths she kept for wiping paint-brushes, Marie wrapped the trout into a parcel, telling Charles excitedly that she would make *truite meunière* that evening, as cook would be away. We walked up the path towards the wood as we had so often done, pausing by the tree with its split trunk and huge girth. "I doubt if you could hide in there now," said Charles. It was a shadow of a joke, which made me long for the natural happiness and ease we found so attractive in his brother.

But it was nearly two years before we saw Edmond again. By that time I had reached my eighteenth birthday, and had been accepted by the Paris Conservatoire. My parents had given me a

Steinway grand piano for the salon at La Chenaie, and to celebrate my success I organised a house concert in aid of the convent school. Everyone was invited, from André Roche to Mme de Valliet, all the farm hands, and the nuns and teachers from both the schools. There were to be no complete sonatas, just short movements, with well prepared introductions so that the audience would have some idea what they were listening to. Marie would play the cello, and I would accompany her as well as performing solo pieces. Her paintings would be on show – I hoped that she would be prepared to sell them if anyone showed an interest – and there would be a *Vin d'honneur* afterwards.

The only person who was unhappy about it was Marie. She felt that she owed it to my parents to play the cello at the concert, but she was modest about her abilities and would have preferred just to listen. As for her paintings, she persuaded herself that no one would notice them.

I remember little of the concert, except that it was well received, that Marie's fears of performing were overcome, and that we both looked well in the dresses that we had bought under my grandmother's supervision in Caen, Marie in a dark red that suited her colouring, and I in blue. What I shall never forget is the party afterwards. There were two unexpected guests in the audience: Edmond, who had returned from St Cyr, before joining the army at Metz, and Robert Cummings.

"I have just heard that our Scottish friends want someone to come here to see how we distil calvados," said my father two days before. "Cummings is sending his son. I've never met him, but if he's like his father he should be an acute observer. We'll have to include him in the party. I can't just leave him in a hotel while everyone else is here."

"One more person will make no difference. The doors will all be open so that there will be some air circulating, and we can even put chairs out on the terrace," replied my mother.

Concerts are given to a sea of faces. They blur and blend, and even applause acquires an aura of mist which only clears when the adrenalin stops pumping, and the longing to be assured cools the spirit – the yearning to be told that the thunderclap was real and not a formality, that the performance had been deep, clear and accurate, and that difficulties hadn't been noticeable. But an uninformed audience sees the strength and not the weakness, and the parade of confidence must go on despite doubts and memories of bad moments.

This audience was also peppered with those who thoroughly knew what they were hearing, and my instinct was to turn to them. I looked for Alice de Valliet, and found her deep in conversation with someone I had never seen before. He was taller even than Charles, with thick sandy hair, an open face, grey eyes, a wide smile and easy shoulders. He seemed like an athlete, with long hands that hung loosely from his arms. What struck me, making me stand still and listen, was that they were talking in English, the first time I had heard it spoken at La Chenaie, except when we were practising with Maman, who had spent some holidays in London as a girl.

"Ah, Anne," said Mme de Valliet turning to me and breaking into French, "you must meet a fellow Scot! M. Cummings comes from the north-east, from Aberdeenshire. He wants to congratulate you on your performance just as I do."

M. Cummings smiled and took my hand. "Bonsoir, Mlle Favoret! I loved your playing of Ravel's 'Ondine'. It must be very hard, but your technique seemed faultless. All those rippling passages reminded me of Scottish rivers. Thank you for reading the prose poem – it made the outline of the story much clearer." He spoke French well, although with a stronger accent than his companion.

"It was very good," Alice de Valliet said warmly, kissing me on both cheeks, and patting my back. "Come up to Ronval and see me – I may have one or two ideas!" She turned to the wall to look at Marie's paintings, while I remembered that I was a hostess. People were pouring out into the evening sunshine in search of champagne and canapés.

I walked downstairs through the cellar, which was cool and silent, neatly stacked with wine bottles, the floor cobbled and swept clean of dust. I breathed deeply and prepared myself for meeting the people outside, emerging unseen at a lower level than the terrace where the guests were gathered. I walked slowly up the steps. The first pair I saw surprised me almost more than the exchange I had just left. Charles was talking to Jean.

"You must ask her again," said Charles. I wasn't certain whether he was saying "her" or "him" as both are *lui* in French, but instinct told me that they were talking of Marie.

Jean caught sight of me and bowed clumsily. Charles started, and then he too bowed. "Congratulations, Mlle Favoret!" he said hastily. "It was an excellent performance – from both of you!"

"Excellent!" echoed Jean. He turned. On the other side of the terrace, Marie was deep in conversation with Edmond. I wouldn't stay to gauge the reactions of the onlookers, because I wanted to return to Alice de Valliet and M. Cummings. Walking back up the cellar steps to the salon, with a glass of champagne in each hand, I again passed Charles and Jean who had the aura of conspirators.

"Thank you," said Mme de Valliet. "I love this picture of the tower. She seems to have caught the winter sunshine. It must have been cold sitting at her easel."

"I'm sure she painted it from memory. Marie has a wonderful eye for detail which she stores in her usual orderly way. Yes, it's one of my favourites, and hers. I doubt if she will be prepared to part with it. After the last exhibition she was sad to sell her work, but it was for a good cause like this evening."

"Let me fetch you a drink, Mademoiselle," said Robert. He returned with a plate of petit fours which he looked at longingly.

"You must be hungry," I laughed. "Does that hotel feed you properly?"

"I'm always hungry. It's being a part-time soldier. It's an active life: out of doors whenever I can be."

"Then are you too are a territorial soldier?"

"I'm surprised you know what that is!"

Alice de Valliet smiled. "Anne knows all about the T.A. My brother and uncles were in the Seaforths."

"Well, I'm a Gordon Highlander. We're all Gordons in the north east, where we keep fit running up and down the Grampian Mountains."

We walked towards the terrace to find Soeur Antoinette filling the doorway. She kissed me, and spoke with enthusiasm.

"Well done, Anne! I was surprised how well you accompanied Marie. A firebrand like you is often too strong to play well with others. You must get into chamber music when you are in Paris."

I smiled and thought of the duets. I had been well taught how to accommodate. "It isn't difficult to follow Marie because the playing is so musical and artistic. She has a natural feeling for where a phrase is going." I didn't add that it was also easier when I had room to move.

"Come and see me before you go. I have something for you." She gave me one of her mischievous grins and turned to my grandmother. I couldn't help hearing her say, "I think she will have a career, that young lady." My grandmother smiled with contentment.

Having squeezed past Soeur Antoinette, Robert and I walked out into the cool of the evening on the wide terrace which looked over the fields to the west of the house. There were blue and pink edges to the clouds which stretched out in fleecy lines across the skyline. It was still warm, but the crowd was thinning. Our friends shook hands with me and my parents, and then walked slowly up the driveway into the sunset.

Marie and Edmond were still engrossed with one another. It was more obvious now that there were only a handful of people left: the de Valliets, my grandparents, and one or two others. Bernard Piot came up to me.

"May I congratulate you, Mlle Favoret? It was a wonderful concert. Do you play much Bach?" We had restricted our Bach to one or two arrangements for cello with piano accompaniment, like the "Air on the G string".

"Of course! But Preludes and Fugues would have been a little dry for tonight's audience."

"I've heard Mlle Favoret play Bach with unusual clarity," said a familiar voice behind me. The sound of it gave me a lurch: a mellowness which had filled my young dreams, which were now as vaporous as evening mist. They were fading, but the horn-like voice revived them and made them hover like a game of make-believe.

I backed away into the drawing-room and walked as in a trance to the piano. There was no other response but to play. The Prelude and Fugue in E Major from the Second Book of the Forty-Eight is particularly lovely. The interweaving lines of the Prelude are melodic as can only be achieved on a piano – whatever the authentic lobby says – and the harmonies of the Fugue are like a chorale. I don't think that there were tears in my eyes – the business of playing is too demanding, but it felt like a lament for my dreams, which now belonged to Marie.

Surrounding me were Edmond, Marie and Robert, whose presence felt like a tonic although I had only just met him, Alice de Valliet, my parents and my grandparents who were staying overnight at La Chenaie. But Charles and Bernard Piot were there too, one like a pall of gloom, judgmental and backward-looking, the other a tonic too, but a different one. Looking back on it, there was a purity of soul in Bernard which was reflected in the music. It was a strange paradox to find spiritual strength in the man who wholly rejected conventional belief. I was aware of the different strains of conviction in my audience, the French republicanism of my father, the humdrum Catholicism of my grandparents and the would-be priest with a streak of totalitarianism. But my heart, injured by the neglect of Marie and Edmond who were caught up in themselves, went out to the idealist who wanted the good things of life to be shared. And that is what a fugue does. Nothing is as democratic as a Bach fugue, so rich in every line that each is perfect on its own.

When I finished, Bernard came up to me with unusual gallantry and kissed my hand, thanked us for the concert and said good-night. I saw Charles breathe a sigh of relief as he left.

Chapter 11 1935 – 1936

I went up to Paris in the autumn of 1935, the year the Germans reoccupied the coal-rich Saar, and reintroduced military service, overturning the conditions of the Versailles Treaty, without a murmur of protest from either the French or the British governments. It was the year that Charles entered his monastery in Bavaria, still blind to the excesses of Nazi gangsterism, and persuaded that Hitler was restoring Germany to its rightful place in Europe.

As a music student I heard little of what was happening on the world stage, although I was later to make friends with players who were very well aware of the political threats that loomed over us. My life at the Conservatoire was dominated by piano lessons, which demanded quick learning and a high level of performance. I went through stages of euphoria at being independent in one of the world's most beautiful and magical cities, loneliness when things went wrong and there was no Marie to listen to my woes, and relief that I could make my own decisions as to how to meet the deadlines set by my teachers.

I clearly remember one warm spring afternoon in 1936, well into my first year, when a discouraging lesson had left me feeling drained and empty. I had coffee and brioche in a café in the rue de la Motte Piquet, forgetting my frustrations in a novel, with the score of the late Beethoven sonatas lying at my side. Picking up the book and the thick volume, I decided to continue the story on the Champs de Mars, and sat on one of the wooden benches, scarcely noticing that it was growing colder, when a gust of wind roused me from my reverie. I stood up and shook myself hurriedly, throwing off the imaginary world that had held me. I had walked a few paces clutching the novel, when a voice said "Bonjour, Mademoiselle, haven't you forgotten this?"

I turned to see Robert Cummings holding out the volume of sonatas. I gave a short sigh, and laughed. "Bonjour, Monsieur Cummings – you surprised me! Thank you for being so observant. I doubt if I would have gone far but – thank you! They were a present from Soeur Antoinette – which makes them all the more valuable – but one of them is driving me mad!"

It was Robert's turn to laugh. "I have been standing here in the park for five minutes, wondering where I had seen that hair before! I was sure it was you, but I didn't like to risk making a mistake. How are you? I hear good things of you from your father. I believe he is coming up to Paris in a fortnight."

"Yes, I'd almost forgotten. Papa is coming with Maman and Marie. It will be good to see them, but there is so little time for me to think about anything except piano practice."

"And a good read from time to time!" We both laughed.

"Reading is an escape. It's one way of recharging before the next battle with concentration."

"May I walk with you back to the rue de la Motte Piquet?" he asked.

"Does your father always come with your mother and Marie?" he continued.

"Not always, but I look forward to seeing them when they do. I am making friends here, but I miss Marie's sympathy when things go wrong!"

"May I suggest another way of recharging your concentration? We Scots believe in exercise as the best way of resting and stimulating the mind when it is overburdened. What about some vigorous walking and sight-seeing?"

"I hadn't thought of that. Of course we did a lot of sight-seeing in Paris when we were younger. My parents have been bringing us up to the flat for the last five years."

"No one will ever run out of things to see in Paris. Just to explore the whole of the Louvre would take days. And there are places like the St Denis Basilica that I have never seen."

We reached the *porte-cochère* of the apartment block, and I let myself in, after saying good-bye. My mind was already focussed on the awkward trills at the end of op 109, another way of practising them and making them sound natural instead of strained and difficult.

As my parents and Marie were to spend four days in the flat, I knew it would impinge on my precious practising time, and I began to chafe within hours of their arrival. Marie looked radiant, and as willing as ever to listen, but she had become secretive, and reluctant to talk about herself. I had to wait for a moment when she was shopping to hear her news from my mother.

"She is receiving letters from Edmond, I'm sure," said Maman. "What's more, she has told Jean that she has made up her mind not to marry him. He of course is unhappy. He asked her again just after you left for Paris in January."

"Well, that's a relief," I replied. "Surely you realise he wasn't good enough for her?"

She shrugged her shoulders and then continued earnestly, "I am much more concerned about her involvement with Edmond de Valliet. On the surface it looks like a brilliant match, but he is a soldier, and an Edmond de Valliet will want his wife to be at Ronval. She risks spending much of her life without him."

"Perhaps he will retire early and come home to run the estate," I suggested.

"Yes, Anne, that is always a possibility. But if there is another war…"

"Of course there won't be another war!"

"Your father isn't so sure. He's one of the few people in France who still sees Germany as a threat."

I laughed. "Papa has too much of the spirit of le Capitaine and the hero of Austerlitz! I can't imagine him keeping a rifle under his bed, but he'll fight tooth and nail for a good business deal." I paused and changed the subject slightly. "Charles de Valliet is sure that the régime in Germany is doing great things for the people."

"Oh, there are rumours of some dreadful things happening in Germany." She sighed. "No, Anne, I'm concerned about Marie. She is happy as long as she has us to please, but I don't think she would manage without us."

"What do you mean? Marie is one of the most practical people I know. She would clean and order Ronval in a trice, and keep all the servants smiling at the same time. Anyway she wouldn't be alone. Alice de Valliet likes her…"

"That's another problem. Alice de Valliet is ill. Her nerves were shattered by the death of her husband and brother in the war. Now I suspect she has tuberculosis. She's painfully thin, and I'm told she coughs a great deal. She has been in Switzerland, at a clinic. Charles stayed with her to make the arrangements, and, I imagine, put Ronval in order, as his mother has been too unwell to look after things properly. As for Edmond, I suspect he is an old-fashioned chevalier who would leave such matters to others."

"And who better to look after them than Marie? Apart from the fact that everyone adores her, she's good at looking after money."

"But what about the strain on Marie, if she has to take care of her mother-in-law as she did her own mother, even in very different circumstances? Marie's early life was unbearably difficult, and nursing her mother – in fact the reversal of roles – was hard for so young a child. On top of that, the change from poverty to comparative wealth – from unnatural loneliness to a childhood free of worry, when she came to live with us – was difficult for her. You were always too self-absorbed to see that sometimes her face would become vacant as if her spirit were cowering behind a mask."

"Yes, I did see it once or twice. I always thought it was my fault. It made me feel guilty for wanting to be independent of her. I know she found moving to Caen hard too. She didn't want to come to Paris because she had had enough of change, but, as always, she has made herself busy with her art and all the other things she likes doing."

"None of those things can compare with security. She has missed you, I know. With us she found safety, and there is a deep fear of losing it. She looks wonderful most of the time, but I have seen her sitting under your tree with that vacant expression on her face. The swing was much more than a childish pastime. It helped to reconcile the hardship of her early years and her new life at La Chenaie." My mother sighed again. "As for change, it isn't going to be easy for her to be mistress of Ronval with a mother-in-law suffering from advanced TB and a husband who is always away!"

She looked at me, slyly. "You seem to be whole-hearted about Marie and Edmond. Haven't you been – a little jealous?"

It was my turn to sigh. "Yes, very, but each time we went to Ronval I could feel that he preferred her. It did make me sad, because I had made him part of my childish dreams. It was his voice that I loved so much – and then everything else…Perhaps the moment when I realised that I had to move on was at the concert, where he spent most of his time talking to her. Since then I have been making my own life here in Paris. Now what I want is for Marie to be happy. I hear everything you say, but I have faith in her ability to manage well. She's had to cope with my independence, and now she will have to cope with Edmond's."

"It's not the same, Anne. Your independence was one of spirit, but not of presence. She could adapt to your ways and make herself useful sometimes, just by wrapping herself in her art, so as to let you have your space. But you were always there – until she decided not to come to Paris with you. I hope she will always be able to depend on Edmond's love, but he won't always be there, and neither will we."

I could say no more. My mother's wisdom, like Marie's sympathy, was something I had always taken for granted. My grandmother may have been the person who insisted on correct etiquette, supervised our choice of clothes and lectured us on how to behave. She was much more successful in Marie's case than mine. But my mother, having thrown caution to the wind when she married my father, had learned much more than Mamie, whose life was ordered by social visits and a strong sense of duty.

Chapter 12 Autumn 1936

Robert and I met from time to time, usually with my father, but our sight-seeing expeditions were infrequent, either because I had to meet a deadline or he had to go straight back to Scotland for army weekends. As he said, it wasn't just a question of practice (with a smile at me), as teamwork, being part of a battalion.

One bright warm October day, we walked north – it seemed for miles – from the centre of Paris to the poor quarter of St Denis, leaving behind us the Louvre and Notre Dame, and the noble symmetry of boulevard and monument, river and bridge that makes Paris one of the world's most beautiful cities. When we entered the Basilica, sunlight was pouring through the windows on to the empty tombs and statues of the kings and queens of France.

"It's like a wall of glass," I whispered, looking up at the blazing stretch of colour which flooded on to the paving stones of the transept. As we crept slowly towards the ambulatory, I turned back to look down the nave at the rose window. The contrast between the rose that fades and the window which had survived for seven hundred years of wars and revolution stirred a protest.

"Why a rose and not a star, or at least a star surrounded by an orb?" I asked. "No rose is symmetrical – it would be artificial if it were."

"It represents the Godhead or divine aspect of the world, calming the human spirit, and drawing it to prayer and meditation. This is the first of its kind in France, older than Chartres or Notre Dame. Sadly, in Scotland most rose windows are empty."

We walked over to the north bay of the transept, and stopped in front of the tombs of Louis XII and Anne of Brittany. "Your namesake, Anne," said Robert hesitantly. It was the first time he had used my Christian name.

"Wasn't there a Scottish king called Robert?" I replied.

"The Bruce! He was one of our greatest kings, who defeated the English at Bannockburn."

We both smiled and continued our search for the names of French kings and queens from Dagobert to Louis XVIII.

The Basilica seemed to be filled with the ghosts of French history. Their tombs had been desecrated, but their presence was still felt, the kings and queens who had made wars and alliances, and been overturned by the people they had neglected. It made me think of Charles and Bernard Piot, each on either side of a line which divided the *Ancien Régime* from the revolutionaries, with my father in the middle, the benign face of the modern republic.

It was Robert's turn to protest as we gazed at the outside of the Basilica with its one tower giving the building a queer asymmetrical shape.

I laughed. "Napoleon wanted to repair the basilica after it had been reduced to a ruin, with the lead of the roof stolen to make bullets, and birds flying to and fro among the empty rafters. His architect built an even taller north tower, so the place still looked lop-sided. Like all soldiers he was in such a rush that he gave the job to someone with more enthusiasm than knowledge. It took Viollet-le-Duc years to restore it to its original design!"

"You may laugh, but we soldiers have to be in a hurry – and we have to work out good plans in advance. Of course you have to be able to improvise – use your initiative on the battle-field." He frowned. "As soldiers, particularly in the territorial army, we hardly seem to exist at the moment. It's bad enough for the regulars – even they have to drill with worn-out equipment. Few people realise that Germany is still a threat…"

"Not you too! My father thinks the same. I can't believe that it could all happen again. I remember a lunch party when I was twelve. I embarrassed everyone when my grandfather said grace, and then I had to play duets with Soeur Antoinette. It was only afterwards that I realised, that everyone except me had lost a close relative as a result of war. It made me feel very humble."

"Can't you see that the only way to prevent it happening again is to build a strong army – to deter rogue nations from taking advantage of us? That means being up to date with armaments – not relying on the left-overs from the past! There are too many dictators in Europe at the moment – and Hitler is the most dangerous, as far as France and Britain are concerned. But the appeasers have let him occupy the Rhineland and he's building up an army – and air-force, with much more energy than we are."

"I can't believe that the governments of democracies like ours would allow us to go to war again. It's strange: before the lunch party I told you about, I was of your opinion – that we must fight for what we believe in. It was Marie who said, 'If there is another war, there won't be anyone left to stand up for what they think.'"

"That's why we need an army. To prevent it happening! It's more important than ever to keep in training!"

"When do you have to go back to Scotland?"

"Tonight, on the train from Gare du Nord."

I had been shocked by his insistence on the possibility of war. Hitherto I had regarded his T.A. enthusiasm as something akin to a pastime – something like music is to the amateur, forgetting that Ben Creighton had died a soldier of a territorial regiment. I now saw that it was much more. "Enjoy being with your soldiers," I said, "and think of a rose window filled with stained glass, not sad and empty like the legacy of war." He bent forward and kissed me lightly on the lips.

"Good-bye, Anne. I shall see you next week."

It was about this time, at the beginning of my second year at the Conservatoire, that I became a member of a trio. Tadeusz Donska and Paul Raven, both a year ahead of me, were two of the most outstanding string players in the Conservatoire. When they heard me accompany a cellist, they asked me how much experience I had of playing chamber music. I told them about Marie, my childhood friend with whom I had played sonatas, and about the duets. I in turn asked them about themselves; they lived together in the rue de Seine on the left bank south of the river; they had known each other for two years. Their relationship didn't embarrass me. There is a magic about Paris that opens the mind, and makes you look at the unexpected with a vision that is clearer, less judgmental. Hearing Paul and Tadeusz play the double concerto by Brahms convinced me, that whatever their life-style, they had much to give to the world – and to me.

Combining the rigorous programme at the Conservatoire with the demands of Paul and Tadeusz was a challenge, but my technique had improved, learning new scores had become less of a strain, and I had just enough energy to cope. Inspired by Robert, I walked – almost ran – in the Champ de Mars every morning, and returned breathless but invigorated. The living room became a studio where we would rehearse until the neighbours knocked on the doors to make us stop. After that the boys would talk until late – usually over a glass of my father's calvados – before taking the metro to Mabillon, and walking back to the rue de Seine where they lived at the top of six flights of rickety stairs.

It was because I had listened to adult conversation at an early age that I found I could contribute to the exchange between two intelligent musicians – who, unlike most music students, were interested in life around them. Tadeusz was a Polish Jew who was constantly worried by anti-Semitism, particularly in Germany. He had a wry and sometimes malicious sense of fun, imitating the strutting of petty German officials he had seen in Berlin, and criticising other cellists either for being too sentimental or for playing out of tune.

Paul, who was as fussy about intonation, and also disliked players who pulled the music "out of shape", as he put it, came from a family of English musicians. As he had sung as a boy in the choir of King's College Cambridge, his musical tastes were firmly rooted in the English choral tradition, and he smiled when I told him that my early training was based on the British system of notation. He led the Conservatoire orchestra. Not only was he an outstanding player, he had played in orchestras all his life and couldn't understand why French students found it so difficult. Paris had given him a sense of freedom – the English can be so stiff! He told me that meeting Tadeusz was the best thing that had ever happened to him.

I liked Paul, and felt more confident playing with him because he was invariably polite, even when he was being critical. Not so his outspoken Polish friend.

"Let's play the last movement, Anne!"

"I haven't looked at it yet."

"Well, read it," Tadeusz would say. "Surely that nun taught you to read!"

"She's probably tired. Anne, do try. The only way to read well is to read!"

"All right, I'll try."

"Well done!" said Paul when we had finished. "You'll find it easier to learn now."

"Let's have all the right notes tomorrow!" (Tadeusz.)

Over a drink they would talk about other things.

"My cousins in Berlin are trying to leave, but don't know where to go. The British don't want them, and it's difficult to get visas for America. The last place they want to go is Poland."

"I find it so strange that people don't like Jews. The upper classes in Britain see them as some sort of threat. They either live in the East End of London or mingle in high society with anglicised names. There are lots of Jews in New York."

"I don't know what the French think. There are no Jews in our corner of Normandy – as far as I know," I put in tentatively.

"The French don't like us either. Haven't you heard of Dreyfus?" asked Tadeusz.

"Only vaguely. I remember praying for the conversion of the Jews, but I didn't imagine what they were like."

"The trouble is that to survive two thousand years of persecution you have to have an instinct for coming out on top. The greatest scientist of our age is a German Jew."

"You mean Einstein?" asked Paul.

"He's in the USA. Let's hope that my cousins can join him! Oh, did you hear that American girl play the Dvořák concerto last week?" He took out a handkerchief (not very clean) and pretended to mop his brow while playing with an imaginary bow and humming out of tune. "Ton-ton (that was one of the teachers) adores her but she makes me think of American 'candy'!" He said "candy" with an exaggerated American accent.

"You've been watching too many American 'movies', Tadeusz," I laughed.

"She's pretty enough to be in one," said Paul. "That's why Ton-ton likes her. Come on, it wasn't all that bad!"

Tadeusz went on humming. This time it was a Negro Spiritual – deliberately out of tune. "Some Americans think they own Dvořák, but it was the music of the despised negroes which inspired him, just like Gershwin. Now there's an American!"

Paul moved to the piano and started to play "I got Rhythm." He had a wonderful ear for harmony. (That was one of the reasons he could be so critical.) Tadeusz sang the melody falsetto.

A knock on the door ended the song.

"They go to bed in America too, Tadeusz," I said. "And talking about that, I have the third movement of a trio to learn by tomorrow."

I made coffee, but when I got back the boys were deep in another discussion. They had gone on to European politics – Britain, where the newspapers were ignoring the relationship between Edward VIII and Mrs. Simpson, although it was widely covered in the press in Europe and America. It was 1936, the year he came to the throne in January, only to abdicate before Christmas.

"Why shouldn't he marry her?" asked Tadeusz. "You British aren't Catholics like most Poles. There would be no problem in France or Poland – if there were still a monarchy. Marry one woman to please public opinion, and have the one you like as a mistress!"

"But he wants her to be queen. The public will never allow it. People were talking about it in the English church where I play the organ on Sunday. If he doesn't make a choice between the throne and Wallis Simpson, he could destroy the monarchy."

"Is that such a bad thing?" I asked. "France manages without one."

"We don't want revolutions in Britain, Anne! Anyway the last king and queen made the monarchy popular. They even persuaded George V – who was very old-fashioned – to speak on the wireless."

"Aren't they all Germans anyway?" asked Tadeusz. I could see another half hour of Germans and Jews looming and I wanted to sleep. I yawned, poured out the coffee and asked them to come at seven the next evening. I looked at my watch and realised that it was nearly one o'clock.

About midday my father rang. There was a telephone in the flat which reached the Mairie in Quinon after delays and frustration, like making calls from my grandparents' house.

"I am coming up to Paris at the end of the week to see Robert Cummings. I'll be on my own. By the way, I've got news about Marie! She is engaged to Edmond de Valliet. They're getting married in the summer. There was some difficulty with that wretched priest – you know, the brother – but Mme de Valliet has brought him round. She's not well, by the way. Marie spends a lot of time up there. That's one of the reasons she's not coming to Paris to tell you herself. She sends her love and will write. *A bientôt!*"

The next day I had a letter, one of the many which I still have. When I reread it, it reminds me how careless I could be of Marie's feelings, especially when I focussed my thoughts on my own future. It showed how dependent she had been, without ever seeming to cling or intrude. Whether it was a finely-tuned nature that could always find the balance between sharing and tact, or a constant wariness which feared to upset, I was never certain. I had always known that she was prone to fear, but I ought to have realised that her heroism in accompanying me to the bridge when we were children far outshone any courage of mine.

La Chenaie
November 1936

My dear Anne,

How good it is to be able to tell you of my engagement, after more than a year of secrecy! I could never tell what you thought of Edmond distinguishing me whenever we met, especially after the concert at La Chenaie. He has always admired me – even before our first visit to Ronval. He had been watching us both coming down to the river for years and drawn me sketching, hidden among the trees of the orchard. When we first went to Ronval he sat beside me while you played, and, somehow, I knew that he was fond of me. It is still difficult to believe. He is so wonderful – talented and distinguished.

After the concert, he asked me whether my feelings weren't engaged to anyone else. I told him that Jean had asked me to marry him, but that I had not accepted him. After that we met several times when you were in Paris, but I was bound to secrecy about our feelings, because he had to persuade Charles that we should be married. He is devoted to Charles, who is much more like his father. Mme de Valliet is more unconventional – preferring honest feelings to social forms – but she too wanted to be sure that Edmond had chosen someone who would promote his happiness – not just revel in being the mistress of Ronval.

Of course I shall love looking after the house that we always dreamed about and didn't visit until we were sixteen, and I shall take pleasure in caring for Alice – she has asked me to call her that. She isn't well, and it will be like looking after Maman. I could hardly look after you, Anne, bursting with health and energy, and heading for a good career which needs a sound constitution and steady nerves. If only you knew how nervous I was before that concert. I was sure my bow would shake so much that I wouldn't be able to control it!

You must forge ahead and forget about my little ways. My life is here, as I always hoped it would be, and I have found how to be useful – as well as unbelievably happy.

Edmond is coming back before Christmas. When your term is over, I look forward to celebrating my engagement with you, you whom I have always loved as a sister.

With much love,

Marie.

I wrote back kindly, I hope, but with a heavy heart. Maman was right of course. I was jealous, and selfish enough to want to take Marie at her word, to shake off the past and become mistress of my own future.

Chapter 13 December 1936

I looked up at Voltaire towering above the corner where the rue de Seine meets the river. That statue was removed by the Germans, and has been replaced by a smaller life-size version with a quizzical expression on its pock-marked face. I wondered what he would have thought of the world two hundred years on. Behind him lay the river and in front of him the teeming student life, the artists, musicians, writers, scientists and philosophers, Parisians, provincials and foreigners – and plenty of rogues too – crowded into shabby apartments, rather like the insects in the oak tree at La Chenaie.

People come to Paris for different reasons. If they don't have a purpose, they suffer the same fate as Dick Whittington, who discovered that the streets of London weren't paved with gold. The bells of Notre Dame don't make extraordinary promises, but if you come to Paris with something to offer, it may well pay you back with interest. You have to take your chance. But don't come to Paris with only your dreams – it can be unkind.

I had promised Robert to show him another *quartier* often missed by tourists, like St Denis. We had proved that we could both walk for hours without feeling tired. I had overdone my piano practice and I needed a break.

"Ugly old cynic," said Robert. "I read *Candide* at school and more at university, but I never enjoyed his wit."

"At least he disliked fanatics. My father admires him because he had balanced views about religion." We walked away from the river down the narrow street. "The violinist and cellist of my trio live near here. I told them we might call on them – that is, if you'd like to meet them."

"Will they mind?" he asked.

"They don't have a telephone, but as it's four o'clock in the afternoon, they should be awake. They live like owls and hoot all night. I'll ring first and if they're too busy we can just go away."

Climbing the stairs in semi-darkness was a hazard. The tread was uneven and I thought of the dangers of carrying a cello with one hand and clinging to the rail with the other. Before I rang, I heard the familiar cacophony of practising, the stopping and starting, the repetition of fast passages, the palpable frustration.

"Hello, Anne! Why aren't you working?" Tadeusz – accusing.

"Come in," said Paul. "We wanted to stop for coffee anyway."

"I have Robert with me. I'd like you to meet him. We won't stay long."

Paul was nearly as pleased to lapse into English as Robert. Paul's French was excellent, and Robert's was good for someone who didn't live in France, but there comes a time when it's a relief to speak your own language – a bit like sinking into a comfortable chair. I chatted with Tadeusz, hoping to escape his cousins. It turned out that it was they who had escaped – to America; and he was now worrying about his own family in Poland. Looking back on it, I think the cousins got out of Germany just in time.

We drank our coffee sitting on dilapidated chairs with uncomfortable broken springs. The whole apartment smelt of smoke and stale air, and everywhere there were papers and scores, overflowing ashtrays and unwashed plates from suppers that had been eaten before yesterday. And yet there was something in the atmosphere of the rooms with the ceilings slanting with the rooftop that had an inescapable charm. It seemed to tell you that living like this was one way to savour the fullness of life. If Robert had sniffed with disapproval at the mess I wouldn't have forgiven him. It's part of the bargain that Paris makes with you – accept the life-style of others and you may carve out your own.

Robert and Paul found quite a lot in common. Robert had been an undergraduate at Cambridge and he spoke of music with the enthusiasm of the amateur who makes the trials of professionals worthwhile. He asked about forthcoming concerts with a freshness that was so pervasive, that Paul and Tadeusz seemed less tired when we left than when we arrived.

Going down the creaking steps was even worse than going up, and it was a relief to breathe the outside air. Revived by the coffee we walked past Voltaire as far as the Pont des Arts, and keeping to the left bank we turned right with Ile de La Cité on our left. It's when you look back that the feminine splendour of Notre Dame strikes most forcibly, with the flying buttresses bending over like the graceful arms of dancers at the barre.

"I shall never tire of this view," said Robert in clear English.

"You sound like my first piano teacher," I replied in French. "She's Irish!"

"Well, I'm not! I'm Scottish through and through – a Celt I suppose."

"And I'm a northerner too – my red hair is probably inherited from the Vikings – through my grandfather." I told him about the Capitaine and he laughed.

"Once a soldier, always a soldier, at least at heart, but I hope I won't ever keep a gun under my bed to keep out intruders." He smiled and looked straight into my eyes. "You talk of your red hair as though it were a misfortune. But when I saw the sun dancing on your head in the park in March, I remembered the brilliant young pianist I met in Quinon last year."

He slipped his hand in mine. It was like an electric current running through me, and yet, like everything else about him, it felt strong and reassuring. I liked him for being straightforward, a man with a keen head for business, as well as a soldier with a mission to modernise an army. He was as realistic and competitive in business as he was energetic in his leadership of men. I imagined that he would pursue a business objective with every intention of getting what he wanted – at someone else's expense if necessary. My father was the same.

"I liked your friends," he said. "At first I wondered whether you liked Tadeusz…"

"You needn't be jealous of them. They have each other!"

"What! That sort of thing is against the law in Britain."

"But this is Paris."

"I see." We walked in silence.

I wondered that he should be surprised. Paul had mentioned composer friends of his parents who were homosexual, but who, like many others, had to hide their private lives behind a curtain of respectability.

"If you were my sister…"

"You don't have a sister!"

"But if you were, I don't know whether I would approve of you playing trios with them."

"But don't you see how easy it is? There are teachers at the Conservatoire who flirt so much with young girls that they can't get on with their work. If you have that kind of hassle or danger in a musical relationship it becomes almost impossible to create a professional partnership. If I played with a husband and wife, there would be the danger of the husband making the wife jealous and so on. With these two I can do something different from the rest of the pianists – and feel free! There might be problems with three women – two complaining about one. I only have one female friend, Marie. I look upon her as a sister, but I am sometimes ashamed that I have neglected her. Still, I can't imagine anyone else being as close."

"You don't have to feel guilty about Marie now that she's engaged to Edmond! When is the wedding?"

"At Easter, but there is to be an engagement party this Christmas."

"I can't remember what his mother's maiden name was. She told me her brother was in the Seaforths…!"

"Creighton. Alice Creighton."

"I knew Creightons at school. There was a Tom Creighton who enjoyed the Corps as much as I did!"

"Corps?"

"Schoolboys playing at soldiers. We were in Perthshire. You can't imagine what army exercises can be like on the Scottish mountains. Of course it's dangerous and you have to be very fit, but it's a life of comradeship and exhilaration – the kind that makes it a joy to be alive." He paused, perhaps a little embarrassed by an un-British burst of enthusiasm.

"I find the same sort of joy when I play trios with Paul and Tad," I replied.

Chapter 14 December 1936 – April 1937

The engagement party was postponed, not on account of any differences between Edmond and Marie, but because Alice de Valliet was so unwell that she was taken back to Switzerland. As Charles was unable to leave the monastery, Edmond made use of his promised leave to accompany his mother to the sanatorium where she had made a significant recovery in the past. Everyone knew that it would only be a reprieve, but we looked forward to her return for the engagement some time after Easter. The date of the wedding was fixed for the middle of August.

Meanwhile the news of the future marriage of an English king, so successfully blocked by the British press, but given full coverage abroad, exploded on December 1st. Within ten days he had abdicated in favour of his younger brother. At La Chenaie the vagaries of royalty were greeted with a Gallic shrug, while our Franco-Scottish neighbours were too occupied with their own problems to show much concern. On the other hand, my father was infuriated by the instability of French government, which had changed fourteen times between 1932 and 1937, and the passive attitudes in both France and Britain towards Hitler's disregard of the Versailles Treaty and the Locarno Pact. Then there was the sinister growth of totalitarian governments surrounding France, in Spain, Germany and Italy. They were a threat to peace – and thus commerce. There were French and British voices which advocated a firm stand over German reoccupation of the Rhineland, but as I remembered Charles saying, democracies follow national opinion more often than they create it. France and Britain were sick of war, and there was, even in the army, a spirit which favoured strong defence but feared provoking an armed struggle.

It seemed to me that my father and Robert were of one mind in more than business interests. In both of them the warrior and the trader combined to make formidable partners and rivals; each of them looked forward with dread to 1937.

But 1937 was a year of waiting for events in Europe, and one of consolidation in our own lives, which I began to see as a microcosm of western politics. Our Christmas was peaceful, with only Marie fretting in her undemonstrative way about the progress of Alice de Valliet's cure; for me it was a respite from hard work, the demands of chamber music partners, and an emotional limbo between the pull of Edmond's magnetic powers and the encroachment of Robert's. His antagonism to Paul and Tad was an irritation I wanted to forget. It was a relief to walk down to the river, and know that the Ronval people were away, that Paul was in England, Tadeusz in Poland and Robert in Scotland. I doubt if I spared much thought for a novice priest who only saw advantages in the resurgence of Germany, or his local arch-enemy whose ideal was a fictional Russia.

When I returned to Paris in January, the demands of my course were such that I had to beg my friends in the rue de Seine to reduce the work-load. Although both of them had concerto engagements, in Britain and in Paris, Tadeusz still complained about my unwillingness to rehearse, but only to make a point. Paul was more practical.

"A friend of my parents has asked us to give a concert the week after Easter – I know it's some time away but we shall have the holidays to rehearse. Madame Brive has a house with a large music-room and a good piano in Neuilly. Supposing we plan a programme now?"

"Let's hope that Anne is less under the weather by then, and doesn't feel overworked," carped the Pole. I heard echoes of Soeur Antoinette's spoilt-rich-girl litany. "What have you been doing during the holidays apart from resting and eating?"

I looked at Tad's generous waistline and smiled. "I was tired, and I now feel like getting on with playing. There is a *concours* in March. I've got to do well!"

"Did you see Robert?" asked Paul kindly.

"No, the only person I visited was Soeur Antoinette, the nun. She's pleased that I'm playing trios, by the way. Otherwise I had walks down by the river and yes, I did rest and enjoy the good food made by my mother and sister - well, not really my sister, but that's how I think of her."

"Sorry, Anne," said Tad. "I'm worrying about my own mother and sisters. If the Nazis invade Poland – and we all know that they are rebuilding their army and air-force for war – who knows what will happen to them?"

What could I say? Both my father and Robert agreed about the possibility of war, but as for the "all" to which Tad referred, most people refused to countenance it. I was one of them.

The *concours* was successful and the coveted *premier prix* within my reach. Teachers who had advised against involvement with a trio at such an early stage gave it their tacit approval and I looked forward to our first concert. As I saw little of Robert that spring, I began to wonder whether the gap between our values was too wide for us to continue with the friendship. Did he see me as belonging to a decadent Bohemia, which would preserve its own peace at any price, while he wanted to fight for justice?

He rang several times, his voice as cheerful as ever, but his visits to Paris were short, and his schedule so tight that it wasn't until the end of March that he asked me whether we could meet – to sightsee or have a meal together one evening. The date he mentioned made me breathe quickly.

"It would have to be a very late dinner," I said, trying to speak slowly. "We're giving our first trio concert in Neuilly."

"How can I buy a ticket?"

It was typical, straightforward, the direct road through tangles of judgment and defensiveness. "The audience is by invitation, and we are asked to bring one or two friends ourselves. Please do come – I think you will like the programme, Beethoven and Ravel, as well as some solos from each of us. The piece that requires so much practice is the Ravel. It's not much played because you have to work together a lot!"

"Is that a hint that you won't be available before then?" he laughed.

"I shall be very busy. When I was at home two weekends ago I told my parents that I can't go back for the Easter holidays – I have important auditions coming up as well as the concert – but I shall be going down to Quinon for Marie's engagement party the weekend of Ascension, and probably stay on until Whit Monday."

"I am planning to be in Normandy in May too," he said quietly. He paused, and then asked for the address in Neuilly.

"Try to get there early or you won't see anything. Be prepared for a squash – I've played at house concerts before. The salon at La Chenaie is larger than most Paris drawing rooms – and don't expect it to start on time!"

My warnings were justified. A man of six feet four and powerful build needs more space than Mme Brive allowed for her dapper Parisian friends. The atmosphere was suffocating. Fortunately there were no speeches, but we had to wait for some of Mme Brive's more distinguished guests to arrive before we were allowed to start. She had a large living room with alcoves, spread across the *entre-sol*, an area which opened on to a small garden, below the level of the street. Up above was a gallery which could be turned into upstairs rooms, but with the curtains drawn apart, it revealed enough space to make the total audience up to a hundred. They applauded enthusiastically, but Paul and Tadeusz had been so cramped that they had wondered whether they would poke one of the guests in the eye with their bows.

Afterwards, Robert stayed in the background while Mme Brive said good-bye to her friends, and sent us away with strict instructions to play there again. I found Robert at the door. He kissed me and shook Paul and Tadeusz warmly by the hand.

"My congratulations!" he said with such sincerity that I forgot his misgivings. "You are so talented – all of you – that it's a privilege to know you. The Ravel was like a – almost like a symphony – I could hardly believe that there were only three players. And everyone seemed to make the same wonderful sound – I didn't know whether it was the violin or the cello in some passages. Sometimes I looked at Anne's hands – the string pizzicato seemed to come from the piano too!" He stopped, but not in embarrassment, collecting his memory. "That opening is magical – almost oriental, delicate. I shall never forget it!"

Paul and Tad suddenly looked like boys standing side by side, schoolboys given an unexpected treat. They were delighted with praise that was as fresh and unstinting as it was apt and intelligent. There had been a certain stock-in-trade uniformity about the comments of some of the guests. This was real listening, the sort of response that professionals long for.

We all shook hands, and the two figures, the slight Englishman with his violin case slung over his shoulder and the round Pole made even rounder by the cello coffin on his back, disappeared into the metro.

"Now let's go and find something to eat! I'm starving," said Robert.

As I am tall for a woman I always wore flat shoes, as high heels made me tower above Marie. So it was no hardship to walk. Still, I had to keep up with the long strides of my companion, who was used to the pace of my sturdy sightseeing brogues as opposed to light evening slippers. It was crisp and cold. The vigour of our steps kept time with the bustle of Paris by night. The carriages and cars passed at hectic speed, between the bright street lights and the glowing windows beneath red awnings, which invited the passerby to come inside.

Eventually Robert stopped and scrutinised a menu.

"I've been here before! Forgive me, but I could do with a good steak-frites. What about you, Anne? Wouldn't you prefer something more adventurous?"

"I'm hungry too. I could eat almost anything. There is *Escalope de veau*, and what about some warm soup to start? *Soupe à l'oignon?*"

Robert laughed. "Sounds good to me, but it's just as well my brother isn't with us. He hates onions and can't believe that anyone else could like them either!"

We sat down to order. Robert shook his head as if trying to concentrate. "I'm sorry, that opening of the Ravel is still haunting me. I can't get it out of my head, and I didn't have to play all those notes. You must be exhausted!"

I wasn't. I had been marched through Paris after my first trio concert and I felt exhilarated.

The wine arrived. He tasted it and asked the waiter to pour. He looked at me with searching eyes. "You are really talented," he said slowly.

"I would have to be to study at the Conservatoire."

"But it's something more than that. Why do you want to play chamber music? Your solo was amazing."

"So are the solos of all the other pianists – and there are so many of them! But few people play chamber music, partly because everyone wants to be a soloist, partly because that's what we're being trained to do, and partly because it's so difficult to organise rehearsals and concerts. The boys have both played concertos this spring. They too are very busy, and no one knows where their careers are going. I know what you think. But playing with them is a unique opportunity, and one which I shall make the most of, provided I can keep up with the demands of my teachers."

He took my hand in his. "And so you shall! I'll come to every concert I can. Anne, you must forgive me for being an old-fashioned Scotsman."

"You're a soldier and a businessman and you say what you think." The soup arrived, and as I took my first mouthful I realised that we had called each other "*tu*". Who had started it? I think it was Robert, but it may have been me – the British are wary of being forward.

There was a bell ringing. It was muffled and blurred by the flow of the conversation about my career, and about the growth of Cummings and Hay in the French market. But it rang clearer when I got into bed, full of excitement about the concert and about Robert, his physical strength and presence, his humour and enthusiasm. It tuned with the music still humming in the background, it chimed like another bell, a long steady sound that wouldn't identify itself. I was nearly asleep when I realised – it was like the moment when Edmond had lifted me up and called me "*vous*".

Chapter 15 Summer 1937

When Robert rang the flat to say that he would be in Normandy for Ascension, I was surprised. Why should he do business with my father over a long weekend, when he usually made such efforts to be back in Scotland? The solution was simple. Papa wanted to show him a new calvados still. Robert had made contact with Tom Creighton, who was going to Ronval to visit his aunt and meet Edmond's future bride. They had decided to stay at the hotel in Quinon which Robert had found comfortable in the past, but when Alice de Valliet heard of it, she insisted that her nephew and his school friend stay at Ronval. So Robert would climb up to the studio in the hexagonal tower, without a lifetime of wondering what it was like! I fell into a mood bordering on resentment.

On the surface, Robert would be the representative of Cummings and Hay, but more would be inferred by friends and family. It was unfair to Marie and Maman, on whose discretion I could always rely, but I felt cornered, manipulated by Robert – and by a premature crossing of lines which hitherto had been sharply defined and kept apart. My life in Paris was one thing, my home another.

When you are a child you imagine the bliss of freedom, of making your own decisions; but once a child, always a child when confronted with your past. I felt pinned down; and Paris didn't wave its liberating wand, or breathe into my heart that people should follow their own paths. (I still wonder whether Paris isn't like one of the gods or goddesses in Homer, rather spiteful and partisan, but magical and helpful when on your side.)

So I was doomed to seem independent and contented, when inside me a cauldron of emotion seethed. I was ashamed of my demons, of pride, jealousy of Marie and being exposed to gossip. We had always soared above it, or so we thought. After all we were the maire's daughters. I would spend the holiday *pont* – Thursday to Sunday – acting a part, and betraying nothing of what I really felt. The *grand pont* would last until Whit Monday; but for the rest of the holiday, Robert would be back in Scotland, and there would be time for the rest from pressure I craved.

The train trundled into the station at Quinon, and I collected my baggage, mustering as much self-control as I could. Fortunately it was my father who met me. We always had an affinity. He wasn't perceptive like my mother, but I could always – or nearly always – rely on his approbation, entering into the spirit of my plans and pointing out flaws with tact. He was delighted to see me, but his news didn't give me any comfort.

"There are going to be eight or more young people at that party at Ronval – and they've invited your grandparents, so we'll have a full house at La Chenaie too. Even that priest, or monk or whatever he calls himself – the brother who was against the marriage – will be there. He's coming back for the wedding in August, but when he heard that his cousins from Scotland were included, he decided to come for the engagement party too."

Worse and worse – a party at Ronval with Marie and Edmond centre stage, and Charles' pale eyes seeing straight through me, accusing me and my family of putting Marie in Edmond's way. I wondered how perceptive Robert would be, whether he would notice my chagrin. Looking back on it, part of me wanted him to understand, while another part hoped that he would blend with the others and not take too much notice.

"Have you seen Robert Cummings?" I asked, and then wished that I hadn't.

"Grand lad, that one, and no mistake. I think he's taken a shine to you." He patted my lap. "Well, he's impressed by the new still and wants to increase the order for calvados. That shows that he isn't just an insular Scot who only drinks whisky! Mind you, I like his Macallan – high class stuff! *Dis donc*, how's Paris?"

"The chestnuts are out in the Bois de Boulogne. But it's been cold for late spring. How are Maman and Marie?"

"Marie's happier than I've ever seen her. Your mother – well, you can never tell what she's thinking, but she'll be glad to see you."

Marie came running out of the house to greet me. "Oh Anne, I've missed you, especially when you didn't come home for Easter. But it's good of you to come this weekend. It's not that I'm not happy, but La Chenaie isn't complete without you. Mme de Valliet came back from Switzerland last week with Edmond. She's not well enough to organise everything, so I've been up there all morning. Tante Cécile has been helping too." She paused. "I like Robert," she added quietly.

My mother emerged from the kitchen and embraced me warmly. "Come, Anne, it's good to have you home!"

It was true that Maman was inscrutable, but I think that I could guess her feelings better than most. She was still worried about Marie, the fear that she was being thrust into a life with which she wouldn't be able to cope. I could see unease behind Maman's eyes. From a practical point of view there were no problems. My father had seen Mme de Valliet, and given Marie a handsome dowry. Mme de Valliet had given no hint that she considered the connection inferior. And Edmond adored her.

"He calls her '*vous*', Anne," said Maman as soon as we were alone. I smiled, trying to stifle that powerful moment when I had fallen and he had picked me up. "It seems so strange, but that is the way with the old families. At the moment she is overjoyed. He has three weeks leave, before going back to Metz. But she was depressed when you didn't come home for Easter. Of course your father and I understand that you're busy. She needs to be busy too, and there has been no need to call at Ronval since before Christmas. When she wanders out to the tree she just sits there. It reminds me of Hervé. You know that he was unstable before the war; he seemed all right when he came home the first time, but after that he was put in a hospital until the end of the war, because he was witless with shell-shock. It is fortunate that he didn't wander away. They might have shot him for desertion."

"But Marie isn't unstable. Yes, there are moments when she sort of switches off, but they are rare. Most of the time she's more balanced than I am!"

"Anne, you have your moods, but they are on the surface. Marie has always regulated her behaviour to please us, and only retreats when she thinks our heads are turned the other way. She needs to be adapting to some one, and as long as Alice is alive, and she can see Edmond regularly she should be fine. But your father waits daily for more news about Germany, and if there is another conflict, Edmond will be away …"

"Nobody talks like that in Paris. I have a friend who is paranoid about Germans and Jews, but apart from that – well, we beat the Boches last time, *n'est-ce pas?*"

She smiled. "It's refreshing to hear you talk, with all that optimism. Don't be hard on yourself, but you'll have to be busy up at Ronval – there's a lot to do!"

She didn't mention Robert, and I blessed her for it. She had driven away my ill-humour with one sweep of her broom. She was concerned about the present, especially about Marie's vulnerability. If Maman was speculating about Robert and me, she was too wise and focussed to mention it.

We were sitting on the west terrace after lunch, when we heard the noise of voices and barking. A black labrador and cocker spaniel came running up the steps, and greeted Marie with a lot of wagging and panting. There are some people animals instinctively trust, and Marie was one of them. I have often wondered whether it was the animals, the farm cats and cows, that comforted her as a child when she couldn't rely on her father, and her mother was too ill to look after her. A party of three men emerged from the trees behind the house, and my mother went down the steps to ask them to join us for coffee.

We all shook hands with Edmond, who introduced us to his cousin Thomas. He was fairer and taller than Edmond, though not as tall as Robert, with the classical features and high cheek bones that I admired in his aunt. His build was also slight, but, I suspected, strong and athletic. Lieutenant Creighton was a Seaforth Highlander; Robert a Gordon Highlander. Edmond's military persona was something I blocked from my mind. What right had he to paint like a professional, interpret Chopin better than most concert pianists, and be a soldier too? I couldn't imagine him in a képi any more than I could imagine the others in a kilt. I wouldn't have to wait long to see either.

Edmond sat beside Marie, facing Robert and Thomas with me between them. We had our backs to the sun and I was able to observe Edmond and Marie together, their quiet manner hiding deep admiration on his side while Marie tingled with joy. She said little, but every gesture betrayed her happiness. I couldn't be jealous – I had given so little to her, and taken so much for granted. She deserved to be Mme de Valliet; my independence and determination fitted me for the rough and tumble of the life of a professional musician.

"You must miss Normandy when you are in Paris," said Thomas in faltering French.

"I am very busy in Paris, but I think of La Chenaie as a haven from the stress of concerts and competitions. When did you arrive from Scotland?" I spoke slowly and his eyes warmed with recognition – of both my words and the effort to help him understand.

"We took the ferry from Newhaven to Dieppe on Tuesday, and

have been guests of Edmond and his mother ever since," interrupted Robert. "There will be a large party arriving tomorrow, including Tom's sisters and Charles."

I turned back to Thomas. "Your sisters are coming from Scotland too?"

"No, one is in London and the other is travelling from Switzerland where she has spent three weeks with a school friend."

The conversation became general and it was decided that we should walk through the woods of La Chenaie. My father was talking about 'la chasse'. There was plenty to shoot in the wood, but I could see Marie recoil from the idea of killing the descendants of the rabbits and foxes she had watched as a child. I have never seen anyone get as near a rabbit as Marie.

The narrowness of the path which led to the tree, made the party break up into pairs and I found myself beside Robert.

"Aren't you pleased to see me, Anne?"

"Yes," I said truthfully, "but I associate you with the Champ de Mars and the left bank of the Seine, not walking through the wood at La Chenaie to this old tree. It's where we had a swing when we were children." Raising my voice I said "We once hid inside the trunk from two boys who were poaching rabbits."

"And when they came back the next day, they found a red-headed Horatio defending the bridge," laughed Edmond. "That was the last time I ever came here to shoot rabbits."

"Well, now you can shoot as many as you like – if Marie doesn't mind!"

The tree looked more gnarled than ever. I remembered how my mother said that it was a symbol of the friendship between Marie and me. It was our innocence; it had widened our horizons in more ways than one. Far above the trees we had been able to see the world spread out like a carpet, a world with fields and farms and the tower of Ronval beckoning in the distance; it was here that imagination had been planted like a seed, and where, unknowing, we had shared the richness of childhood. One day the tree would keel over in a storm, but not until Normandy had been devastated by war, and it had served other purposes.

We walked slowly down to the river which was swollen by recent rain. The blossom in the orchard was past its best and I felt a pang that I had missed it for the last two years. Even Paris has no magic like apple blossom in spring, the white tinged with pink and the promise of apples in the autumn. The buds had begun to flower that early morning when we defended the bridge. I sighed. Soon the poacher would take his prize to Ronval.

Chapter 16 Summer 1937

I remember the engagement party for several reasons, not all of them festive. It was my first experience of Scottish Country Dancing, and I took to it like a duck to water. It is elegance and exercise, complex and exhilarating, with the rhythmic symmetry of German folk-song, the clear geometric multiple of four bars. It is danced on the toe, unlike most country dancing which is earth-bound, recalling the threshing and treading of the harvest on thudding heels. Scottish dancing is light and airy. You have to keep your wits about you; the banshee who inspired it didn't suffer fools gladly.

The first thing that struck me was that nearly everyone was speaking English. Marie had been reading and practising with Maman and Mamie, as well as my grandfather, who read her passages from *Treasure Island*, which he had enjoyed as a boy. But everyone tried to speak French to us in a way that was touching, and we in turn joined in the English conversation. There were ten young people, ourselves, the Creightons, the de Valliets and two schoolfriends of Edmond's, as well as my parents, grandparents and Alice de Valliet, who didn't dance, but played the reels seated at a chair with a back, and supported by soft cushions. When she tired I took over, much relieved to play rather than concentrate on another complex formation. My mother courageously took my place, as there was a shortage of girls; she had some experience of the eightsome reel when she was a girl. It came back more quickly than she realised. Even my grandmother danced "The Duke of Edinburgh" with Charles, who seemed to forget his hauteur, invigorated by the movement, and happy in his home surroundings.

Marie picked up the dances very quickly. She moved with the same grace with which she swam and ran, her narrow feet weaving through the water or bouncing over the ground like an otter or hare. She danced with Edmond as though they had always been partners, and by the time it was her turn to be in the middle of the set, she had mastered the pas de bas with the poise of Veronica Creighton. If you really can control the pas de bas, the feet move but the body stays erect, only swaying slightly like a birch in a gentle breeze.

I liked Veronica and Elizabeth as much as their brother, both slim like Tom, neither of them really pretty, although their faces were animated and their dancing so assured that they were able to steer us through the complicated formations with little fuss, while concentrating on their own moves. They spoke quite good French, as they had been to finishing school in Switzerland. I think they were a little envious of Marie too, as Edmond was a favourite. Before I relieved Alice at the piano I danced with both Tom and Robert, recognising in each the characteristics of fine British officers, self control and good manners, reflecting inner confidence and good will. It took me some time to get used to seeing them in kilts.

Perhaps I should have started with the kilts, but the dancing was the most vivid memory. The only people not wearing one were my father and grandfather; even Charles wore a kilt, making him appear less, not more, self-conscious than usual. The people who were really astonished were the maids from La Chenaie who had come over to help. I wondered what they would say to their friends. But the dancing made sense of the kilt, and by the end of the evening I was thinking of the Greeks who considered Persian trousers effeminate. You have to be a man to carry a kilt.

The evening was warm, and we all went out on to the grass for air and refreshment. I found myself talking to Charles, who took me aside in a way that was warmer than I expected.

"I hope that you are pleased to see your friend looking so well, Mademoiselle Anne," he said.

"And your brother too."

"I will admit that I was opposed to the marriage to begin with, but I can see why he admires Mademoiselle Marie. I hope that they will find fulfilment in one another. No one knows her better than you do."

"She is one of the kindest and most obliging people imaginable. She will do everything to promote his happiness. She has been a wonderful friend to me."

"There is one thing that worries me; I wonder to what extent her early experiences have affected her. Your mother, your grandparents and the nuns have had a remarkable influence, but it's impossible to eradicate the past – especially the years of early childhood. The Jesuits say 'Give us a child until he is seven, and he will be saved'."

"Marie was brought up and loved by her mother only until she was nearly two. When her father was sent home at the end of the war he was a stranger to her. I think she was frightened of him." I could see that he was genuinely concerned, and I had my mother's presentiments in my mind. But I couldn't be disloyal to Marie. I said something that I had often thought. "Marie's sufferings have made her resigned – they haven't strengthened her, but she will always respond to the needs of those around her."

"So long as all is well she will cope – is that what you're saying?"

I didn't like the tone of his voice.

"I think that Marie will always act in the best interests of those she loves."

Charles pulled himself up to his full aristocratic height. It was as though a ghost from the *ancien régime* were speaking. "She will take my mother's place. She must aspire to that dignity. My mother has always been worthy of the name de Valliet, in spite of her non-Catholic background. She comes from a very old Scottish family."

"Marie is a Catholic. She is a fine artist. Your mother is a distinguished musician. I can't alter Marie's family background. The crucial thing is that she was loved by her mother until she died. After that she was as much loved by my parents as I was."

"I hope that the influence of your mother was the stronger."

I was furious. "You cannot be unaware of how generous my father has been – not only the dowry which we all want her to have, but offering her all the advantages that he gave me. It was she who didn't want to come to Paris to study art."

Charles sighed, and relaxed. "Forgive me, Mlle Anne." It was said with such sincerity that my anger evaporated. "Your father has indeed been generous. I happen to know that he was also very kind to Marie's father – he may well have saved his life. I came across a letter from my father to my mother – she showed it to me. He asked her to care for the Millet family in his absence." It was then that I learnt the story of Hervé being tried for desertion, and how Papa had pleaded on his behalf.

"My mother did look after them. She tried to make life easier for Mme Millet and she took care of her daughter's early schooling. It wasn't nearly as much as your parents did, but it was kindly done. You can see how much she likes Mlle Marie. If she has any reservations she has never expressed them." He stopped and looked at me earnestly. "I had always hoped – you are so strong, and you share my mother's great talent. You know that she hardly ever played again after she heard that her brother had been killed."

I understood. It was my turn to sigh. "I have found another life in Paris."

"Would you play to us? I know my mother would like it."

"Only if it's what the guests would want."

"They won't mind – but I'm speaking for my mother and my brother, and me."

"Won't it be difficult to go back to the dancing if I play Beethoven? I wouldn't play Chopin in front of your brother. I think his B flat minor Nocturne is the most natural and beautiful I have heard."

Charles moved towards his mother, who was talking to my grandparents. I thought of the lunch party when they first met, of the Mozart duet which had tortured my right arm, and the Invention and Arabesques.

"Please do, Anne," said Alice de Valliet. She stood up slowly to address the guests; my grandfather helped her, offering his arm. "I should like Anne to play something. You can dance again afterwards."

I walked to the Blüthner – the piano Edmond had played when first we visited Ronval. Then I thought of meeting Robert in the Champ de Mars, of how Paris had brought us together; of the city like a Greek goddess, sometimes capricious and sometimes kindly. That day op109 had eluded me, and it was as though mastering it were her gift. It's one of my favourites; it's not heroic and outrageous like 106, or sublimely adventurous like 110, or serenely valedictory like the arioso of 111. 109 is human, lyrical, the opening gentle, the outbursts like a cry for help, the middle movement almost warlike in its vigour, and the slow theme and variations of the last movement searching deep into the soul of humanity.

Afterwards, Edmond, aware of his duties as host, sat at the piano and started to play a Strathspey, a slow stately rhythm – an andante as opposed to the driven pace of the reels. Robert, Veronica, Tom and Elizabeth came to the floor while the rest of us stood back and watched. The Foursome is much less well known than the Eightsome, but it is a beautiful spectacle when the dancers are experienced. I stood spellbound, admiring not only the performers, but the skilful way Edmond had restored the party atmosphere.

There was a supper and more dancing before my parents and grandparents left in my father's car. He had enjoyed most of the evening. It took him time to accustom himself to the kilts, although he told me that he was relieved that "the priest hasn't appeared looking like a scarecrow. You fight in a kilt, you argue in a cassock," he added. All the same he strolled out on to the grass for another glass of wine more often than my mother would have liked. At two o'clock she took him and my grandparents home, insisting that Robert drive the car. Mme de Valliet had already retired and we sat talking. The plan was that those who were not too tired should walk back to La Chenaie at dawn for breakfast.

Robert returned breathless and alarmed. "There's someone out there. I was followed all the way back from the bridge. I've a good torch and plenty of field skills. I should have taken your parents' car, Anne, but the night is fine and I enjoyed the exercise. Now I'm worried about your parents and grandparents too. Why don't you both stay here with your mother," he said, looking at Charles and Edmond, "and Thomas and I can go back with Anne and Marie in your car?"

We went out to find the car, but it wouldn't start. It was a question of walking now or waiting until dawn as we had planned. It was better to wait, but I had plenty of time to worry about my parents, realising how isolated and unprotected they were when I was in Paris. There was no telephone, no means of calling for help. Soon Marie would be at Ronval. I had never given much thought to danger before. I kept going out on to the grass looking towards the east – away from La Chenaie which lay to the west of Ronval, searching the horizon for a glimmer of light. When dawn came, Robert and Edmond took us back. We gave them a good breakfast, insisting that they rest before they walked home.

There was no more sign of the prowler, but Papa started talking in earnest about setting up telegraphic communications in the area. After all, there was a telephone in the Mairie.

I decided to take the longer break, and rang the Conservatoire to make my excuses. I was beginning to wonder if Robert had been imagining things – Edmond's car started perfectly well the next day – but I had an encounter on Tuesday after Ascension which made me realise what had probably happened. In some ways it calmed my fears, but it also made me wary.

I had gone into Quinon with my father, intending to shop for Maman who was tired after all the exertions for the party and the worry about the prowler. Having filled the car with provisions, I called at the convent to see Soeur Antoinette. She chided me for not being at the Conservatoire, but when she heard the reason changed her tune and implied that I had a fine time in Paris while my parents lived in fear of intruders. Bit by bit I guided her back towards reason, via Mme de Valliet, Beethoven and Marie's engagement; and she was finally pacified by the thought of having a telephone in the convent. (I didn't ask her whether she would have dispensation to use it.)

I left her in a good mood and walked out into the market square where Jean Belliot was propping his bicycle up against a wall. He turned and said with his usual mocking smile, "So you have had a prowler, Mlle Anne?"

"Yes. We were all frightened. We thought at first that someone had tampered with M. de Valliet's car."

"The seigneur should take good care of his car – especially now that he will have a beautiful wife. And what about you? Will you marry a man in a skirt?"

I was furious. "The kilt is what Scottish soldiers wear. It's not a skirt, and I am not marrying anyone!"

"It doesn't stop them running fast whatever it's called."

I stared at him. If I accused him of doing anything to Edmond's car he would deny it and there was no proof. He was my father's trusted tenant farmer. He worked hard and he gave my parents a good return on their land. I decided to say nothing, but I felt sure that he had been jealously skulking outside while we were celebrating Marie's engagement. It's quite possible that he had tampered with the car and then quietly mended it, satisfied that he had spoilt the end of the party. He knew everything about farm machinery – what little there was in those days – he looked after my father's car, and sometimes drove for him.

I waited outside the Mairie, wondering how many people felt uneasy about Marie's engagement.

Chapter 17 Summer 1937 – 1938

There were no unpleasant incidents at the wedding in August, no ill omens for the future. My mother said nothing to me about her fears, more Creighton cousins arrived with Veronica and Elizabeth who joined me as bridesmaids, The curé conducted the Mass and Mme de Valliet was well enough to enjoy the whole day. Jean Belliot made a token gesture of acceptance when he raised his glass with a cheer at the *Vin d'honneur*, which my father arranged for the people of Quinon in the square outside the Mairie. The civil service was conducted by the maire himself, full of his importance and basking in his generosity. He even managed to say something friendly to Charles, in spite of the cassock.

It was the first time I had ever seen Edmond in uniform. Capitaine de Valliet had invited several of his fellow officers to his wedding; they all looked imposing if not as handsome and dashing as the groom. I was not usually prone to reflection, like my father who was content to live in the present and plan for tomorrow, but I did wonder whether the uniforms brought back memories and heightened forebodings that he would rather forget. It was the contrast between the healthy well-bred officers and the wreck of a common soldier, gazing witless at Marie during her early years that struck me most. I had seen Hervé Millet once or twice. A vacant mind disfigures the human face almost as much as an injury. Hervé had only died the year before, but my parents decided that Marie shouldn't visit him in the asylum. To his credit my father did so regularly.

If my father was able to shelve his fears amid the toasts and cheers, the uniforms jolted my own insouciance into a sense of reality. France needed an army. Perhaps Robert's warnings had penetrated my mind. Like most French people, I thought that having conquered the Germans at great cost to ourselves, we should now enjoy the exciting possibilities and innovations that science was offering – as well as improving social conditions, without major upheaval. I had learned to drive my father's car, ugly telegraph wires were beginning to make our Norman villages look messy, radio and recording offered opportunities for performing to a wider audience. The last thing we wanted to think of was war. Of course people talked endlessly about communism and fascism – which was the more evil? Most of us looked upon communism as a caricature of the ideals of our own revolution. My father, more critical and less inclined to be philosophical, was aware of the communist groups in Normandy, to one of which Bernard Piot belonged. I don't think that he realised that Jean was a member, partly because he didn't want him to be. He liked Jean Belliot. He also continued to like Bernard.

To a man of the church like Charles communism was the work of the devil, the most evil thing (apart from the revolution, the separation of church and state, and suppression of the aristocracy) that the world had ever known. He may have been right, but I wonder whether he was aware of the Nazi persecution of the Jews which so frightened Tadeusz. Whether Charles had any suspicions or not, none of us could have foreseen the industrial slaughter of man, woman and child that would stain the near future.

After the wedding I returned to my life in Paris, self-absorbed and more ambitious than ever. I achieved my *premier prix* and started thinking of life beyond the Conservatoire. As Alfred Cortot was teaching at the Ecole Normale, I left the Conservatoire to study with him – one of the few pianists I have ever heard who could interpret Chopin. That year with Cortot, 1938/1939, so ominous in retrospect, was one of the most stimulating of my life.

I continued to see Robert, and in time we became lovers. It all happened so gradually that I seemed to be in the middle of a love affair before I realized that it had started. It was probably the loss of

Marie that made me want to reach out for something deeper in my life, for human contact and fulfilment. Robert was very attractive. I had to stretch up on to my toes to kiss him, and his hands were so long and strong that if they strayed across my back they seemed to enfold it.

He lightened dull moments with flashes of humour, and taught me to be philosophical about setbacks. "Always treat problems as opportunities! Sometimes it's difficult to see beyond your frustration, but there's always a lesson to be learned!" he would say. If you are ambitious, you attract setbacks like bees buzzing round highly coloured flowers in search of pollen.

It might have started in one of those Paris storms when the rain comes down in sheets, and the water rebounds on the street like pebbles tossed across the surface of a lake. If you get caught you are drenched, but you know that it's coming when the day becomes dark violet, and a whispering breeze grows into an angry murmur. Everyone rushes for the cafés, and you wait for the first clap of thunder, the lightning flash, and then the heaving water unleashed from above. Robert and I were caught walking in the Champ de Mars. We ran towards rue de la Motte Picquet, and walked up to my flat leaving pools of water on the stairs.

The only thing to do was to take off our sodden clothes, and have a bath. I emerged covered in a towel, my hair washed and tousled. He took the towel gently; then we became locked in our own storm, and, in the peace which comes after love, he asked me to marry him; but I was undecided.

Few people questioned our relationship in Paris, and we told no one in Normandy and Scotland. Robert kept asking me to marry him, but I wanted to be free – and I was to a certain extent; but I now know that freedom is comparative, that a love affair is another kind of bondage, one with self-imposed rules about loyalty and a future which is always obscure. Of course life has changed since then, but I don't think people are any happier – we flounder in uncertainty and the future is murkier than ever.

I had grown to love Robert and I made myself forget Edmond. It wasn't difficult because I went home less and less, as opportunities for giving concerts with the trio were found in England, where Paul's parents had influential friends. 1937 merged quickly into 1938. Robert talked more and more insistently about weekends with the Gordon Highlanders and fighting for his country in case of war. I felt that I had scored a point when Chamberlain came back from Munich at the end of September. Robert was less hopeful; he was ashamed of the price that was being paid for peace.

"Chamberlain's bargaining for time," said Robert one morning. His visits were short, but as frequent as he could make them; the colonel of his regiment knew that he had business in Paris.

"They are trying to catch up with arms manufacture, but it's been neglected. Recent governments have been concerned about social deprivation – and with the depression it's easily understood. But our tanks are rusty and outdated, and so is the army attitude. I've heard of one old colonel who says that a cavalry charge on horseback still has its place in battle!"

"Poor horses! They wouldn't have much chance against a tank! What about aeroplanes? Isn't that the safest way to fight – up there in the sky?"

"Not if you're being chased by another plane! A lot depends on the quality of the machines – as well as the experience of the pilots. If they are caught, the plane burns like an inferno – the lucky pilots manage to bail out with a parachute!"

"I wouldn't like to jump out of the sky!"

"Let's hope you don't have to."

"What about you?"

"It's unlikely. There are paratroopers and airborne divisions specially trained for parachute jumps – like jumping off a fourteen foot wall, I'm told."

"That sounds even more dangerous than falling off a horse!" I sighed. "Ever since I've known you, you have been talking about war. Even the first time I met you at the house concert at La Chenaie you spoke of the army as part of your life. I still can't believe that France and Britain would want to repeat the events of twenty years ago."

"It won't be a repeat! That's what's wrong with the army in both countries, imagining how they could restage the last war with fewer casualties. Another war would be much worse – unless we face reality now! We've pledged ourselves – and the French too – if Hitler invades Poland. I very much doubt if Chamberlain trusts him an inch." His voice became more insistent. "When war does break out, my battalion will join a territorial division, and I shall fight for my country. I can't do anything else. But I want to be married by then, and I shall want to know where you are. It would be the only security I'd have."

I frowned. "I want to stay here and finish my two years with Cortot. I can't just give up because you believe in a war that most of the French don't think will happen. Anyway, France is well defended. Aren't people talking about the invincible Maginot Line north of the Vosges?"

"It certainly seems invincible, but again it's a question of time and science – which side has the most up-to-date machines, and the strongest morale."

"France must have the best machines. We've always been interested in inventions."

"But the French have neglected their army as much as we have. Nobody wants war, so no one wants to think about it." He sighed with exasperation. "I meant what I said about marrying you."

"And I want to stay here and work! I know that seeing each other from time to time isn't ideal, but I've a good chance of having a career, and the best place for me to be is Paris. Anyway I'm still a student. I had a wonderful lesson with Cortot yesterday. When he plays I am reminded of Edmond: of course technically there is no comparison, but they both understand Chopin, and make it sound flowing and natural, unlike the business-like performances of so many professionals. Chopin's music is so elusive."

"Why won't you see reason, Anne? Heaven knows what is going to happen, but I sense that you might be a little safer in Scotland than here. In the last war with Germany they nearly reached Paris."

"And what would I do in Scotland? Play chamber music with the local amateurs – after working with Paul and Tadeusz?"

"If the Germans invaded France, Tadeusz would be in great danger – he knows it, because he said so himself." Tadeusz had gone back to Poland that summer of 1938 and been stopped by unpleasant guards on the way back through Germany. He was more worried about his family than ever, and I was slowly beginning to realise that his fears were justified.

"Please let me finish this year with Cortot. I'm going to give two trio recitals in London at the end of this term. Paul and Tad are freelance musicians – at the moment Paul is leading an orchestra in Switzerland, and Tad is playing concertos – one in Aberdeen. They come back in November, and we are planning some new programmes."

"Anne, I want you to meet my family. I want you to be part of it. My brother is a rather old-fashioned doctor, but my mother is an educated woman with a broad outlook – she regrets not having had a career in medicine. She would appreciate your professionalism and independence."

I paused. I didn't want to marry anyone but Robert – not now that Edmond had married Marie – and I felt safe with him. Married women with careers become used to compromises and juggling with priorities, but I disliked compromise. "I want to do one thing at a time. Let me finish this year. Can't we get married in July?"

"It might be too late," he said quietly.

"Surely not! We must both hope that it isn't."

Chapter 18 Christmas 1938 – 1939

In February 1939 Alice de Valliet died. I had been home for Christmas and seen Marie at Ronval looking after her mother-in-law, as she had tried as a small child to care for her own mother. She looked pale and drawn. I urged her to spend a few days with me, and allow my mother to nurse Mme de Valliet. She agreed reluctantly after Edmond returned to the army at New Year.

"I see so little of Edmond," she said. "He's always in Metz and I am only sometimes allowed to join him. Every time we meet I feel we have to get to know each other, and just as we are beginning to relax I have to come back here. But Alice has been wonderful. I know she's ill, but she has so much strength and wisdom, and I am happy looking after her. Charles has been home too. He's kinder than you think, Anne – and he's glad I'm looking after his mother. And he's so helpful. A priest or a monk is always a protector and friend – even when he's stern. It must be comforting to Alice that her son is in the church. She has finally become a Catholic – it was such a happy day."

"You need rest, Marie. Nursing the sick is always tiring."

"What I dread most is losing her; being alone at Ronval, with no one to look after. I wish I could see more of Edmond."

"Have you had a holiday since your honeymoon?"

"Not really. He's always in demand. And when he's free he wants to be here with his mother."

"I understand. Do you have time to paint?"

"I go up to the tower and take out my paints, but somehow I feel lost. It's not the same as when we were girls." She paused. "I miss you," she said, and added "I shall miss you more when the end finally comes. You're so strong. I have always loved being with you – I need to be with someone strong like you or Edmond. Even Alice is stronger than me."

After the funeral I knew that she shouldn't be alone at Ronval, and we persuaded Edmond to bring her to La Chenaie, where we made her comfortable in the room which we shared as girls. Edmond promised her that they would have ten days' holiday in the south of France at Easter.

She lay on the divan in our salon, and we sat quietly with her. It was then that I saw what my mother had mentioned, her eyes go blank as if she were detaching herself from a life which was too painful to bear. I would rouse her with conversation and she would respond to begin with, then lapse into silence. When I knew I should tear myself away to go back to Paris, she clung to me. "Don't go, stay with me, Anne. Don't go." I made excuses at the Ecole Normale, but I had a concert to give and eventually I left. My mother did everything to comfort her, and bit by bit she regained strength, looking forward to her holiday with Edmond.

When she returned in happy spirits at the end of April I told her that I was going to marry Robert in July. It gave her something to focus her thoughts, something to look forward to.

"I have always liked him," she said, "but where are you going to live?"

"We haven't yet decided. He's afraid of the outbreak of war and wants me to be in Scotland, but I want to stay in Paris. I'm not making any decisions until my course is over."

"It would be very strange not to go where your husband decides,

Anne. I think that Edmond is afraid that there will be a war too. It's one of the reasons he's so busy."

"Oh, Marie! Robert and I have been arguing about it – almost from the moment we first met in Paris – but I still tell him he's exaggerating. Think of the people who were killed in the last war!"

"I don't want you to go to Scotland, Anne, but you must obey your husband. Wives have to."

"Marie, I'm going to have a career, war or no war!"

"I wonder what Tante Cécile thinks?"

So did I. My mother had followed her heart and disobeyed her parents, but she had been an excellent wife to my father. His views were distinct. He also was afraid that there would be war. He wanted me to go to Scotland, and to take with me the title deeds of the properties in Normandy and the south of France, as well as papers concerning shares and investments. But he wasn't going to bully me. Both my parents admired my independence and were unwilling to interfere.

But Robert grew more insistent and we had several more rows.

"You talk as though France were going to be invaded! It's ridiculous."

"If you stay here I shall hardly see you. You will be my wife!"

"If, as you say there is going to be a war, and you join your Scottish Division, I won't see you anyway. Poor Marie hardly sees her husband. I might as well be doing something, not just housekeeping in Scotland. Robert, I'm going to work whatever happens! Our trio has been invited to make a recording in October."

"October! Heaven knows what will have happened by then!"

"You sound as though the world were going to end. I don't believe it, and neither do most of the French."

We reached a compromise and decided to take a house in London, while I could still make use of my parents' flat in Paris. I had set my heart on the recording, and wouldn't countenance the talk about war, although I know I was wilfully deceiving myself. We found a small house in Wimbledon, famous for tennis, but also the home of many musicians, including Paul's parents. It would be my home, on and off, for nearly five eventful years, years that would sweep away my youth, and with it faces and places that were part of its kindly panorama, devouring the good and the brave with the flawed and the cowardly.

We were married with all the splendour that the maire could afford, toned down by the good taste of his wife, who persuaded the curé to conduct the church ceremony with coherence and authority in front of a man who terrified him. (I don't think that bottles of absinthe helped.) As Edmond was coming back for the wedding, Marie was doubly excited. She moved back to Ronval to make preparations for his arrival. Relations from Scotland poured into the hotel in the market place at Quinon, and we received Robert's mother at La Chenaie. I had met her in London in April and found her as perceptive and welcoming as Robert had described. I couldn't say as much for Dr Hugh and his wife, who wore an expression of xenophobic suspicion throughout the day. Betty Cummings was an ardent Presbyterian who refused to come to the church ceremony. Her husband disliked "fancy food". Neither of them made any attempt to speak French, whereas grey-haired Emily did everything she could to help my mother with the preparations, speaking slowly and grammatically, and remembering her school-girl French with dignity and amusement at her mistakes. My grandparents spoke to her in English.

Most of the details have faded from my memory, but I remember overhearing a conversation the night before my wedding, which chilled me at the time, and later helped me to understand what happened to our community in the war years – and the wider sphere of national life. The whole family party, except for Hugh and Betty, was gathered at La Chenaie. My mother and Marie were talking to Emily, who was laughing and wading into a deeper topic than her vocabulary could cover. Marie, recognising another intelligent Scotswoman, was taking trouble to explain, fetching a dictionary, and thoroughly enjoying being useful. Edmond and Robert were talking to my father. I walked down the steps into the night air, musing that tomorrow I would only be Anne Favoret when I gave concerts. Soon I would have a British passport. I would leave the corner of the world I loved most – even more than Paris.

I heard voices in the wood and walked towards them, not out of curiosity, but because I was distracted. They stopped. There was nothing conspiratorial about them. The conversation was earnest, not secretive or frightened. I instantly recognised Jean Belliot and Bernard Piot.

"Thousands have disappeared," said Bernard.

"So it isn't just the Jews."

"They've always hated the communists and the trade unionists; other minorities too. I have contact with cells in Germany and Austria. In the week after the Anschluss thousands were rounded up."

"And now Czechoslovakia. They weren't content with the Sudetenland. Where do they take them?"

"Concentration camps. They don't live very long."

"The same will happen here if they come."

"It's more likely than not. We've got to be ready, but we've got to be patient. Let the Nazis and the capitalists fight it out, and when it's all over, we communists will rule France. Real democracy – real equality, state farms like the Soviet Union. Our party is well organized, but we need to be brave too. Bad times are ahead, *mon vieux*. We need intelligent operators like you, whether there's peace or war. Our leaders are afraid of war, and if they let the Nazis in, they may take advantage of National Socialism to destroy us. That is when we will have to go underground." They walked on and I heard no more.

It made me realise several things. Tadeusz was not paranoid. He had gone back to Poland that summer to visit his family. He never saw them again. And Robert was right about the coming war, but the issues weren't clear. I had always known that Jean and Bernard were communists, or at least Bernard was, with Jean taking advantage of association with a political party. They threatened to leave France defenceless so that they could change her. I returned to La Chenaie, my head spinning, wondering what to think. I almost envied Charles the moral and doctrinal certainty that would persuade his mother to join the Catholic Church when she was dying.

Chapter 19 Summer and Autumn 1939

A snake sheds its skin naturally, discarding the old one as easily as we throw away old clothes, forgetting their significance, the special occasions or humdrum tasks for which we wore them. But I had done something more dramatic than shed a skin, an outer layer, which is a natural process. The rite of passage from a rural childhood, and the years as a music student in Paris to womanhood, was marked by a change of passport. I was the wife of a British army officer in the Gordon Highlanders. Nothing would be forgotten, but nothing could be retrieved as it was. An idyll had passed; a new life had begun.

The memory of that summer is a blur of beautiful highland scenery in Loch Torridan, a visit to Lechen where we had a royal welcome from Emily Cummings – and terrible British food. One night in a Scottish hotel was enough. We found a cottage through the help of the Creightons where amenities were no more primitive than in Normandy where, before the war, we had had no gas or electricity, and water was heated by a stove which had to be lit every day. An old Scotswoman with intelligent eyes and slow clear Highland speech looked after us. I cooked with wine and bought fresh vegetables when I could. Meat is never a problem in Scotland, nor is fish, although the choice is limited, but I have always sighed when people like Hugh boast that the Scots beef is so fine that it doesn't need to be prepared with anything other than potatoes.

I made plans for our little house in Wimbledon. There would be herbs in the garden, every vegetable that I could cultivate, and a stock of good wine (and whisky for Robert – whisky is part of the

Scotsman's daily ritual) in the small cupboard under the stairs. The house was tiny by comparison with La Chenaie or the magnificent Scottish house where Robert had grown up, but I wanted to work, not to socialise. I was now convinced that hard times were ahead, that a large garden would be more useful than a large house. As soon as we got back to London, I engaged a gardener and set about preparing the soil for planting in the spring.

Robert gave me a Bechstein piano as a wedding present and I loved it for many reasons. It was German. It reminded me that whatever happened, you could never eradicate the wonderful legacy that German musicians have given us. No! The best German is not a dead German. The best German is J. S. Bach, and he is as alive today in the recordings of Andras Schiff as he was in the playing and teaching of Edwin Fischer. I made a point of playing Bach every day that I was at home during that terrible war. I memorised most of the Preludes and Fugues from the Forty-Eight, and every night of the blitz, I thought how the real greatness of Germany would never be blotted out by bombs and tyrants. When I shed the French skin of my youth I put on a tougher one – it was only British on the surface. It may seem far-fetched, but in the horror of war I became a European. Europe is where my culture is rooted. Every bomb emphasised it, making me all the more determined to find and express all that is best in our European heritage, from Burns' love of man and nature (who else could address a poem of compassion to a mouse?) to the Preludes of Chopin and the delicate shades and geometric perfection of Piero Della Francesca.

And I loved my piano because it was Robert's recognition of his wife as a musician, not a useful appendage, the "other half" of a respected army officer. You mustn't misunderstand me! I may have been confused about the issues of the war on the eve of my wedding, but I never doubted that the two soldiers of my story were fighting for the best of motives. It was not just for the defence of France and Britain, but for all that makes life worth while. I was proud that my husband was a soldier, but he was also proud of me.

We were in a ferment of anticipation the first weekend of

September, listening to the wireless and waiting for the inevitable. Would Hitler be deterred from entering Poland by British and French threats? On Sunday, we went to the morning service in Westminster Abbey. Listening to the choir reminded me of Paul, the exquisite tuning and perfect togetherness of each phrase ending. In the measured English voices I heard the tones of Alice, Edmond and Charles. My thoughts strayed from London to Paris and then back again. I thought of visiting the Basilica of St Denis when I first knew Robert, and then of the coronation of our Norman Duke William here in the Abbey after his brutal invasion, and the following imposition of French culture on a Saxon civilisation. Such a mesh of wars, treaties and upheavals had marked the succession of kings and governments in Europe! Would this be any different?

The service was interrupted. France and Britain were at war with Germany. We had kept our pledge with Tadeusz's beloved Poland. I thought of Chopin, of Cortot and Edmond's B flat minor Nocturne. And then all reverie was driven out by a sound like a crash of thunder as the organ played Bach.

War was declared on the 3rd, and on the 4th, Robert took the train to join his regiment at Bucksburn, not far from his home town, where an old and experienced manager of Cummings and Hay was entrusted with the war-time running of the firm. I stayed in Wimbledon preparing for my return to France to record the Trio by Ravel and the sonatas for violin and cello by Debussy.

The British began to ship soldiers and armaments immediately to Cherbourg, Nantes and St Nazaire, so as to avoid enemy air attack; but as no such attack occurred during the winter months, soldiers were sent to nearer northern ports. In October I crossed the channel from Newhaven, in a boat full of soldiers laughing and joking and exchanging cigarettes, but when we arrived there was no cheering or welcome in Dieppe. The Normans didn't want this war; in Paris it was hardly mentioned. I had other things to do. For three weeks I suspended reflection as I prepared for the recording.

It was gruelling. Recording in those days was both haphazard and frustrating. There was none of the bar-by-bar editing of today. A perfect performance could be ruined by technical errors in the machines; they in turn behaved impeccably when there were wrong notes or faulty balance from the players. To make everything go well at the same time seemed impossible. There were frayed nerves, angry silences and outbursts – especially from Tadeusz – before we were finished. Even Paul's sang-froid risked rising a degree or two.

"You played that wrong last time, Anne." (Tadeusz.)

"No, last time it was the microphone."

"We've got to get the music absolutely right each time – just in case that cretin knows what to do with his infernal machines."

"Calm down, Tad. We've been playing for two hours. Let's have a break." (Paul)

"You British have no staying power, and the French always make mistakes. Look at their scores – littered with errors!"

By this time the technician had stalked out and I had to smooth things over.

"He's worried about his family," I told him. "I know you're doing your best. And we're all tired, including you."

"*Sale Juif* – filthy Jew," he replied under his breath. I was shocked. This was France. "They think they know everything."

I eventually had the recording made into a CD so as to avoid all the stops, as you didn't get much into one side of a 78, and even then, you had to speed up or slow down so as to have breaks in convenient places. When I listen to it, I recognise the quality of each player. Paul had that wonderful British precision. You can feel his mind searching right down to the bass of the harmony and reaching up to the top of each phrase. My part is good. There was a Favoret tenacity about my practice, and I was probably more concerned about accuracy than many pianists before the Second World War. But Tadeusz's playing is in another league. He despised sentimentality because he had a well of inner warmth which he was always trying to control, unlike his temper. The sheer beauty of the cello sound and the natural flow of his phrasing and rubato make me realise why I was prepared to endure his volatility, and why Paul loved him.

"Why don't you move to England?" I said when it was all over. The voice of the technician was much in my mind. I can still hear the venom behind it.

Paul looked at me. "We'd have to part or risk breaking the law."

"Isn't it better to be alive? I still find it hard to imagine that our army combined with the forces of the British Empire can't defend France, but, as Robert says, so much depends on which side makes better use of powerful and up-to-date arms. It's also a question of morale, of innovative thinking. Britain and France still cling to the mind-set of the last war."

Tadeusz looked at me. "I'm sorry about my impatience, Anne. I'm always wondering about my mother and sisters." Poland had already fallen, a victim of the German blitzkrieg. I have since seen pictures of Polish cavalry charging against tanks. Hitler's attack was like a knife plunging into soft butter.

I took Paul aside. Soon we would have the records. Surely musicians in England would want to help someone of Tad's talent? Paul's parents eventually persuaded the British to let Tadeusz come to London. He would justify their grudging admission of another Jewish immigrant before the war was over.

In the meantime letters arrived from Bucksburn and then Aldershot. Robert was in his element. I think that he would have made the army his career if he hadn't taken over the family business when his father retired. Hugh had chosen to be a doctor, and Robert was happy to combine his love for the army with the life and travels of a wine merchant. He enjoyed nearly all the drills and exercises and the training of his men, making special mention of the Scottish country dancing which was compulsory for everyone of the rank of major and below! He had such a well-balanced nature that he could tolerate the foibles of his fellow men, knowing when to turn a blind eye and when to enforce rigid discipline.

His sheer strength and love of outdoor life enabled him to lead from the front, climbing up and down knobbly Bennachie in record time. Hugh's children called it the "mountain with the mumps" – they had more imagination than either of their parents. Robert's only regret was that I wasn't with him. We missed each other, but we were lucky that we were fully absorbed, one by music, the other by soldiering, and that for each of us physical love was a bonus and not a necessity.

Letters came slowly to London from Normandy too, and I wrote to my parents to say that I planned to go down to Quinon in November after the recording. While I was in Paris I received several which had gone to England, before being forwarded to me in the rue de la Motte Piquet. I opened the letter in Marie's handwriting which had the oldest post-mark, with news that made me all the more eager to see her. She was going to have a baby in March.

Chapter 20 November 1939 – February 1940

"I've been looking forward to this for weeks," said Marie, "ever since you wrote to say you could come."

"And I've been looking forward to a rest," I replied. "It was exhausting. You look tired. You're too thin!"

"And you're as bad as Tante Cécile! I've been busy up at Ronval. The weather has been fine and they've been repairing the roof. The kitchen needed redecorating and I have put in a new boiler to heat the water. I hope Edmond approves. He's coming home for Christmas. Where will you be?"

"In London, I hope. I don't want to go to Scotland!!"

We were walking through the wood and stopped by our tree. The browns and reds had been swept from the path and the branches spread widely, with spindly fingers on the twigs weaving shadows on the mulch below.

"I've just remembered," said Marie. "I once found a brass model of a horse on the path and I picked it up and put it in the tree. I wonder if it's still there. I don't know why I did it! Perhaps I was afraid I might be stealing, but as I found it in the wood I thought I'd better leave it there." She put her hand into the cleft of the trunk and felt upwards into a crevice. "It's there, Anne, but it's got stuck."

I put my hand into the crevice, felt where it was and pulled. It came away in my hand covered in moss and mould. It was green, but with a good clean it would be almost as good as new. The crevice must have been fairly dry because the moss was hardly damp at all.

I have often wondered why she thought of the horse at that moment. Maybe she was thinking about the baby, or maybe she just wanted mementos of a past that was fading, to relive the childhood we had shared, groping for threads of memory – while she shrank from the unknown.

"We'll clean up the horse when we get back and you can keep it for the baby. You're so slim. I was beginning to wonder where you'd put it!"

"It's there all right. It began to move last week. I'm sure it's going to be a boy."

"Then it really will like the horse. But seriously, Marie, you mustn't overdo things. Just let the baby grow!"

"Will you be able to come back in March?" she asked.

"How can I promise? Nobody knows what will happen. Tad and Paul are coming to London, and I have some solo concerts. Apart from that – and Robert coming home for Christmas – I try not to think too far ahead!"

"But I have to. Tante Cécile says I can come back to La Chenaie to have the baby, but I think that Edmond wants me to have it at Ronval. It would be so much easier if you were with me."

"If it's at all possible I'll come. I love this place more than anywhere else in the world, but I wish I could take you all back with me to London. My house is far too small, but we'd manage somehow. But then – who knows? The Germans might leave France alone this time and invade England. Has it ever struck you that the last person to invade England was a Norman?"

"I hope that they're not going to invade anywhere! Edmond is involved in the only fighting so far – just skirmishes north of the Maginot Line. Of course he can't tell me much, but his letters are always full of hope."

We walked back to La Chenaie. It looked so friendly, so familiar with its half timbered slanting walls and terraces at the top of the steps. The evening was fine and my father was sitting reading the paper, drinking Pernod. The smell of my mother's cooking made me breathe deeply. I wished that time would stand still, that Robert and Edmond were here, that there was no war, that we could all get on with our lives and the baby would be born into a world at peace.

"Mesdames," said my father smiling. "Venez, un verre de vin ou un porto?"

"Sit with Papa," I said to Marie. "I will help Maman."

In the kitchen, I asked my mother how Marie had been. She made sure that we were out of earshot. "She was very depressed when you left, and early pregnancy made it worse; but after two weeks here with us she felt well enough to go back to Ronval. She perked up when we had your letter saying that you would come after the recording, and another arrived from Edmond promising to be home for Christmas. Of course she's better now that the first three months are over, but at the beginning of September she was as bad as she was when Alice de Valliet died – listless, vacant. She needs us all. Has she asked you to come back in March?"

"Yes. But I couldn't make a firm promise. Who knows what will happen?"

"You are better off in England, Anne."

"I will come if I can."

"What will Robert say?"

"Nobody can predict anything, but I suspect that he might be in France then too. The British have sent two divisions over here already. Robert's battalion is still in training in Aberdeenshire, but …how can anyone tell?"

Robert was no wiser when I saw him in December. No firm directions had been given to the battalion, as far as he knew. They could be sent out to India to replace regular divisions with more experience. The 5th Gordons were now at Aldershot, and it was said that they were now up to the standard of the regulars, but rumours were rife and had to be ignored. The 1st Gordons (a regular battalion) were already in France.

We did spend two days in Scotland over Christmas, travelling in cramped sleeping cars with tea brought by an attendant at the moment when I had finally fallen asleep. We returned, vastly overfed, in time for New Year which we celebrated quietly together. I hadn't yet mentioned Marie's request.

"You know that I saw Marie and my parents when I was in France in October and November."

"So you said. Well – you've made your recording – and persuaded that pair to come over here. At least you can play trios on this side of the Channel now!"

"They're coming in January – with the records. I was pleased with the result…"

He put his arm around me. It was always wonderful. He was so warm and strong. "Come, Anne. I think I know what you want to say. You want to be with Marie when her baby is born!"

"I didn't promise. You know what she's like."

"That's why I don't want you to go. Even if this phoney war is still lulling us all into a false sense of security, even if Hitler decides to sue for peace, I don't want you to go, but I can't stop you. Marie is a lovely woman but she depends on you and she will beg you to stay. What did your mother say?"

"She said I was better off in England."

"She's probably right. I want you here too – permanently. I may be selfish, but I want you to be safe because I love you. What if you find that you are going to have a baby yourself? Would you risk losing it by making all that effort to go back to Normandy? Travelling will become more and more difficult as more British divisions are shipped into France – and, what is quite likely – Hitler might have invaded by then. Be sensible, Anne! Marie will have your mother to look after her. You know that it was your mother who helped her overcome her last depression."

It was a relief to talk to Robert, and find that although he was opposed to the scheme he was not adamant. It was the most I could expect. The week passed too quickly and I found that we drew closer and closer to one another. I didn't want to go against his wishes, but caught between two loyalties, I realised that life as a woman was more complicated than the child or the student had anticipated. I wasn't being wayward or independent. Yet the idea of going to Marie's aid, of unselfish giving, felt like something bordering on defiance.

Meanwhile, in January, waiting to leave for France, the 5th Gordons were staging their own protest over unwelcome orders. In September the War Office decreed that the kilt was unsuitable for modern warfare. Each Highland battalion was to hand them in before embarking. Many men were relieved. The memory of appalling leg sores caused by mud-caked kilts in the trenches still lingered. But for Territorials like the 5th Gordons, proud of their Scottish heritage, it felt as though the English had succeeded in enforcing a ban which the Scots had been resisting for two hundred years. The Commanding Officer, Alick Buchanan Smith, arranged a parade on the town square at Bordon, in which a kilt was ceremoniously burnt. A little stone memorial was inscribed "We hope not for long."

At the end of January the 5th Gordons disembarked at Le Havre with the rest of the 51st Division to join the British Expeditionary Force. The onlookers at the quayside stared at them with fear and suspicion, in marked contrast to the ceremonial greetings with bands and fanfares of 1914. Robert and I had exchanged countries. It was more than shedding a skin. I had swung round in a semicircle. I was in Britain. Everyone I loved was in France.

Chapter 21 March and April 1940

The decision to throw caution to the wind was made on impulse. A letter came from Robert saying that he was billeted near Bolbec, about a hundred miles from Quinon, and another came from my mother with news that Marie was well but suffering nightmares and too tired to do anything. I had no engagements. I packed my bags, and gave detailed instructions to my daily help. She proved loyal, even looking after the gardener when he came back after the long hard winter. I took a train to Newhaven. I had crossed the Channel with soldiers before, but this time I couldn't move for them. It was a struggle to persuade the authorities to let me go, but when I said that my husband was in the army, and my family in Normandy, they reluctantly let me board an army transport ship. At Dieppe there was less difficulty. I was French, in spite of having a British passport. Before I left, I wrote to Robert, hoping that I would see him.

But by that time Robert had left Normandy. The billet near Bolbec was uncomfortable for the officers, while the men had to clear filthy byres to find shelter for the night. In freezing conditions they were moved north to Gonnehem where at least there were hot baths. In spite of floods and continuous rain, they provided a smart guard of honour for General Fagalde when he visited the divisional headquarters at Béthune. There were lighter moments too; football matches against the French, with the 5th Gordons winning the final, and brawls between rival battalions, another Scottish tradition, fought out in cafés and bars. Reading Robert's letter in my sitting-room in Wimbledon, I laughed at a description of a "wee fight" between the Black Watch and the Argylls, ending with an empty beer-bottle being hurled at the man sitting at the piano. It made me think of the feud between the de Valliets and Favorets. "Wee fights" between rival clans had always been part of life in the Highlands – very much in the spirit of my red-headed grandfather.

By the beginning of March the 51st Division, strengthened by three regular battalions replacing three of the territorials', was moved to the Belgian border where many of the men were digging fortifications, a poor imitation of the Maginot line, which did nothing to deter the German onslaught in May. But the Scots dug with a will, showing the sort of tenacity with which they would fight. The Argylls, some of whom had been recruited in mining areas of Scotland, enjoyed the work, and moved earth and rubble with a speed and energy that amazed their officers.

I arrived in Quinon on March 2 and was met by my father. Maman was at Ronval with Marie, and he wanted her back.

"Why can't Marie come to us and have the baby? It wouldn't be the first to be born at La Chenaie!"

"Don't fret, Papa. I'll go straight there and then Maman can come home. Does Marie have a competent mid-wife?"

"Cécile has everything under control except poor Marie's nerves. She worries about de Valliet …"

"And?"

"She thinks he'll come back like Hervé. We can't tell her that he was a bit like that anyway. She hates the war – don't we all?"

Marie greeted me warmly. "Thank you for coming. I'm so feeble, Anne. I'm always thinking about my own father. I didn't call him Papa. I should have been kinder to him, but he just looked at me without recognising me, and I wished that he hadn't come back."

"But Edmond is quite different. How was Christmas?"

"Wonderful. He was so pleased to see me like this."

"Well, you're not hiding the baby any more! It should come soon. Then you'll have someone else to care for. That's what you like best. Was Edmond pleased with your renovations?"

"Very! But we had a joke that Charles might prefer the old stove – just because it's old! He's so backward-looking that he imagines he's doing the maids a favour when they have to bring up hot water in jugs. It stops them thinking! They still have to work hard, as the boiler has to be lit in the morning or kept alight, but at least we have hot water coming out of a tap!"

"I'm looking forward to a bath after that journey in a boat full of British soldiers. When did you last have a letter from Edmond?"

"Yesterday. He still trusts in the strength of the Maginot Line. With you here I can almost believe it."

"Well, I'm staying until the baby comes. So you'll have to be cheerful. Have you had the pianos tuned?"

"Yes! When you wrote to say that you were coming it was the first thing I did. The tuner complained that no one was employing him, so I sent him to La Chenaie too. So you have a choice of three pianos."

With this sort of banter her demons vanished. While she was resting I walked round the house, which was neat and orderly, without losing any of the homeliness that had surrounded Alice de Valliet. There was the smell of dogs – one of the bitches had just had puppies – and tartan rugs still covered the heavy sofas where they dozed during the day; but the sun shone through sparkling windows with frames which had been painted inside and out. Even the studio in the hexagonal tower had been cleaned and tidied. I slept in the room next to the one Marie shared with Edmond. It had been decorated for the baby. In the corner was an antique cot which had been cleaned and polished, and I wondered how many generations of de Valliets it had cradled.

Three nights after I arrived, I was woken by Marie.

"I've been having contractions since two o'clock. At first I thought they were the usual little twinges, but I'm certain that this time the baby's coming. It's a week early."

I told her to go back to bed and I rang my mother.

"I'll contact the doctor as soon as it's light," she said. "Babies, especially first babies, don't arrive in a hurry."

Francis Charles de Valliet was in no hurry at all. Marie suffered most of her labour with Norman stoicism, but towards the end she became too tired to fight the pain and she looked like a helpless animal. I thought of the wounded rabbits she had nursed; baby birds thrown out of their nests which she had taken home and cherished. The doctor and midwife were reassuring, but it seemed much more painful – and messy – than the birth of calves which I had watched since I was very young. Marie lay on piles of newspapers, which crackled as she moved, and we lit her new boiler so as to have plenty of hot water to wash the bedclothes which covered them.

Maids came and went in hushed excitement, and I was pleased to see how much they too loved Marie. Her unusual combination of practical intelligence, artistic perception and charm touched everyone from the seigneur to a thrush with a broken wing. Her weakness was that she needed to be surrounded by strong people who loved her, and to whom she could be useful by way of recompense.

We all resolved that she should come back to La Chenaie to rest. Her nursemaid was made comfortable in one of our maids' rooms, and the baby slept in a small room, no bigger than a cupboard, off the one that we had shared as children. Marie would be cared for by my mother, and I could plan my return to London. I didn't want to go, but other loyalties called me back. I wanted to write to Robert and reassure him that I was home and, as far as he was concerned, safe. But it seemed illogical to leave my parents, my friend and a tiny baby in conditions that my husband thought would be unsafe for me.

My letters took a long time to reach Robert. They followed him from Bolbec to the Belgian border, and then to the Saar where he was stationed near a small village just north of the massive Maginot fortifications. This part of the war, before the invasion in May, was more like playing boy scouts. Robert was sent forward to make contact with a French regiment who were sniping at the Germans, not far from a village called Betting beyond the *Ligne de Contact* with the enemy. There was a tacit agreement between the two sides to break off operations at mealtimes! Robert came across one group of Frenchmen having a civilised (French) picnic – tables spread with good food and wine on white tablecloths. In the middle of them was Edmond.

He stood up. "Bonjour, Robert Cummings! How wonderful to see you!"

"Félicitations, Edmond de Valliet! I have just heard from Anne that you have a son."

"It was kind of her to go back to Normandy to be with my wife. Francis is nearly two months old. I am told that he is growing fast. I wish I could see him."

"The war isn't treating you too badly. This is better than life on the Belgian border. Nothing would surprise me. Do you have a grand piano here too?"

"Ah, Robert, you're not wrong. I have friends not far from here. They have a Steinway piano like my mother's. What news of Mrs Cummings? I look forward to hearing the recording." Typical Edmond! I was always "Madame" or "Mrs Cummings". He called everyone "*vous*". The first time I heard him call anyone "*tu*"– apart from the dogs – was when he spoke to his son.

"She tells me she's playing Bach and growing herbs. She doesn't like our British food!"

Robert told me this anecdote four years later. He said that

Edmond was the same as ever, polite, controlled and civilised. I still wonder if he realised how vulnerable his wife was. She was so practical, so able to meet his needs without a murmur, that he imagined her as the woman in the Old Testament who rises before dawn to attend to her household. It was Charles who saw her as she was. He understood her, and, I think, had sufficient compassion to fear that Edmond might destroy her by marrying her.

I looked at Marie sitting on the divan in our salon with her baby eagerly clasping the narrow fold of a breast, and then subsiding into sleep.

"Don't go, Anne," she said. "Soldiers can look after themselves. They have guns."

"I have to go. I promised Robert. It's you who said that a wife has to obey her husband."

She sighed and looked far away. I never saw her again.

I based this part of the narrative on Robert's diaries. They were brought to me by an officer who spent five years in Laufen Oflag.

Part 2

Chapter 22 May 10 – 15 1940

The drone of aeroplanes overhead roused Robert from sleep. He had been dreaming of Anne, of Edmond, of a picnic, of the house where Edmond had played Chopin two nights ago, and where he had spent a pleasant evening at the invitation of a French colonel. Part of him wanted to believe the dream; the pianist became Anne; another part of his subconscious mind screamed at her to go away. Here on the German border, war was masquerading as peace – a treacherous tranquillity, alternately taunting and soothing him, mocking the heaviness that had accompanied him from Wimbledon to Aberdeenshire and from Aldershot to the Saar.

The hum intensified. The Luftwaffe – were they heading for French airstrips, to bomb and destroy the only cover the 51st could expect? Where was Anne? He shook himself awake. He had been dreaming. Anne was in London. The Germans were attacking at last.

The Gordons were in reserve back at the *Ligne de Recueil*. Last week they had been up at the *Ligne de Contact*, playing games with the enemy, stopping for lunch, leaving a space in the wire for the

Germans. The rules of the game were a tacit arrangement between German and French platoons. The French left a space in the wire so as to know where the enemy was. They had explained their logic to a Gordon Highlander, who left two Mills grenades on a trip wire hidden beneath the gap. There was no explosion in the night, but in the morning they had found two German hand grenades instead.

Robert had enjoyed his few days up there. There had only been danger at night, and even that had been more like training. He had thought of the distant days at school in the Corps, crouching behind boulders and crawling through the heather. These woods were like the lower reaches of the Grampians, a few conifers among the beech and oak, alder and birch, shadows of sunlight, a carpet of dried leaves, the scent of moss, grass, sap and resin.

Two days later, two days of waiting while other battalions fought, Private Macrae approached him as he was shaving, to the sounds of planes like tigers purring, amid the whine and scream of Stukas, and the thud of bombs falling on Metz.

Macrae stood to attention and tried not to notice, but he had to raise his voice to be heard. "Message from Colonel Buchanan-Smith, sir. They want to send up an advanced party. He says we're to be ready to leave at 14.00 hours."

Robert looked at his watch. It was half past six: time for breakfast, and to gather the platoon. "Thank you, Macrae, make sure that everyone is awake – now! We'll spend the morning training."

Army rations were generous. There would be a good Scots breakfast to instil courage into the hearts of men going into battle for the first time, porridge, bacon and eggs, strong tea. Yes, and into me too, thought Robert, as he ate. Apart from Fraser, I'm as much a novice as anyone. The only difference is that I have to pretend that I'm not. How much pretending was there in war? Only a few of the senior officers had fought between 1914 and 1918. General Victor Fortune, who commanded the Division, had emerged from the war unwounded – as well as decorated for bravery.

At 11.00 they stood to attention in front of the colonel. "The Black Watch are holding the *Ligne de Contact*. The whole battalion is to relieve them tomorrow evening, but I want you to go up there today, so that when the rest arrive someone knows what's happening." Colonel Alick Buchanan-Smith looked ill and tired, as he gave orders to eleven officers and more than a hundred men standing to attention, their faces taut with apprehension.

Two miles separated the lines, one a place of rest, the other a theatre of war. The noise of exploding shells could be heard from the moment they set out. There were British soldiers running and crouching, and stretchers taking wounded men back to the *Ligne de Recueil*. The first casualties had been coming in for two days now, with stories of men captured by both sides, and the ground covered with dead and wounded, mostly German.

Robert and his men reached Battalion Headquarters at Rémeling, a village with a ghostly air bereft of normal life. The Black Watch Colonel looked at the young lieutenant, glad to see someone fresh, unjaded by the events of the last two days, which had seen the enemy repulsed at great cost, only to attack again with renewed vigour.

"We've lost contact with one of our platoons. The radio link has been destroyed, and we've tried to get a message through to them, but it's been impossible. Take two men and find out what is happening. Sergeant Petrie will act as guide."

Robert looked at the tired face of the commanding officer, and then at the nervous Petrie, who should have been with his platoon. Wondering what their chances were of succeeding, Robert picked Macrae and Sergeant Fraser, and together they crept north. Like Petrie, Robert and Macrae were armed only with rifles, to give them mobility, but Fraser had a Bren gun which he carried as though it were a featherweight.

Fraser was built like an ox, a blacksmith who had fought with the Division at the end of the First World War, and then gone back to his forge in Lechen. Robert had known him first as a child, when he took his pony to be shod at the smithy, which was dominated by the sergeant in his blackened apron. When he joined the battalion, it was Sergeant Fraser who was in charge of drilling new recruits. With Fraser beside him, Robert felt again like a child with a strong father-figure to support him. The fact that he was an officer, and Fraser still a sergeant made little difference.

The woods had been raked with firing from both sides. Skeletal trees, blasted by shell, gave nature a sinister appearance, and provided little camouflage for a tall German sniper, who shot at the three approaching Highlanders. Robert fired back. The German fell forward, his arms flailing.

"Leave this to me," said the sergeant at Robert's side. A wounded man could still be dangerous. One blast of the Bren gun was enough to silence him.

Robert shouted. They could see the platoon post, but he was wary of approaching without good warning. There had already been a tragic incident; a young officer had been killed by nervous firing from his own side.

"Hello, we're Gordons." They crept nearer and nearer, but there was no reply. The post had already been overwhelmed. Robert, Macrae and Petrie fought their way back, with Fraser and his Bren, in the rear.

Exhausted, they reached the relative safety of Rémeling, only to be told to go out with the rest of the platoon to give cover for a Black Watch company, which was falling back without their equipment.

Robert's platoon had to fight their way to the front, countering machine-gun fire, rifle shots from snipers, and the advance of infantry pouring through the wood. With Fraser's help they found a clump of bushes from behind which to fell oncomers. Germans dropped thickly on the dead ground between the Highlanders and the trees of the Heydwald, but many more seemed to spring up in their place. Three of Robert's men were wounded. Macrae and Private Allan dragged two of them to safety. The third was able to run, clutching an arm streaming with blood.

They had to wait until dark on 13 May before the rest of the 5th Gordons moved forward to replace the Black Watch. There had been a disagreement between Colonel Buchanan-Smith and the Brigade Commander. The Colonel didn't want his men to go to Rémeling, only too aware of the dangers. A sensitive man with an academic background, a Territorial with a deep affection for men recruited from near his home town, he couldn't face such sacrifice. Buchanan-Smith was ill. He would soon retire, and a regular officer, trained to be more objective, would succeed him.

Then orders for a general retreat, to a line south of Rémeling, came from Brigadier Burney. Later, General Condé made the two French flanking divisions, as well as the Scots, withdraw behind the *Ligne de Recueil*.

But the day's work was not over for Robert and his men. The withdrawal from Rémeling was a panic. They were asked to go up again to face the enemy.

"We've managed to help evacuate a company, and we've sustained injuries. What more can we do?" pleaded Robert. "My men have had enough. We'll cover the roads for you." They were the last to leave.

Chapter 23 May 18 – 20

Sergeant Fraser was humming "A Gordon for me" while cleaning and oiling his rifle. There would be an inspection before nightfall when the patrol would venture out again into the woods. Rumours were rife. A French Division had been withdrawn west, and the Seaforths and Camerons had been spread out to cover the gap. It was said that German Panzer Divisions had forged through the Ardennes, crossed the Meuse and crushed the ill-trained and ill-equipped 9th French army. There was a danger that the 51st Division might be stranded here in the east of France.

But that didn't stop the burly Fraser remembering the song loved by wives and families of Gordons; nor did it stop him looking forward to another night prowl. There had been less activity from the enemy during the last two days. If the main thrust of the enemy were to the west, then perhaps the 51st could attack in the east. He was an optimist, and a soldier at heart, although he had returned to his forge in 1919 to forget the slaughter of the last war. On the rough earth floor beneath the blackened wooden roof held up by three stone walls, with wind and weather driving through the open front, he had immersed himself in the work he loved. He could feel the strength and swing of his arms as he beat molten iron, his hammer clanging against horse-shoe and anvil. He was good with horses. They stood still when Fraser matched the red-hot shoe to the upturned hoof, filling the smithy with fumes and smoke.

He was aware of Robert at his side. "We'll not be retreating tonight. It'll be near the boundary with the French we'll be heading as soon as it's dark," said the tall lieutenant.

"Thon Frenchies canna fecht," replied Fraser. "I seen them rinnin, at the first burst of fire ower yon hill."

"Not all, there's a Breton company I met up at Betting last week – they were as fierce as any Gordon! And there are Normans too…" Robert thought of Edmond. He hadn't seen him since the evening when he had played Chopin. It seemed like years ago.

It was a well-fed and cheerful band, with a life-time of experience crammed into two days' fighting that set off under a canopy of stars through the wood of leafless branches, silver in the moonlight. They walked stealthily in twos with more than five yards' distance between each pair, their ears alerted to the slightest sound. Somewhere a nightingale was singing.

A shot rang out to their right. One of the men in the lead fell headlong, while his partner, Macrae, crouched down and aimed at where the shot came from. Robert ran up to him, his long body bent double. Three Germans like wraiths, their grey uniforms silver-trimmed, ran into the open. Robert fired. Two of them fell, but the third, aiming wildly kept running. A shot from Macrae stopped him. There was more firing from the right and Robert signalled to his men to spread out and find cover. Fraser was beside him. Macrae ran forward as another shot came from the right. It missed him, but he in turn fired as he ran. There was a cry and a thud. The shot had gone home.

There were more wraith-like figures running towards the Gordons, who had hidden as well as they could. Shots rang out and men on both sides fell. Two Gordons ran forward, but they were greeted with a burst of machine-gun fire. Robert signalled his men to creep backwards, but there was more firing coming from the south. There were Germans on three sides.

Beyond the wood to the left was a hilly space where the French had held the *Ligne de Contact*. The line no longer existed; the Germans had cut away the wire, but Robert knew that this was the only place to run. The firing on the right became heavier. His men lifted the two wounded men, leaving the dead soldier where he lay, and ran. There was a house in the distance, a silver outline. Shots rang out in the dark and Robert could see Frenchmen and Germans fighting for possession. Robert signalled to his men to crouch down while he ran. "*Ami,*" he said.

"*Bienvenue!* You are welcome! We can get rid of them together."

The exchange of fire lasted twenty minutes, but the Germans were outnumbered.

"Where is your commanding officer?" Robert asked the nearest man.

"In the building. I'll take you to him."

His surprise at meeting Edmond de Valliet was only matched by the fact that they were in the salon of the house where they had met ten days before – where Edmond had played Chopin and they had drunk champagne. Now there were shards of glass on the floor, and wrecked furniture strewn across the room, the grand piano unscathed, but covered with the broken remains of photographs and lamps.

"Have they all gone?" asked Robert. "I'll go upstairs and see."

He crept up the stairs as noiselessly as he could. As he straightened up he saw a German with a pistol aimed at him. The shot missed, but Robert's rifle rang out true. The man fell dead at Robert's feet.

He came downstairs to find several wounded men being attended by a French medical orderly.

"We are only safe here until dawn," said Edmond. "The enemy are to the south as well as the north. I came up here, like you, on a night patrol, but they will be back in daylight in sufficient numbers to capture us all."

"Is it true that they've broken through the Ardennes?"

"I'm afraid it is. We shall all be leaving the Saar, but where we will be sent I don't know."

"How did they do it?"

"The ninth army was under-equipped. The Germans found bridges that hadn't been demolished, and constructed pontoons as well. And they knew what to do with tanks, surging forward in large numbers and meeting little opposition."

"I've seen tanks up here – but they got stuck in ditches." The Lothians, a well-trained tank regiment, had lost several in two misadventures on unsuitable terrain.

"There are roads through the Ardennes – they were enough."

"We Highlanders want to find the rest of the British Expeditionary Force – and we want to fight."

"So I can see. My men want to fight too. They wouldn't have come on this patrol, if they didn't. But alas, many of our soldiers have already given up. And we're all afraid of being surrounded by Panzer Divisions."

"We don't want to be surrounded by tanks either!" Robert thought for a minute. "We'll have to go back the way we came. If we improvise stretchers, we should be able to carry our wounded. The rest will have to take turns in carrying them."

"I suggest that we go together. Let's stay at the edge of the wood. There are enough of us to keep groups of attackers at bay and still carry the wounded."

They found water and food, and made their way back before light without further incident.

Chapter 24 June 4

A line of French soldiers, like the poilus of the trenches, straggled forward in untidy uniforms covered by long coats, smoking Gauloises, calling to each other in raucous voices, scuffing their dirty boots against stone and tussock. They didn't want to fight. The war was already lost. Robert looked at them aghast. Sergeant Fraser could hardly contain his fury.

"There's the Seaforths and Camerons takin' a hammerin' and that lot are supposed to join them. What a shambles!"

He was right. The last ten days of May had been a shambles, the withdrawal from the Saar, directions and counter-directions to Varennes, to Etain, to Pacy and now to the stretch of woods, fields and villages which lay between the Somme and the Bresle. Six battalions of the Division had been detached and sent in the wrong direction, only to join the rest after angry protest from General Fortune. There had been a spirited attack by Général de Gaulle on May 30 against the German bridgehead at Abbeville, but the supporting Highlanders had no time to prepare or reconnoitre. The French were to hold the Scots in reserve, only to be used for rearguard action, but they had been thrust unprepared into the front line and repulsed. General Fortune was furious, his faith in his allies seriously shaken. His Division was thinly spread over eighteen miles, with a mandate from the French to hold the line. The 31st French were supposed to stiffen the defence, but he was as unimpressed by them as were Robert and Fraser.

The thump of drilled marching broke the chaos, which subsided as a company of soldiers, heads erect and eyes in front, filed past the Gordons. A huge sergeant called a halt. Capitaine Edmond de Valliet looked at his troops with grudging approval, and cast a look of disgust at the men who had stood aside to let his company through.

He came up to Robert. "I can't believe it," he said in English, "the lack of morale in the 31st. I was asked to join the division by General Condé because I'm half Scot. At least I was able to take my company with me. Perhaps you will remember one or two of them from our scrap in the Saar? They are good soldiers – real Frenchmen; but most of those scoundrels seem to have decided to give up before they've started."

Robert had never before seen Edmond ruffled. An inner confidence and competence usually regulated every move, every action and reaction. But his patience was exhausted. Men were dying – largely because one compatriot army was unwilling to support the other. He looked at Robert straight in the eye. "General Condé was a friend of my father's. He can't praise the Highlanders enough, talking of the spirit of Beaumont-Hamel – of friends on the day of battle. But what are we doing – or rather what are these Pyreneans doing? Why did they join the army – to ski?"

Robert smiled. "Not all Scots are brave, but the faint-hearted are the exception. In the past the clans fought one another – almost out of duty to keep the family feud going! You won't find a Campbell and a Macdonald fighting side by side."

It was Edmond's turn to smile. "A bit like the de Valliets and the Favorets. I know a very fine woman who has put an end to that." He spoke to his sergeant. "We will move up to the front now." He turned to look at the sheepish bystanders. "And you will come with us."

The sergeant glared at them and shouted "Quick, march!" The shufflers picked up their feet and followed. Edmond shook Robert's hand.

The scream of diving Stukas was disheartening. Within an hour many of the same disaffected troops were back at the village where Robert was stationed. There had been a counter-attack, they claimed – but they had probably only seen their French walking wounded, and tank crews withdrawing.

There was no sign of Edmond and his men. At 16.00, orders came for an advanced company of Gordons which included Robert's platoon to relieve another depleted battalion. In theory French troops were to replace the Scots, but their commander refused to take responsibility. At 21.00 the rest of the battalion moved forward, hoping they would be flanked by the French.

It was chaos. There were wounded men being brought back in carrier trucks and prisoners being rounded up, undaunted by capture, sure of ultimate victory. Some were being questioned, others willing to talk to anyone who spoke German. Robert heard a Scots voice and was surprised to see the grey uniform of a German lieutenant.

"You're brave, but you can't win," said the prisoner. "We should be fighting together against the Bolsheviks, not against one another."

Robert smiled. "Where did you learn to speak English like that?" he asked.

"At school in Scotland – my mother's country. I'm not surprised that you Highlanders fight so well. There were thirty of us captured, and only then did we realise that we were being shot at by half that number. They managed to kill quite a few of us too. But you won't win. There are too many of us – and the French don't want to fight."

"Don't be so sure!" said Robert. "It's difficult to beat the 51st! You didn't last time, and we won't give in easily. And don't write off all the French. There are some fine soldiers among them."

The German was taken to headquarters. Robert waited for orders to advance. He saw a truck bringing in three wounded Seaforths and recognised Tom Creighton among them. He sat up when he saw Robert.

"It's my leg," he said and groaned. "I hope that they can get the bullet out and let me go back. It's not serious."

Robert smiled. "You'll have to fight with a crutch in the meantime, and let the Gordons get on with the shooting!"

"The Seaforths are being mown down but they won't give up, even if we need a little help from the Gordons! The trouble is that we aren't able to concentrate in one area. There's too wide a line to defend."

Meanwhile some of the 1st Gordons, who had made good ground against the enemy nearer the Somme Canal, were ordered to withdraw from the very place which they had won at great cost. They had taken prisoners who had talked of long marches from the north, and of motor transport columns heading for the Somme area. The previous day Dunkirk had fallen. Of the one hundred and sixty thousand British troops (mostly non-combatants) left in France, the Highland 51st Division was the only British formation still in the front line. They could expect the full might of Hitler's attack over the coming days.

Chapter 25 June 6

The 51st Division fell back westwards from the Somme to the River Bresle which lies on the border between Picardy and Normandy; and from the Bresle across the rivers which flow down to the Channel on the Upper Normandy coast. They fought each yard with tenacity, ceding ground, yard by yard, to superior forces. They went slowly, first yearning to turn the tide of defeat into victory; but by the time they reached the Bresle they had begun to think of embarkation, a miracle like Dunkirk. Only a few would realise that dream, among them the Argylls, two battalions reduced to less than one, in their struggle backwards from the Somme.

June 4 had scythed through the Camerons and the Seaforths south of Abbeville on the east wing of the straggling line of Highlanders, a line thinned hourly by injury, death and capture. June 5 was one of the blackest days in the history of the Argylls, who were defending the area nearest to the sea. They continued to fire when surrounded, refusing to surrender until the ground in front of house, shed, school and copse was strewn with their enemies. But out of tragedy sometimes steps a hero. His name was Lorne Campbell. He led two hundred men racked with thirst, stranded behind enemy lines, by night, with only a compass to guide him, changing direction seven times, to join the remnant of their Brigade on the other side of the Bresle.

The Gordons were in the middle, flanked by the French, among them the 31st Division, part of the tenth army. It was their general, Altmayer, who nominally commanded, but his army was cut in two by a surge of enemy forces driving westwards from the interior.

The remnant, the ninth corps, would be commanded by Général Ihler. Yet neither general could stomach the reality of France being overrun, neither could make decisions, neither could challenge the intransigence of their commander in chief who could only rail at the Scots for leaving the Somme. In the end it was General Fortune, with no clear mandate, except to support and defer to his allies, who directed the motley crew which dragged backwards at the speed of packhorses, while Rommel's tanks forged from the south towards a seaside town called St Valéry.

Robert crossed the Bresle on June 6, before the sappers destroyed the bridges, but the Bresle was a narrow river, steep-sided in places, and in others, only three feet deep, with shallow mud banks. Over two hundred Germans had already reached the west bank, gnawing at the relative tranquillity of the exhausted Scots, who longed for food and rest which had been denied them since the chaos of removal from the Saar. On either side of the Bresle there were woods, ideal places for an enemy to lie in ambush.

Robert and his platoon were patrolling not far from battalion headquarters, where a bridge had been destroyed opposite a small hamlet. Fraser was aware of other soldiers nearby, and signalled to the men to lie down. Robert edged towards the river, and saw that there was a French company creeping near the bank looking for enemy activity. It was then that he saw Germans lying in ambush among the trees waiting for them. He was sure that there were more on the other side of the river.

"If I take four men upstream and cross over we should take them by surprise," suggested Fraser to Robert.

"You might get across, but what about getting back?"

"It's a risk worth taking. We'd have to wait until dark. Och, but there's a company of brave Frenchies walking into a trap and we could spring it the other way!" he chuckled.

"I'll keep the men here and spread them out. We'll try not to fire until you do."

Fraser, Macrae and four others drew back and crept along the edge of the wood upstream in the opposite direction from the ambush. They waded across the river unseen, and edged their way downstream. The woods gave protection to the ambushers, but also to the Scots. Fraser had natural field skills, and a taste for adventure. Rivers and trees, mud and the unevenness of a bank where the ground was soft or stony, without a foot track, were no impediment. He had a feel for danger, a sixth sense of approaching peril, which heightened his awareness and caught his breath. He knew which men to choose; he knew that Robert would wait as long as he could, and that the men would have the courage to obey him. Robert was a leader. Where he went, men followed.

There were five lines of men, each with the scent of the hunter and the hunted. The French were looking for the Germans, who in turn were waiting for them, while the Scots lay behind them, well aware that they themselves could be snared. In an ambush, the sound of your own breathing has to be controlled. One minute seems like an hour, an hour an eternity. Self-control is paramount. A shot rang out – but from which side?

The Germans were firing at the French who were running, some upstream, some down. There were shots from the other side of the river. French soldiers were being mown down. Then the German firing across the river became intermittent, as they suffered casualties and turned to look for attackers behind them. Fraser and his men kept moving, shooting from different places, giving the impression of being a platoon of men. And the Germans on the west bank were holding fire, as they in turn were being attacked. No one dared throw grenades for fear of killing an ally, neither the Germans, nor the Scots.

The French stopped running, aware that they were being supported, crouched, fixed bayonets and started to probe through the undergrowth in search of the enemy. At that moment the Scots charged, yelling through the trees; Germans dodged and tried to fire but the trees made shooting almost impossible. It was hand to hand fighting such as soldiers learn in training, hard work with the bayonet; Robert blessed his sergeant who had drilled the Gordons in Scotland and in Aldershot, demanding an ever higher standard of skill and determination. A few German prisoners were taken but most ran into the forest, cowed by the ferocity of the Gordon attack and the French recovery.

Robert was less than surprised to be facing Edmond de Valliet.

"You have saved our lives, Robert. We would all have been killed or captured without you."

At that moment there was a splash and the sound of German voices. The men on the east bank had found a fordable crossing and they were shooting as they waded, waist-deep, across the Bresle. There must have been thirty or more. Several were hit from behind. Fraser and his team were good marksmen. Robert and Edmond responded immediately. They shot several dead in the water, but more kept moving up towards the bank. The two leaders, one Scot, one French-Scot, fired at the vulnerable Germans clambering up the muddy slopes. The Gordons and French fired from either side; shots from the east bank well aimed at those still in the river felled more. The attack faltered, but one huge German plunged onwards, dodging to and fro, defying bullets from all directions. He hurled himself up the bank and fell on Edmond, the slighter of the two leaders. Robert hacked at the German with the butt of his rifle and stunned him. Edmond, regaining his balance, shot him.

They shook hands, but knew that there was no time to be lost. The attack could be renewed at any time; there were wounded men to be helped to safety. Robert's thoughts were with the Gordons on the other side of the river, but his first duty was to lead the men with him back to headquarters, providing fire-cover for those dragging the wounded. Two of his men had been killed.

Robert waited until nightfall and there was still no sign of Fraser or Macrae. He cursed himself for letting them go, and then he corrected his thoughts. The skirmish had been successful. The Germans had suffered a tiny defeat, and the Auld Alliance had proved its worth. The Scots were reassured that there were brave soldiers among their allies. But he groaned all the same and longed to see the burly Aberdonian who had been both friend and tutor.

"Lieutenant Cummings, sir!" said a voice he recognised. Robert turned round. It was Macrae.

"Where are the others?"

"Mackay is here and Hay. Miller and Allan were killed…."

"And Sergeant Fraser?"

"He was badly wounded. He wouldn't let me carry him. I tried to lift him with Miller and Hay and then Miller was shot. Then Sergeant Fraser spoke to me. 'On you go, back to the lieutenant. That's an order. Tell him we shot over thirty Jerries before they got us.' He let me give him a morphine injection, and then said I was to do what I was told. I only got away in time. We had to hide and wait until dark before we crossed the river."

Robert felt a great cloud of misery descend over his shoulders. Fraser was gone, the best friend a soldier could have. But he didn't forget Macrae. Macrae was exhausted and fighting back emotion. He too had lost comrades; and the men had loved Fraser, even though he was a stern disciplinarian.

"You did well, Private Macrae. I shall recommend you for promotion."

Chapter 26 June 7

A pause in a battle is hardly a reprieve. There is time to rest, but there is also time to think, to wonder what the morrow will bring, to remember lost comrades. As the army regathered its strength on June 7, there were disturbing rumours that they had been outflanked, that tanks were thrusting through France to cut off the army's slow trek west.

If the 51st Division had known to what extent they were a pawn in the game of politics played between allies, they might have lost heart. One ally was demented by fear and humiliation, the other planning for a future battle where the outcome was a terrifying uncertainty. But even if they had known, it would still have been difficult to dishearten the Scots. Their history is one of defeat and oppression, of major setbacks and heroic last stands.

Their defeats, Flodden and Culloden, stay firm in the memory. Betrayal is part of their folklore. The sacrifice of one of Britain's most famous Divisions in June 1940 is another chapter.

The Battle of France had already been lost in the mind of the French Prime Minister, Reynaud, when he telephoned Churchill on May 15, but political posturing and the optimism of the British leader demanded that the drama should be played out to the bitter end. The French wanted support from the British. Above all they wanted it in the air. Churchill needed the RAF to defend Britain. He, in turn, wanted the French to fight on, if only to play for time. The French were clutching at straws, unwilling to make the separate peace which the treaty between the allies forbade, looking for excuses, a let-out, a scapegoat. Général Weygand, the Commander in Chief, ranted that the British had deserted him at Dunkirk, and that the 51st Division had betrayed their trust in retreating from the Somme. His scapegoat was General Fortune – in front of the appalled Churchill, Weygand screamed that his name should be "Misfortune".

But the French also had their memories, and they were recent. The lack of fighting spirit among many – but by no means all – French soldiers, was not only the legacy of 1914 – 1918, with its two million dead and wounded, leaving a population of orphans and widows, but of the Franco-Prussian War when the Germans defeated France and proclaimed their first emperor at Versailles. And there were communists who disdained both sides, "imperialist and capitalist," eroding national pride and the will to fight, like a canker. The Battle of France was won by modern machines and fighting methods, but lost through indecision, divided command, outdated strategy – especially in the use of tanks – and, after Dunkirk, lack of air support. If the Highlanders were bitter about anything it was that. Nevertheless – and the Scottish mind, which refuses to compromise, uses the word "nevertheless" like a breath of resignation – they would not give up. They marched and fought their way to defeat at St Valéry, with pipes skirling and heads held high.

For Robert, June 7 was a day of reflection, deepened by the loss of Fraser and the dread of impending defeat through encirclement. He was alone. He was a leader and men would look to him as a child looks to an adult for guidance. His loneliness grew more unbearable as the day passed. He fought with himself for control and mental rigour, suppressing his misery as he cajoled and encouraged his soldiers.

In the evening he was reading Anne's last letter, when he was aware of footsteps. It couldn't be Macrae, who walked with a firmness born of obedience and determination. The footsteps had a different confidence, a measured slowness that made an economy of effort, where courage was implicit, not worn like a badge. He looked up.

"I have come to thank you." Edmond spoke in English.

"It was all in the day's work," smiled Robert.

"Your sergeant is dead, isn't he?"

Robert sighed and refused to speak, until his breath could control the words without breaking them. "Yes," he said slowly. "Fraser was a great man. I have known him since I was a child."

Edmond was also a Scot, his education had been English, and his grace and manners looked back to an age of chivalry. There was no effusion, no outpouring. "I am so sorry." The tone of his voice gave the banal words meaning. They hung in the evening air like a tribute. Robert's gaze was more than an acknowledgement.

"Have you heard from Mrs Cummings recently?"

"I was reading one of her letters when you arrived. She is happily playing trios, and she is thinking about us all in France while she is stranded in London. Of course she continues to play Bach. It's a sort of protest. She refuses to hate the Germans, even if we are fighting them." He paused. "I can't hate either. Fraser is dead, but I can't hate his killers."

"Neither can I. My thoughts are at Ronval and La Chenaie, where M. and Mme Favoret are caring for Marie and Francis, but they are also in Bavaria where Charles is praying for us all. He was with me the first time I met Marie and your wife. I can still see the river, the tree where two young girls had their swing, the defiance of a fiery red-head. What spirit – and yet she bound us to her, and broke a hundred years of feuding. No, I can't hate; it's hatred that we're fighting, not Germans, but I fear we are outnumbered, and will be surrounded."

"You don't have to hate to fight, you have to be loyal. We may be outflanked, but the men under me will fight as long as they can, and I think yours will too." There was another gap in the conversation. Edmond nodded.

"If we have to be evacuated, will you join us?" continued Robert, broaching the subject which his mind had kept at bay all day.

"Only if I can do no more here."

"The Scots have taken an awful hammering. I wonder how much longer they can last without proper sleep or rations."

"War is war. We have to endure what it brings. If you get back to England, please send my warmest regards to your wife. Tell her that I want to hear her play one of the Preludes and Fugues which haunts me – in D sharp minor – or is it E flat minor? Do you know, I think that he wrote the Prelude in flats and the Fugue in sharps!"

"I shall get her on to it as soon as I see her." Robert's face relaxed into a smile. Here they were facing death, injury, capture and defeat, and they were talking of Bach, of a world which transcends violence, but comprehends the whole of humanity, its strength and suffering.

"Good-bye, Robert, and – good luck!" They grasped each other's hands; Edmond held on to Robert's grip. He looked into the fair blue eyes beneath the thatch of sandy hair. "I shall pray for the soul of Sergeant Fraser, and for the others who died with him. They gave their lives for my men." There was no more to say. Both of them were bound by codes of honour and self-control. They were soldiers.

Chapter 27 June 8 – 9

Robert suppressed a groan. It was the worst thing that could have happened. No! It wasn't the worst thing. Losing Fraser was the worst thing – the loss made every tottering footstep more painful. He felt he was carrying the whole British army on his shoulders. Fraser would have made light of it. Robert could hear the hearty Buchan bark "Yar no carrying yar mother's stove. Yar in the army and ya'll carry whataver the army wants!" And he would have ferried the heaviest equipment across land and stream without a murmur.

But Robert wasn't Fraser, and his job was to set an example of fortitude with a smile. As an officer, he didn't have to shoulder two Bren guns and several loads of ammunition; but every man counted; the battalion, although less depleted than others, had had its losses, and the fewer the bearers the heavier the loads. The order to move west from the Bresle to the Eaulne had come too late to organise transport, and the 5th Gordons were carrying all their equipment themselves, picks, shovels, guns, and ammunition. Men were falling, sergeants were swearing, everyone was exhausted, but they had to keep moving because the army said so. Robert hummed "One more river". They had just crossed a shallow stream, struggling through water with their equipment, and up the muddy banks, slithering and sliding like helpless children.

It was dark, but as they weren't molested by the enemy they were able to steer a straight course. As far as each of his men was concerned, it was a case of following the shadow in front, but Robert had to use his intelligence to be aware of everyone in his platoon and keep up their spirits. The temptation to let his mind wander was intense, to dream himself into Anne's arms, to relive the past and imagine a future at her side. He almost envied Tadeusz and Paul who would be giving concerts with her in spite of the war. The thought brought him to his senses – envying that pair? He had never accustomed himself to their lifestyle, and he disliked Anne's acquiescence in something which made every nerve scream with disgust. He had known of soldiers sent to prison…where hell awaited them.

"How are you doing?" he asked Macrae as he passed him.

"Fine, sir!" The words came out in a burst of effort. He was carrying his rifle, two shovels and a pick-axe.

"Good man!" said Robert, trying to sound encouraging.

He looked back at his men and smiled. There were few complaints and when one man fell, another would help him to his feet. Not all were heroes. Two had been reluctant to join the patrol at the Bresle, and one of them was glad to have Sergeant Fraser off his back. Menzies was known to have said that the sergeant would have put his grandmother on a charge. But Robert knew about Menzies, as Fraser had done, pitying the boy who had been beaten by his drunken father and neglected by his stepmother. The battalion was the only real family Menzies had ever known. Perhaps it was the advantage of a territorial battalion – you knew your men and you understood their weaknesses. Perhaps it wasn't an advantage. Perhaps it would be better to be impartial, to think of the men as cogs in a wheel, not people with feelings. Stop thinking, keep going, find something cheerful to say, forget the blisters on your shoulders – everyone else must have them.

Eighteen miles through the night, each yard a journey in itself. The will to keep going induced darker thoughts. They were retreating. There would be no victory at the end of the trudge, only another walk backwards – and to what? Rumour runs through an army like any other community. Thousands had been rescued at Dunkirk. Surely there would be a rescue for the 51st! But the withdrawal was too slow. This night of misery was just a mistake. With proper organisation

– and the 51st was a well ordered unit with high personal standards and a fine leader – the division could be moving in trucks and carriers to Le Havre. But loyalty made them stay with the French and their pack horses, which moved no faster than the Gordons stumbling towards another river.

The river! That's what Anne talked about, not the Bresle or the Eaulne but the river which divided Ronval and La Chenaie, a river in Lower Normandy, Calvados – how many miles would he have to walk to reach it? His feet were drying after dragging through the last stream. To take off boots and dangle bare legs in cool water, to rest, to stop. Yes, just stop and rest. He could see Anne's tree, the huge trunk, part of it hollow. The swing-tree. It was part of Anne's childhood, a burst into freedom, a bond of friendship. To swing freely, not carry the world on one's back.

The tree had bound her to Marie, but also to Edmond de Valliet. Had she loved him? Surely not! Anne was his. And what of Charles de Valliet, the shadowy would-be mystic, who only emerged from the black shroud of his habit to dance reels in a kilt? How could a man deny himself the fullness of life? What drove him to such extremes – self-rejection in search of God? Why search? Didn't Christianity teach us that God had found man? Why not accept it like everyone else, follow the flow of nature, and live generously and openly like Anne, who laughed at the nuns, but boarded a ship full of soldiers to support her friend? Yes, friends are good… what would be the end of the blood-letting battles improvised by a retreating army that longed for respite?

He heard Macrae's voice through his reverie. "Menzies has fallen and refuses to get up. He's twenty yards back. Sergeant Grant's at him but it's no good – he says he can't go on."

"I'll deal with Menzies." Robert put down his load and almost staggered with the lightness of relief. He walked back, rolling his shoulders and breathing deeply.

"Get up, man. Take off your rifle and stand up straight. Do you want to be a prisoner or do you want to stay with the battalion?"

"I canna git up. I'm killt."

"You're not even wounded. Men have run with wounds, and here you are giving up, when we've gone most of the way already." Robert hoped he was right. He gave Menzies his arm and pushed him upright.

"Pick up your gun – and now your shovel. What else were you carrying?"

"Naethin'."

"You should be ashamed of yourself. You're carrying less than most of the men. Now get on with it!"

"But I'm tired and ma feet are killing me."

"Do you think you're the only one? Forget about your feet, and just follow Sergeant Grant. Look how much he's got to carry!"

Menzies limped forward. Robert walked back to his load. It wasn't his feet that were killing him, it was his shoulders. They were raw and sore, and now he must make them even sorer. The pain of lifting the guns on to them was almost unbearable. He stifled a moan, and was glad that no one could see him. He struggled onwards, catching up with Macrae. "He'll follow. If not, he'll be caught," he said through gritted teeth.

"Thank you, sir." Macrae was fighting back his own discomfort.

They reached the Eaulne long after daybreak. That evening orders came to fall back to the Béthune.

Chapter 28 June 10 – 12

History is full of "What ifs?" Why retreat to Le Havre when Dieppe was at the mouth of the Béthune? In spite of bomb damage and mines at the harbour entrance, it was still partly usable. General Fortune had received orders to fall back to Le Havre with the French. He obeyed. They were to reach it in stages by June 13, a plodding retreat, mocked by the lightning speed of Rommel and his tanks. Even these directions were less than firm; Weygand still raved that they should go south to cross the Seine at Rouen by ferry. Was it spite, or the rambling of a leader maddened by defeat?

At the War Office in London the fate of the 51st Division was treated with ambivalence. Without directives from the French, there could be no second Dunkirk because the fragile alliance would be shattered. Orders were inferred from a vague statement made by Admiral Platon on the afternoon of June 11. By then it was too late.

Voices of sympathy were heard among the British Navy. Two officers met General Fortune as early as June 9. They were still with him at St Valéry; one of them would make a dramatic escape. The War Office sent ships to Le Havre to rescue the garrison, but gave them no mandate to save the Highlanders. Other vessels hovered out at sea waiting for orders from Britain, among them a flotilla of small boats, manned by volunteers who had set out in the spirit of Dunkirk, but had had no sleep and little food or water for some time. Radio contact was so erratic that messages didn't get through. And then the bombardment from the top of the chalk cliffs started. Few nowadays blame the fog that descended early in the morning of June 12. Ships returned to Britain empty, while thousands waited.

On June 9, General Fortune had divided his men into two forces, pairing off many of the troops who had joined his Division from elsewhere, along with the Argylls, reduced to half their numbers, and the 4th Black Watch, sending them west to Le Havre in well-organised transport. They avoided Rommel's 7th Panzer Division by only hours.

And what of the rest, the larger number, two of the three Highland Brigades and all the other Divisional Regiments, Norfolks, Lothians with their tanks, Artillery, Engineers, Pioneers, Signals, Medical Corps, and more? And what of their French allies?

On June 11, the 5th Gordons were stationed at St Pierre-le-Vigy about five miles east of St Valéry. Shortly after midnight they received an order to move nearer the town, but their commanding officer was suspicious. He had met a colonel from the French army who said that Général Ihler had surrendered. The Scottish colonel refused to go anywhere, until he was certain of the facts. The Frenchman might be wrongly informed; he might want the Scots to be more pliant; he might be a spy.

Robert was reporting to headquarters when he heard a calm voice penetrate the darkness. It was unmistakable. He greeted Edmond warmly, and asked him if he had any news.

"My commanding officer thinks we have surrendered," said Edmond. His tone was bleak, but he still retained that easy control and economy of words which makes the emphasis of each important. He wasn't convinced.

"What will you do? It may be just a question of time."

"I shall obey orders until I am sure that we *have* surrendered, and then I shall try to escape with those of my men who won't admit defeat."

"It would be easier to escape while it's dark. If your colonel wants to give up you would be better to go now."

"It seems undutiful either way. If I stay, I shall be unable to continue to fight for France. If I leave, I could be disobeying orders."

"Why not go now? I must stay because the Scots want to fight on, but you and your men could escape to Britain. I still hope to embark at St Valéry with the Gordons, but it will be difficult. If the Germans follow us to the cliffs we will be easy targets, and so will the boats sent to collect us. But I refuse to give up hope."

As they talked, day was beginning to break through pouring rain, the first to fall for days. A group of French soldiers streamed past in disarray with white handkerchiefs on their bayonets. It was the second time Robert saw Edmond's self-possession leave him. It wasn't the raising of a visor, the uncovering of hidden anger, the revealing of another side to his character; it was Edmond as he always was, a brave man whose sensitivity and intelligence enabled him to understand rather than condemn.

"It's not their fault," he whispered angrily. "Most of my fellow officers want to surrender, and their men are running around like a herd of lost animals. Mine are no different from anyone else, some honest, some scoundrels, but they still have a sense of purpose, and I know I can rely on them."

Returning to his company, which had gathered on the west beach in hope of embarkation, Edmond led a group of six to the harbour, past the blazing town and on to the beach beyond. He had heard a rumour that there were boats at Veules-les-Roses, two miles east of St Valéry. The tide was out; they crept along the shore protected by the thin light of early morning, and the fog that followed the rain. They clambered in and out of caves like catacombs, which protected them from the Germans firing above them on the cliffs, and waded into the sea chest-deep where they were among nine hundred French and thirteen hundred British to be picked up by small boats, and ferried to a destroyer.

The Gordons moved closer to St Valéry and stopped at Manneville, a mile and half to the east of the town, resisting attack, while Generals

Fortune and Ihler wrangled about a cease-fire. The French general wanted Victor Fortune to send a telegram to the British government informing them of their surrender, as all communication with the French High Command was cut. At first the Scot refused. Instead he set about deploying his battalions in a last-ditch effort to defend the Division until help came. The French put a white flag on the church at 8.00 a.m. General Fortune had it torn down.

Robert fought on, Macrae at his side with the remains of the platoon which Fraser had drilled, pressed back step by step towards the town which burned like a furnace, as mortar and shell-fire were thrown at a surrounded army. Men fell, others dragged the wounded, medical orderlies tended the badly injured, but there wasn't enough food, water, or ammunition to sustain the 51st Division for another day's fighting. At 10.30 the cease-fire call was blown on a bugle. The men couldn't believe it. They had imagined death and injury, but not surrender. Exhausted and ashamed, some broke down. Robert refused to bow to despair. He made his platoon walk in marching order, holding their heads high, as if they were on parade. Pushing through the mêlée of men being herded towards the sea-front, they looked for Col. Clarke, and refused to stand at ease until they had found him. There would be pride in defeat as well as victory.

Ten thousand Highlanders and their supporting regiments were sent into captivity, along with thousands of French, some of whom were released when the armistice was signed. Robert and his friends stood in angry stupefaction at the sight of French officers in full dress, waiting with packed suitcases to be taken to the moderate comfort and complete safety of captivity. (They were given hell by the villagers as they marched by.) For most of the Scots, it was a different story, five years of hard work and poor food, some dying of malnutrition, of accidents and some trying to get away. The fury at being captured created an energy and determination which inspired many escapes. Out of two hundred and ninety British prisoners of war who had returned safely from German POW camps by the end of 1941, one hundred and thirty-four were members of the 51st Highland Division. Their stories are full of twists of fate, of setbacks and difficulties. One adventure went as far as Palestine. Robert's turn would come later.

Part 3

Chapter 29 Summer and Autumn 1940

And what of those left behind? Why didn't Edmond try to return to Ronval, while Calvados was still unoccupied? Didn't he think of his wife? Wasn't he worried about her? The answer is simpler for a soldier than a mother. Mothers are soldiers now and the issues are even more complicated. But we are talking about a generation where the roles of men and women were clearly defined. I was unusual in my demands for an independent career. Edmond was a successful officer because he put his men first. The traditions of the army were deeply imbedded on both sides of his family. While his mother had looked after her home and her children, her husband had fought for France. He would do the same.

He overestimated Marie's strength and he could hardly foresee the consequences of Nazi occupation, but I think that he would have acted in the same way, even if he had been weighed down by hindsight. In England he contacted his Creighton cousins. There was no difficulty in his being accepted by the British, although, like me, he was blamed by frustrated people for France's easy capitulation. He could reply with confidence that he – and thousands of others – hadn't capitulated and were continuing to serve the allied cause. I could only stammer that not all the French had given up the struggle – my best friend's husband had escaped and joined the Free French. He found my telephone number, and let me know that Robert was alive on the eve of the surrender at St Valéry. It was a relief which I shared with Robert's family; but we had to wait for months before we had a postcard from his camp, Oflag VIIC near Salzburg. Even the standard letter, confirming that Robert wasn't missing but a prisoner, took agonisingly long to arrive. During the weeks of suspense, I took a train to Scotland and spent a week with my mother-in-law.

I found a community in shock. People shopped in silence. You would ask a question, and wait for the words to register before they could form a reply. The eyes were dead, unbelieving that the Gordons, heroes of the Great War, admired by the young Churchill in the Boer War, known to be foremost in fighting spirit and skill of the British Army, their reputation stretching back to the eighteenth century, had surrendered. Confirmation of the numbers killed came first. No one knew whether they wanted news or not. The waiting was unbearable, but until the letter arrived there was still the possibility that a son or husband or brother was still alive.

Suspense draws comfort from little things, routines like wearing old clothes and eating simple meals. Every evening we made the ritual tour of the many windows of the house, checking that each was covered in the blackout. No chink of space escaped Emily's beady eye. It took a long time, but it felt like playing a part in the battle which Britain was fighting alone, a small contribution to the war, a tenuous thread of contact with Robert. It was only when the letter arrived – my kindly daily help rang to say that she had posted it, but hadn't opened it – I saw Emily lose her Spartan self control. Strangely, she reminded me of my own mother. It made me wonder how Maman and Marie were coping with the loss of communication between us. In spite of my relief I felt dispossessed, unused – and foreign.

"You must play the piano, my dear," Emily said, only partly understanding my feelings. "There are some people coming in this evening. Would you let them hear one of your pieces?"

It was the last thing I wanted to do, to be shown off as a local attraction when I could be giving professional concerts. I thought of Wimbledon, where I would find Tadeusz and Paul, and a link between the past and present. The picture of disarray in the rue de Seine, contrasted with the ordered grandeur of the Scottish house made me want to burst out laughing. Emily misread my smile; an evening with the quality of Lechen had to be endured, comments on my clothes, worried platitudes about British isolation, and the barely hidden accusation of French betrayal. I have often looked back, and wondered whether they could ever realise that their own government had also betrayed Robert. Le Havre could have been another Dunkirk. There would have been terrible casualties, but the Division would have survived.

Some local musicians had been invited, justifying, I thought, my insistence on living in London; but they turned out to be the most agreeable of the guests, aware of the demands of my professional life, and cosmopolitan in their outlook.

"I heard Tadeusz Donska play the Dvořák concerto in Aberdeen two years ago. He's a wonderful cellist," said a Doctor Murray.

"Where does someone with a name like that come from?" whined Betty Cummings, the most insular Scot I ever met, even worse than her husband.

"Poland," I replied.

"We went to war because of Poland," she continued accusingly, "and now we're on our own."

"Tadeusz has been as concerned about his mother and sisters as we have been about Robert," I said.

"They aren't in the army," she blundered on.

"No, but they're Jews."

There was a stunned silence, broken by the outward-looking doctor. "Then I can understand why he's worried." He changed the subject valiantly. "Will you make more recordings? I would love to hear the Ravel Trio. It's far too difficult for me. The most I can manage is the Mendelssohn D minor."

"Then we must play it!" I said with an edge of venom in my voice. "I doubt if it's being performed in Europe."

The doctor smiled. He took me aside. "You don't have to play with us – although of course we would love it. My wife, Mary, is a better violinist than I am a cellist."

We played the Mendelssohn two evenings later. Dr Murray apologised for Betty Cummings' narrow-mindedness. "She takes uncommon care of Hugh, and she is a good doctor's wife, but we all know her ways."

"Don't worry. Robert told me. We're all worried about the future, and I don't suppose that there are many Jewish musicians in Aberdeenshire. I shouldn't have told her. It was wicked of me – I couldn't resist it! But her reaction makes me understand how the ordinary people in Germany feel, especially when they're constantly told that the Jews are to blame for their problems. It's a bit the same in France, although I was unaware of anti-Semitism until I met Tadeusz. He opened my eyes to many things." I paused, and changed tack. "He wasn't the first cellist I worked with. I played the first movement of the Brahms E minor sonata with my childhood friend. That's why I was able to play with good string players, when I went to the Conservatoire."

The Murrays complimented me on my English. I said that I had grown up with it at piano lessons, and we laughed when I told them about Soeur Antoinette and the duets.

"Don't go telling Betty that. She hates Catholics too!"

"I know – from my wedding!"

It was a good evening, much more relaxed than playing with Paul and Tad, and all the more enjoyable, because I found out how much people liked and respected Robert.

"We all miss him. He was such a dare-devil. If any one tries to escape it'll be Robert."

There was a brother of Stephen Murray's staying with them, a major who had been wounded at Dunkirk, convalescing in the brisk Scottish weather, which is often at its best in early autumn. He was as interested in music as Stephen and Mary. With the battle of Britain raging in the south, he longed to be back in action, and he sympathised with my frustration and feelings of isolation.

"Have you heard of ENSA?" he asked. "Why don't you and your trio enrol? You'd have to be auditioned – but that's no problem. They have groups of classical and variety musicians playing to the troops. There's plenty to do – in fact it's probably very hard work, but it would give you the opportunity to perform at a high level."

"It would be helping with the war too," I replied eagerly.

"It's organised by Basil Dean. They operate from Cambridge Circus in central London. Contact them as soon as you get back to Wimbledon."

I couldn't wait. It was something to do at last, something to help me forget that I was a foreigner, something for soldiers like Robert and Edmond.

Chapter 30 1940 – 1941

"Every Night Something Awful" – pianos with half the keys missing – signposts on the roads deliberately misplaced to confuse enemy agents, making everyone hopelessly late etc – but not usually the performances, although these too must have varied, especially when the players were exhausted. Entertainments National Services Association covered a wide range of shows, from classical to popular music, and light comedy to the tragedies of Shakespeare; and there were artistes like the well-known Vera Lynn, Gracie Fields and Joyce Grenville, as well as young musicians like us. The finest national performers – the sort of people who played at the National Gallery like Myra Hess – belonged to a different association called SEMA. I went to hear some of those concerts, which continued all through the blitz. The paintings were stored under the gallery, leaving gaps on the walls where Rembrandts, Turners and Monets had hung. I have a wonderful memory of Myra Hess playing the Mozart concerto in C – K 467 – the life she brought to the outer movements and the serenity of the Andante.

There were already three teams of eight classical players when I enrolled with Paul and Tadeusz, whom they accepted, in spite of his Polish background, as soon as they heard him play. We formed another group with a solo pianist, two singers, a clarinettist and horn player. I can't remember the organisation being less than excellent – perhaps ENSA was more relaxed about variety shows. At first I felt jealous of the soloist, but when I thought of the opportunities for chamber music, the trios with clarinet by Beethoven and Brahms, and the Brahms Horn Trio, I realised how lucky I was. We seemed to go everywhere, sometimes doing "pot-pourri" programmes, sometimes full works, and, as the allies progressed from North Africa to Italy, we were flown out to play to the troops behind the front line. I remember a concert with a wonderful piano in Sicily.

It was hard work. We wore army uniforms and we stayed sometimes in private houses, sometimes in dormitories in barracks, with the three women together in one room and the five men in another. I never felt really clean, and I was always glad to get back to Wimbledon where I had hot water heated by a coke stove, and electricity which was more powerful and efficient than in Paris, where two pins stuck into holes in the wall gave a feeble light. (Hot water in Paris was heated by gas which lit up when you turned on the hot tap. Not everyone had such luxuries. In rural Normandy there was neither gas nor electricity.)

The worst thing – apart from worry and danger – was the food. At home in Wimbledon I had chickens and vegetables, herbs and wine. I gave eggs to my gardener when I was away, asking him to take the onions, potatoes and other vegetables for his family, provided he left enough for me. I had no qualms of conscience about making the most of my home produce – and drinking the wine which Robert had imported from France before the war.

But on tour the food was dreadful – spam fritters, powdered eggs, and puddings made of sago and semolina, as well as the suet which surrounds an ox kidney! Nothing will make me eat Christmas pudding, which you prepare in September to serve three months later. Everything was washed down with strong tea, which I diluted with water and drank without powdered milk. I missed the fresh dairy products which were always available in Normandy, but I lived well at home, and always hoped that I could share my minor successes in the garden, like courgettes and asparagus, with Robert.

You may think how spoilt I was. Houses, especially in central and east London, were bombed daily; but I think that my determination to live well was more than self-indulgence. It was a way of saying to myself that I was French, and nothing was going to put me down – a little like the cockneys who kept up a cheerful banter wherever you went. I shared my asparagus with my neighbours, but I wasn't often there to enjoy it as the season was very short.

There were three concerts which I remember distinctly. The others simply flowed past, one tiring schedule following another. I became used to hearing my colleagues toss off the Mendelssohn Rondo Capriccioso, and Liszt's "Un Sospiro", and I was always playing the piano part of "The Shepherd on the Rock", a favourite of the soprano and clarinettist, and the Mendelssohn trio in D minor. I don't think that Betty ever found out who or what it was, let alone the race of the composer. Her loss! – and listening to Tad phrase that wonderful opening theme, the gain of thousands of soldiers, sailors and airmen, whether musically literate or not. They loved it.

I was so tired that it hardly registered that we were to play to the Free French in the late autumn of 1941. My only concern was to sustain enough concentration for another concert. I was young and could cope, but when I slept, I sank into oblivion, abandoning all thought of Robert, home or Marie. I would wake with a guilty conscience, reproaching myself for forgetting them, and start another gruelling day. It was hard work but a lot of it was fun – apart from the food.

You can imagine my joy when we discovered that not only the audience, but our hosts, were French. We played as we always did, but at the end I heard a voice sing the Marseillaise. I have perfect pitch. I knew what key he was singing in, and I started to accompany him. Our singers didn't know it, but it was enough for Paul or Tad to have heard something occasionally, to know the tune and the harmony. They had lived in France for four years, and they knew our National Anthem. It was encored again and again, until the soldiers were in tears – and so were we.

When the audience had gone I returned to the indifferent piano to calm myself with a Prelude and Fugue.

"So you still play Bach, Madame ?" said a voice I knew.

I looked up. There was a tree and a child and an army of insects. Somewhere there was a snuffly labrador running with eagerness towards someone I loved, a world of security and comfort and lovely things, like the smell of *Poule Normande* in sizzling cider, flambéed in calvados, and a strong Norman accent saying "Bravo!" There were two houses, one half timbered and the other bathed in a grey mist, a hexagonal tower full of paintings and, in the salon beneath it, strains of the Chopin Nocturne in B flat minor. The voice had teased and deceived me, but it still held its magic.

"Edmond!" I blurted out. Then I took hold of myself, "Forgive me, Monsieur! Yes, I play Bach when I'm at home."

"Anne Cummings," he said taking my hand and kissing it, "you have given us much pleasure. Please tell me, what is the news of Robert?"

"He sends postcards, telling me nothing except that he's alive. I'm sure he's tried to escape, but that's just guessing. And you, do you have news of – home?"

He looked grave. "No, I have no contact with my wife, and I have never seen Francis. I know that they're in good hands. Your mother is a remarkable woman."

"He must be eighteen months old by now – into everything. He had a shock of dark hair when he was a baby. I think of them all sometimes, but I have been working hard for ENSA and…."

"Unfortunately I have had too much time to reflect, but there is a rumour that we won't be idle for long. We may be leaving for one of the French colonies in Africa."

"When I think of it, I feel so helpless, with Marie and my parents in France, surrounded by enemies, while I am free. And – there's Robert a prisoner…" I felt that I was going to cry, and fought for self-control, but when I looked up from the piano where I sat counting the keys – anything to hold myself together – I saw that there were tears in his eyes too. He too looked away.

"I am a soldier. I must fight for France. I hope that the struggle will bring benefit to my family in the end."

We walked out into the night. Edmond lit a cigarette and offered one to me. Apart from the stars and a crescent moon, it was quite dark – and cold. We stood in silence as there was nothing to say. We couldn't talk of the future. It was like a locked door at the end of a long corridor, dark and narrow, veering one way and then the other, in a succession of tomorrows which were always the same, colourless like my uniform.

"Do you pray?" he asked.

"No," I replied. How could I tell Edmond de Valliet anything but the truth?

"You and your father are practical people. Your paths are marked out with decision and clarity, and you thrive on plans and successful outcomes. But there is more to you – and to everyone – than that. You have to focus on something beyond the demands of the world to understand it fully. It's only then that the balance between ambition and duty – sometimes conflicting duties – can be found."

I came to my father's rescue. "Papa may be a republican and an ambitious one, but he has a very strong sense of duty, to the family and the community. He visited Hervé in the military asylum… it couldn't have been easy."

"I know, and I respect him for it. But it doesn't mean that you can cut yourself off from God."

"The nuns taught us to pray, but they always seemed such hypocrites."

"It isn't easy to be a nun! You have to forgive them – and think what Soeur Antoinette did for you!"

"Sometimes she made my life very difficult! But I see what you mean. All those women living together – and no hope of change – except growing old."

"Try to pray, Anne Cummings. It's all that you – we – can do for Marie and Francis – and your parents – and Robert."

I didn't see him again until late autumn of 1944. I tried to pray, and I found that it was a way of remembering them all, even when I was stretched to the limit. But neither my prayers nor his were enough to save Marie.

Chapter 31 1941 – 1944

In December 1941, the Japanese attacked Pearl Harbor, and America entered the war against Germany. Six months earlier, Hitler had made a fatal mistake. His armies invaded Russia, where they were defeated by conditions which had driven back invaders of the past, like Napoleon and Charles XII of Sweden. The autumn rain turned roads into quagmires. The mud clogged up tanks and artillery, and frostbite chilled and maimed an army of three million, stranded amid the vastness of the Steppes west of Moscow. In Britain the key to the future turned in the lock, the door at the end of the corridor began to open, and the possibility of victory lay behind it.

For nearly four years I played for ENSA, returning home for occasional breaks, always tired, but trying to pray, as the nuns had taught me, for those I had left behind in occupied Normandy. Edmond left for French Equatorial Africa, where there were setbacks for the Free French as for everyone else. They had to learn to keep secrets.

I have said that three concerts remain vividly in my mind: playing to the Free French when I met Edmond, a second at Aldershot in March 1944 – it nearly turned out to be the last – and the third in Paris, six months later.

In the spring of 1944, our leaders were preparing for the invasion of France, with a huge network of espionage and counterintelligence to inform the allies and deceive the Germans – as well as making plans for D-Day. There were now American forces to be entertained, and our schedule became more and more demanding. The details of this second concert are all the more firmly imprinted on my memory, on account of the events before and after it. I happened to be at home for twenty-four hours when I was told that Robert had escaped. He was in neutral Portugal. Then a letter arrived. Robert was coming home. I ached to be with him again.

Dearest Anne,

I'm free and I'm on my way home. I don't know how many weeks it will take, and I can't give details. I long to hold you in my arms, after four wasted years! Keep well. I love you more than I can say.

Robert.

It was difficult to concentrate with such a change just over the horizon, a change from the drabness of the last four years, with the punishing schedule of concerts; as well as loneliness, missing the bright colours of my childhood, the sounds, the smells, the warmth and comfort of home, my parents – and Marie. In the shadows of my mind there lurked fear, which made me long for Robert's reassurance and optimism. I wondered if the army and ENSA would contrive to let us have some time together. When would he be back? How could it be planned? The future tantalised, one moment prosperous and defined, the next a web of questions. In the meantime there was a concert to prepare.

We were met in a rather grander way than we were used to, with the Colonel's wife inviting us to dine with them. I had almost given up hope of getting a decent meal and this was no worse or better than the usual fare – except that the dreadful food was presented with style. We had a thimbleful of sherry before dinner, which was served by a butler in uniform, spam fritters and rice pudding (made with powdered milk) and water to drink. Afterwards there was coffee which was unrecognisable except for the colour. I was taken aside by Mrs Jamieson with the invitation to "wash" which I longed to do – not just a splash of tepid water after going to the lavatory.

"My dear," she began imperiously – I wondered what entitled her to call me that – "my husband tells me that Captain Cummings has escaped. He was at the British Embassy in Geneva last week and is on his way to Lisbon."

"I know. Why do you call him Captain Cummings?"

"Escaping officers like your husband are usually promoted, especially when they save other people's lives in the process. He got out of Austria last autumn with another officer, who fell and hurt himself. Your husband more or less carried him up the side of a mountain, where they spent the winter in a Swiss chalet. He, I mean the other officer, knows my husband and has been in touch with him. Apparently Captain Cummings distinguished himself at St Valéry too. I shouldn't wonder that he'll get some medal. You should be proud of him!"

"I am," I replied, amazed, but still wary of Mrs Jamieson's patronising tone.

"Now," she added, "do you think that it's appropriate for the wife of a British officer to continue like this – with ENSA? You'll need to look after your husband when he comes home, not traipse around playing to soldiers – Americans too, I presume!"

British snobbery! It made me feel sorry for the Americans.

"I'll talk to Robert when he comes home," I said.

"Oh," she said with a faintly prurient smile. "He'll want you at home with him, for as long as the army gives him leave. Yes – the war hasn't spoilt your looks. I once had hair your colour. Mm…. I can see why he married you ….You're French, I believe. You don't sound it! ….Catholic too no doubt…," she sniffed.

Insufferable woman! "Musicians are often good linguists. They have good ears too." I replied. "And I owe my early musical training to an Irish nun."

"Well, whoever taught you, I think you should play your music at home from now on. The Colonel agrees with me."

I wondered who commanded the battalion, the Colonel or Mrs Jamieson. "I shall have to think about it. But thank you for the news of Robert's promotion."

The concert entertained Mrs Jamieson with a well-worn programme. We couldn't try anything different or contemporary. I have often thought that we had the players, the expertise – and the musical rapport after four years – to learn Messiaen's *Quartet for the End of Time,* but we didn't know of its existence, or its extraordinary first performance at a Prisoner of War Camp. Four thousand men, standing in the freezing cold of a Polish January, listened to one of the greatest works of the twentieth century. Messiaen himself played a piano with keys missing, and the cellist coped on three strings. When I think of Mrs Jamieson and her narrow mind, I compare it to the breadth and spiritual stature of Messiaen. I doubt if she would have liked him. He wasn't an officer, he was deeply Catholic, and he was French.

At the reception afterwards, I was approached by a Major Dunbar. He congratulated me on the concert in the usual way.

"I believe you're French," he said. He was much less condescending than Mrs Jamieson, but it struck me that I was accused of being French for the second time in one evening.

"Your English accent is so good that I would have thought you were British, possibly from Scotland."

"My husband is a Scot. He's escaped from a prison camp near Salzburg."

"My congratulations!" He bowed slightly. He then added, "My colonel wants to meet you."

"I've met him – and his wife." I didn't add that that was quite enough.

"Oh, this isn't my regiment. My headquarters are in London."

"And who is your colonel? Does he like music? If he does, I hope that he's interested in contemporary repertoire – or Bach. I never tire of Bach."

"He may like Bach. He's certainly heard how well you play. I believe you will be at home in Wimbledon at the end of this week."

"You seem to be well informed," I replied.

He bowed slightly.

"Perhaps you would both like to come to my house to hear some Bach – when my husband gets back. There seems to be some sort of conspiracy to stop me playing for ENSA!"

The conversation faded into the back of my mind. I went home for a rest, in eager anticipation of Robert's return. When the telephone rang the following evening, I wondered whether it was Robert, but a strange voice – very English – said "Is that Mrs Cummings? This is Colonel Grey. I believe you spoke to Major Dunbar after your concert at Aldershot."

"Yes, Anne Cummings speaking," I replied. "Do you have news of my husband?"

"I'm told he's still in Lisbon. I have other news that will interest you, though. Perhaps we can meet for lunch."

I didn't hold out much hope for the lunch, but I wanted to hear any news – any at all.

"Where would you like to meet me?"

"What about Prunier's in St James' Street? It's a fish restaurant. The food is excellent."

Perhaps Colonel Grey knew more about me than I realised. "Certainly, with pleasure – especially if the food is as good as you say."

It might seem very trusting of me, but this was war. Girls could travel by night in a compartment of soldiers without any fear of being molested. There was a spirit of comradeship, a feeling of everyone pulling together for a common cause that made you feel safe – anywhere – provided there were no bombs.

"Tomorrow at one. I look forward to seeing you!"

Chapter 32 March 1944

Colonel Grey was tall, commanding and suave. He offered to hold the conversation in French, but spoke it with such a deliberate and affected Oxford accent that I nearly told him not to bother. I would have preferred my father's Norman patois to the flow of perfect grammar with no nuance – except the sort of mockery in which the British upper classes excel – grandly articulate, like beautifully presented food with a synthetic taste.

So we spoke English and he was polite enough to say that my English was good. I didn't return the compliment.

"What would you like? The turbot is excellent. What about wine? Would you prefer Sancerre or Muscadet?"

"Sancerre. My husband imported quite a lot before the war. It's lighter than Muscadet."

"Ah yes, your husband has escaped. I believe he was captured at St Valéry – they ought to have got out at Dunkirk. And you – are you enjoying ENSA?"

"It's tiring, but everyone's worn out by this war. We have to produce the same repertoire over and over again. The only composer I never tire of is Bach. You said you had news for me?"

He poured out the wine and I lifted my glass to my lips. It was cool and fruity, dry enough to be served with fish, but lovely to drink on its own. I couldn't believe it – 1944 in the middle of London!

"You come from Normandy?"

"Yes, near Quinon. Have you news of my family?"

"Do you know Marie de Valliet, née Millet?"

"C'est mon amie. Marie, comment va-t-elle?" I gasped.

"I don't know. I have reason to believe that she has made some drawings which have been hidden, and would be of some use to – my people."

"Then is Marie in danger?"

"Who knows? I had clear radio messages from our agents in that area until the end of last week, but since then I have only had one rather strange one."

"Please tell me about Marie. Is she still with my parents? What about her son?"

"I believe your parents are in Paris."

"Marie is alone at La Chenaie?"

"Your parents' house?"

"Yes. Please tell me about her!"

"I can't give you much more information, because I haven't had any messages for some days. We want to find her drawings."

"If I could see Marie, I would be able to get them for you."

"If you tried to see her she would be – in considerable danger."

"So what can I do for you? How can I – we – save Marie from danger?"

The turbot arrived. The first mouthful was delicious. I hadn't tasted food like this since before the war.

"You can help me discover the meaning of this message."

"Surely you can decipher anything! Tell me about Marie."

"Not a 'horse in a swing'. There are no swings near your house."

"I know exactly where your drawings – Marie's drawings – are."

"Oh," he said nonchalantly, "where?"

I took a piece of paper out of my handbag, and started to draw. I looked up once and saw a curious glint in his eyes, and then the supercilious visor went down.

"There is a wood near our house, and in it, an ancient oak tree, so old that its trunk is split, but the broader side was strong enough to support the swing which we had when we were children. Before Francis was born – that's Marie's son – we went for a walk and she remembered that she'd hidden a brass horse in a crevice of the tree. She'd found it on the path, and hadn't wanted to take it home because it might be stealing, so she hid it safely in the tree. It was green and covered with mould when she took it out – probably years later – but it was quite dry." I looked up. He was interested. "This is where you can find your drawings."

He took the piece of paper, folded it and put it in his pocket. "It's where you will find them!"

"What do you mean?"

"The drawings will have to be found by night, and I can't send that sketch to our agents without it being intercepted."

"Then you can show it to one of the soldiers in your regiment."

"How does one distinguish one tree from another by night?"

"What are you saying?"

"That you will have to go. If you don't, your friend will be in danger. The Germans have ways of solving puzzles that wouldn't appeal to her."

"Even turbot and Sancerre have their uses," I said coldly. "How do I know you're British anyway? I wonder what your German's like?"

"Not bad. But I do work for the British government. I can easily prove it. Mm….you're an intelligent woman. And you're strong. The operation shouldn't be too difficult."

I was furious, I felt like a trapped animal. "You've planned this all along. It would have been more difficult if Robert were back! He wouldn't let me go."

"Ah, but he's stranded in Lisbon. The Channel is mined and Portuguese ships are wary of danger. As for flights, there should be no difficulty – when you get back from France."

I sighed. "What do you want me to do?"

"Fortunately, I'm quite certain that we are not being overheard, but I should like to continue this conversation after lunch. We will go to my office. Now what about a crème renversée? Light but very satisfying."

"I'll have coffee. I seem to have lost my appetite."

I sipped the coffee – real coffee – my own store had run out in 1941. "Will you promise one thing in return?"

"I make no promises, but I can listen to a woman – of spirit."

"Will your people – your agents – protect Marie, if I get the drawings?"

"They will try, but only if you don't attempt to see her. It might be… dangerous for you both – as well as for the operation."

I had walked into Prunier's full of hope, and left in deeper turmoil than I had known since Robert was reported missing.

Chapter 33 March 1944

Robert had escaped from prison, from confinement and indignity, but he had been respected by his captors because he was a northern European, and an officer. The Nazis recognised the tenets of the Geneva Convention, as long as it didn't interfere with their insane racial policies; and they aspired to be on a footing with the officer class of the western allies, aware that they were despised by their own aristocratic army elite.

It was my turn to be a prisoner, at the mercy of the British Secret Service, a victim of blackmail, what we French call *chantage* – being made to "sing" to protect my friend. I suspected that the Geneva Convention didn't specify what happened to the victims of spies and secret agents – and that I had entered a murky world where you depended on your wits, and would be sacrificed if you proved inconvenient. My fears were soon justified.

I didn't know it, but ENSA had already been told to replace me. There was a strong possibility that I wouldn't survive the mission, and the return of my husband was used as an excuse for withdrawing me from our group. Tad and Paul were furious. They made life difficult for my replacement, but there was nothing they could do about it. They were at the disposal of the authorities. War was war.

The next three days passed in a sort of twilight trance. I had to learn how to parachute from a thousand feet, and I remembered talking flippantly to Robert about jumping out of aeroplanes before the war. Fortunately I was athletic. I learned to fall in a somersault quite quickly from fourteen feet, keeping my legs together. When

I jumped out of a plane the first time I was terrified that the straps wouldn't work, and the canopy refuse to unfurl above me. At the end of the second day, I was told that we would be dropped into France the following evening. The weather was forecast clear and there would be a half moon.

I remember seeing someone at Knightsbridge and being met in Northampton by a lady with a cello in the back of her car. All the time I worked with a young para called Marcus – I've no idea if that was his real name. He was quietly encouraging, but he didn't invite me to confide in him, and became impatient if I betrayed any fear. We were together on a mission, and he looked upon me as less of a liability than a more hysterical woman would have been. It was a question of exercising concert nerves at all times – very, very tiring.

In March it gets dark about seven and we were to leave at eight. I suffered from a bout of concert tummy, and left feeling drained and empty. I remember walking over to the aeroplane, a funny-looking machine called a Lysander with short wings spreading out from on top of it. My whole being was jolted as we lurched into the air, and, paradoxically I felt sleepy. (Living on adrenalin wears you out in the end.) I must have dozed for half an hour, when I was gently woken by Marcus who said that we were approaching the French coast, and we would jump in ten minutes. I felt sick, but had to keep my head. The sleep had revived me a little.

When I jumped I expected to die, and suddenly I remembered Edmond. He'd asked me to pray for the others, and suddenly I realised that I could ask for help for myself. It's strange how childish we are at heart. I reasoned that with all the prayers that I had offered for the others, I had clocked up enough credit to say one for myself. What would the nuns have said about that? But there wasn't much time for theological arguments at a thousand feet, floating towards the ground under a huge white umbrella. I fell on uneven earth, and was grateful I wasn't tangled in a tree.

We quickly unravelled the parachutes, folded them up with our boiler suits, and hid them under a high Norman hedge. Then we set out to walk along a road I knew well. The road to La Chenaie.

"If you pass anyone, you're to behave like a couple out for a walk. Make it look realistic," said one of our instructors – Colonel Grey had disappeared into the mist as soon as I reached his office, leaving me in the care of his minions.

Marcus put a hand, which was cold and clammy in mine. He was as apprehensive as I was. There was a roar in the distance, the buzz of a motorcycle bumping along the uneven road, which had been paved years before the war, but was now little more than a cart-track. The buzz slid down a third, a whining diminuendo to an aggressive purr as the cyclist slowed towards us.

Marcus started to kiss me, clawing at my arm and taking care not to knock off the black beret which hid my distinctive hair.

"Fiancés, eh?" said a guttural voice.

"Mais oui," replied Marcus with a perfect French accent (which he hadn't learned from his colonel). He tried to sound as amorous as he could. The cyclist laughed and went on his way – possibly to some tryst of his own. There were plenty of willing girls wherever the Germans went.

We walked on, until we came to the place where the road veered right towards Quinon, and left to La Chenaie. I guided Marcus, telling myself that from now he was relying on me. We slowed down as we saw lights in the windows; my heart beat with longing. We followed a curving footpath away from the house, round towards the wood. Most of the overhanging branches hid the moonlight, but I knew the way and didn't need a torch. I walked noiselessly to the tree, our tree where we had our swing, and where Marie had hidden the brass horse. The outspread branches were wearing the pale green of early spring, when the leaves haven't quite unfolded. The moon could peer between them. A shaft of light reached faintly into the split trunk. I put my hand in the crevice, and there, wrapped in oilskin was the packet we had come for. I handed it to Marcus, who put it securely inside his coat.

He put his arm firmly in mine, and we followed the path back the way we had come. There was my house. I pulled at his arm. I couldn't resist it. Marie was there. I wanted to see her, to know that she was well, not frightened.

He pulled me back and hissed into my ear, "You mustn't approach the house – it's full of Germans." I pulled at his arm, and he gripped me with strong hands like a vice.

"What would you do if I did go near the house?"

"I would have to kill you."

As we passed, I thought I heard the sound of raucous singing and a piano being played in the background, my piano, the Steinway my father had given me for my eighteenth birthday. We walked on quickly, undetected. "Where is she?" I asked.

"She left three weeks ago."

So that was it. Marie was beyond my help, and I had risked my life – for what? The Colonel had fooled me. Marcus put his arm round me. It was a gesture of humanity, but if I had given way to my feelings, the cold-blooded killer would have resurfaced. I was in his power. We crept towards the fork in the road, back to the field where we had left our parachutes. We would have to wait under the hedge until the plane returned. I was too numb to feel very much. Would I have tried to enter La Chenaie, if he hadn't stopped me? Possibly. Of course I would have betrayed the whole mission. I knew I had been used, considered disposable, like a theatre ticket which you mustn't lose before the show, but is discarded afterwards – unless you want to keep it for sentimental reasons. I smiled to think that the Colonel could be sentimental – but then my red hair would have been recognised, and the Germans would have been put on the alert if they had found me with a knife in my throat. No, it was more convenient to bring me back alive – on balance – and soldiers like Marcus are not wanton killers. They prefer clean missions, but they kill without compunction when it's necessary.

We waited in silence – what was there to say? – until we heard the drone of the Lysander coming back for us. Marcus looked at his watch. It was half past midnight. I saw a smile crack across his impassive face. Mission nearly completed. He was handing me – good manners when all is well – into the plane when we heard the roar of a motorcycle. Agile as a cat, he jumped in beside me and the small aircraft started up again. There was the crack of a rifle. I crouched into the belly of the plane and lost consciousness. When I came to, we were over the Channel, and Marcus' arm had been roughly bandaged. I still wonder whether it would have been my arm, if the cyclist had approached half a minute earlier; one minute sooner, and I might have been left behind. The drawings were important. I was not.

I was too angry to speak to him, too unnerved to ask him if his arm was all right. I suppose he had done what he had to do, and a surface wound wasn't much of a price to pay. We sat and looked at one another.

"You did well," he said.

"Did you?" I replied.

"I did what I had to do, and I have the drawings. My arm will be fine."

"Where is Marie?"

"I don't know."

"You knew that I was being fooled, manipulated into going because I thought I could help her?"

"Yes, but the message was for you. It took us some time to find you, and quite a bit of research to realise that you were her friend. She wanted you to find the drawings. She put them in the tree, and left. The message came from another transmitter, but it was sent by the same person who contacted us three weeks ago."

"How do you know?"

"Because I received the messages. I know the code-name of the member of the Resistance who sent it."

I had a flash of inspiration. "Was it Jean Belliot?"

"We only deal in codes. Real names are too dangerous."

"How did you know Marie's?"

"More research. It was a question of finding out who could draw."

We touched down with an unexpected jerk, and I was sick. "Dear God, where is Marie?" I wailed in my weakness.

The next day Robert rang. He was back. He had three weeks' leave.

Chapter 34 Calvados 1940 – 1942

Where was Marie? The story of our patch of Normandy between 1940 and 1944 is a tragedy where one by one the lights are turned off, and hope and happiness sputter out like a candle burnt down to the end of the wick. There were those who survived, but everyone was changed by the events, not least Soeur Antoinette who told me much of what follows. She was one of those larger-than-life characters who thrive on drama; confinement within the walls of a convent where most of the women were narrow minded and ill-educated, was a terrible penance for someone so gifted and intelligent. She may have infuriated me when I was a child, but I was the one to whom she gave every ounce of her inherent artistry, and when I had gone, she hovered round those I left behind like a guardian angel.

The first – and most astonishing – change was the arrival of Charles de Valliet, a fully fledged priest, having left his Order in Bavaria. He took up residence with the tottering curé, allowing him to sink into the oblivion he longed for, while an active young man performed his duties. I say astonishing, because when I heard that he had returned to Quinon I could hardly believe it. But to the people of the parish it was a welcome change. Anyway, how could a Frenchman bear to live in Germany, the country of the occupier? He became popular with the local Catholics, making an effort to involve himself in their round of domestic problems, always advising patience in adversity, and urging humility on those who were prosperous. Not that there was much prosperity to boast about, but life wasn't materially hard for the people of Quinon until the invasion of 1944. My father was just as active in the interests of the community. That was his undoing.

Soon after the armistice was signed, German soldiers began to infiltrate the area, making their headquarters at Ronval, where they installed makeshift electricity dependent on an outside generator, and introduced a second telephone line. (The first had appeared just in time for the birth of Francis.) They kept Marie's maids – those who were willing to work for them. Marie had been at La Chenaie ever since I had left. She supervised the inventory which the Germans made of her furniture, and they promised to look after everything carefully – especially the pianos and the paintings. They even had the pianos tuned.

The occupation of Ronval didn't undermine her as much as the absence of Edmond and me. When she returned from supervising the inventory, she had had a good morning, making arrangements and seeing that her husband's things were in order. What she found much harder was coping with the continual demands of the baby. She was helped by the nursemaid who adored Francis and got on well with my mother. Between them he was well looked after, but my mother noticed that she would slip out into the wood, sit under the tree, and talk to the rabbits, leaving the squalling Francis, who was teething, behind. Marie would come back in a fit of conscience and then sing to him, but she would clasp her hands over her ears when he cried and beg him to stop.

When Charles heard about this, he reprimanded her so soundly that she stayed in for a week while Francis was ailing. She respected Charles, looking to him for support. He was most insistent that she should take good care of his nephew and, I am sure, made use of the confessional to lecture her about her duties as a mother.

Then troubles began for my parents. My father was responsible for the sale of dairy products, some of which were exported to Germany, where people were living extravagantly after the fall of France. Milk, butter and cheese were provided for the officers and men at Ronval. My father made them pay well for it. On the other hand, as 1941 turned into 1942, life began to be hard for the people in Rouen and Paris, and my father was asked to lower his price for some of the shops which supplied poor areas. He was also prepared to lower his prices for the people of Quinon. Someone who was benefiting from his generosity informed the Commandant at Ronval. My father was told to leave the area. He lost his position as maire of the district, and he and my mother set off for Paris, hopeful that they could live reasonably in their flat in the rue de la Motte Piquet.

Imagine their consternation when they found that the flat had been taken over by a German family attached to the Ecole Militaire. They looked for somewhere else, but the only place they could find was a tiny apartment in the rue Gramme with no bathroom, no hot water and a privy outside. There was little to buy in the shops and no fuel in the winters, which were particularly severe during the war. The cold, frustration and lack of country air undermined my father's health, but my mother did her best to keep him cheerful. She read when she could, but Papa was used to the constant coming and going of business life, and was ill-suited to any kind of idleness or reflection. Eventually he became involved with the Resistance in Paris, joining a group of Gaullist supporters, who, towards the end of the occupation, were as wary of the communists as of the Germans.

When she wasn't worrying about Papa, Maman thought about Marie. She hoped that Charles would provide a rock, someone on whom she could rely and make her feel useful. When my parents left, he started coming to La Chenaie most evenings. He took a great interest in Francis, who was a little frightened of him, but he would read to him and play with him, while Marie was preparing the *diner*.

"I often wonder where Edmond is," she said to him one evening. "When this war's over I'm sure he'll come back. The trouble is that I begin to forget what he's like. I have to look at my wedding photograph to remind me."

"I suppose that he's still in England. It surprises me that the Germans haven't defeated the British too."

"And Anne is in England. I wish she were here."

"You should be wishing your husband were here – not Mrs Cummings."

"But I feel that I've known Anne for so much longer. You know that she came back when Francis was born. Edmond has never seen Francis … I wanted Anne to stay. Now Tante Cécile and Papa have gone too…"

"But I visit you every evening, and you have Francis to care for. You are also looking after a property that used to belong to our family."

"I know. Anne told me all about it."

"You must tell me about the people who come to the house, and be careful about letting them in."

"Oh, just Jean Belliot. He cuts wood for me, and gets provisions in his cart from Quinon. He runs the farm and makes himself useful now that Papa is away."

"You mustn't allow him into the house," said Charles abruptly.

"Why?"

"Because he's most likely a communist, and a very bad influence on any one."

"But you can still let him cut the wood. I need it for the boiler – for heating the water."

"I don't want him anywhere near Francis, and you must talk to him as little as possible."

But Jean often called and made himself useful, mending the boiler when it broke down and refitting several doors of the outhouses, which had warped in the unusually severe winter frost. She tried to discourage him from coming into the house, but as spring of 1942 finally burst upon the frozen and desolate countryside, the torrent flooding the banks which divided Ronval and La Chenaie subsided, and the mud on the paths began to dry, she would walk out to the tree with her easel, or down to the river leaving Francis with his nurse.

"Bonjour, Mme de Valliet."

"Bonjour, Jean Belliot."

"Do you have enough logs?"

"We're running low. Can you bring some by the end of the week?"

"Can I get you anything else?"

"Yes. I need more paper – and some paints. I'd have to get them from Caen. There's a special shop there for artists. When you come to the house with the logs, may I give you a list?"

"Volontiers, madame!"

There was nothing mocking about Jean now. He still found her attractive, but he had deeper reasons for wanting to be useful to Marie. The Resistance in France was a tiny movement, not very well organised, and split into different factions, the communists being only one. I don't think that Jean wanted to involve Marie with their activities, but he was suspicious of Charles, whom he had seen going to Ronval from time to time. He wanted to keep an eye on him.

I know that it was during the summer of 1942 that Jean started to supply Marie materials for her painting and drawing. Soeur Antoinette happened to be in Caen with another of the sisters one morning, visiting a nun who was in hospital, when she met him, with a large pad of drawing paper, and a basket full of pencils and tubes of oil paint.

"Have you taken up art, Monsieur Belliot? You never had much talent for music!"

Typical Antoinette – outspoken as ever!

"Non, ma Soeur, I have bought all this for Mme de Valliet."

"Tell her to ask me to get them next time. You stick to your cows and your cheese!"

Soeur Antoinette wasn't being unkind. She had heard Charles talk of Jean, and she was genuinely concerned about Marie. She had her own thoughts about them all.

Chapter 35 1942 – 3

"I told you to have nothing to do with that man!" said Charles when he next saw Marie.

Marie was in tears. "Edmond never spoke to me like this. Neither did Anne and her parents. Oh, why have they all gone away?"

"M. Favoret was cheating the Germans. Whether you like it or not, they run the country now, and you have to do what you're told. They are trying to restore order to France – to get rid of dangerous elements – communists and so on. You mustn't talk to, or have anything to do with, Belliot. The Commandant at Ronval doesn't like him, and neither do I!"

Marie ran out of the house into the wood, crying with disbelief. She leant against the tree and started to moan quietly. Then she sat still staring into space. It was her way of detaching herself from pain. She couldn't reason with herself, take note of Charles' awareness of what the Commandant thought, and wonder why he should be on such terms with the German authorities. Charles was Edmond's brother and a priest; she must respect him. But she wanted to feel secure, needed, loved. The stern priest had begun to frighten her.

"What are you doing?" said a friendly voice.

Soeur Antoinette had had to ask permission to come to La Chenaie, and travel with another sister. She had spoken to Reverend Mother about Marie, and they were both concerned for her well-being. Each had their reasons for wanting her to have nothing to do with Jean. The narrow-minded Reverend Mother was anxious for her purity. Antoinette, too wise to disagree, had no doubts of Marie's loyalty to her absent husband. She understood Jean's intentions and feared for Marie's life – and Francis' too.

"Charles is angry with me," she said looking into the distance. "Where is Anne?"

Soeur Antoinette took her hand. "Come into the house, and make me some tea the way Mme de Valliet used to. Anne will come back one day, and so will your husband. But now you must visit us in the convent – as you did when you were a little girl."

Marie kissed the sister, and they walked together to La Chenaie where Francis was playing with his nanny.

"Maman," he said as he tottered and fell. Marie picked him up, and held him close to her.

"He's very like his father," said the other Sister, who had made herself comfortable near the fire.

Marie made tea and they all sat round the old stone fireplace. There was no sign of Charles, and she chatted quietly to the two nuns, who begged her to visit them often.

"I shall come into Quinon when the weather's fine. The cart goes there most days. I shall have to ask someone to take me."

"Don't ask Jean Belliot," said Antoinette. "He's too busy especially now that M. Favoret is no longer here."

Marie sighed. "Why have they all left me?"

Marie took to visiting the nuns, who sent her on errands of mercy which she was delighted to perform. Charles continued to come in the evenings, and for a while she saw nothing of Jean. André Roche, who helped on the farm, brought her logs and drove her on the cart to Quinon. He also drove her to Caen, when she needed materials for her painting.

But Marie became increasingly lonely. It must have seemed to her that the past was a sort of dream that had never existed, a dream between the world where she spent her early years, and the isolation of her present. There are those who look for comfort in food, in drink, in drugs, in sex, but Marie found a far-away place in her mind, where Edmond and I were close to her and where she could escape from the pain of feeling we had all abandoned her. She would go out to the rabbits without her easel, and just sit looking into the distance, without drawing anything, just staring as her father had done.

Then the evening would come, and she would make herself busy preparing a meal for Charles, and sit in silence while they ate it. He would ask her about Francis, and she would reply truthfully that he was well and that his nanny was looking after him.

And so 1942 stole into 1943 without definition or ceremony, beyond remembering the birth of the Christ-child as December ended and another bleak January began. Francis was three and running about in the wood, his nanny constantly in attendance, and always worried that he would hurt himself.

One day he came back with a toy horse that had been carved out of wood.

"C'est un cadeau," he said showing it to his mother.

"Who gave you the present?" she asked.

"Jean. C'est beau, n'est pas?"

The nanny interrupted. "He was playing on the path, and M. Belliot came up to us. He gave the toy horse to Francis. I couldn't stop him."

It wasn't only Marie who was forbidden to talk to Jean, but small children don't know anything about such embargoes. "We must give it back," said Marie.

She waited for Charles that evening, but he didn't come. It was sometimes like that. She would wait until nine, and then eat her meal silently, sometimes taking a book to the table with her, trying to fill her emptiness with the sort of stimulus that she'd shared with me. There was a knock at the door. She opened it quietly. It was Jean.

"You mustn't come here. It's forbidden – and you shouldn't give presents to Francis. Please go away!"

"Your brother-in-law is at Ronval." he replied.

"But it's his home – my home – and he speaks German. I just wish he would tell me if he's not coming!"

"He's dangerous."

"That's what he says about you. Please go away."

"Do you want to help your husband?"

"My husband isn't here. I don't know where he is."

"He's with the Free French."

"I don't know what you mean. Please go away." She was terrified that Charles would arrive and find her with Jean.

"You can help the Free French – you can help people who think like your husband, if you could do some drawings in Caen."

Marie became more and more agitated.

"No, Charles would be angry with me. Please go away."

"I shall see you tomorrow afternoon in the wood – by the tree – at three. Please come! Your son will be resting."

"I can't. Please go away."

The following morning, Marie went to the convent to look for Soeur Antoinette, but she wasn't there. She returned with her provisions, in the wagon with André, and helped to prepare lunch for her household. She didn't know what to do. Would she be helping Edmond if she went to see Jean? How could he think differently from his brother? Charles was here in Normandy. He had to get on with the Germans like everyone else, and it was easier for him because he spoke their language. If Edmond were here it would be the same…but Edmond had left her, and so had Anne. They would advise her. What was she to do?

She walked into the wood at three and met Jean. He didn't seem dangerous, and she had missed his practical intelligence. André wasn't as good at mending things as Jean, nor could he make useful suggestions for making life easier – it was becoming harder for them all. It wasn't just luxury items that were difficult to buy in the shops, and even she, who had quite enough money found that everything was more expensive.

"I'm glad you came, Madame."

"Please tell me what you want quickly."

"You go to Caen about once every month?"

"Yes. To buy things I can't get in Quinon. I need paper and paints, as well as clothes for Francis."

"The town is heavily fortified and we need drawings or photographs of the guns – where they are, where they point to. Can you draw from memory?"

"Yes, I have a good memory for detail."

"Then have a good look when next you go to Caen and see what I mean."

"I shall look, but I can't make promises."

"Don't tell anyone."

"If Charles knew, he would be furious."

"Just look! Don't do anything else, but remember that you could be helping the Resistance. Your husband is fighting for them."

"I don't know anything about my husband. He's gone away. They've all gone away. I wish Anne were here."

"She's in England. The British want to free France from the Germans. She'd want you to do this."

It was the most insidious of his arguments. She was uncertain of what Edmond would want her to do, as he had been replaced by Charles as an authority. But I remained alive in her mind. I had come to her when she needed me – when Francis was born – when she was forced into a world of responsibility without a husband to support her.

Chapter 36 Winter 1943 – February 1944

Marie was now caught between Charles, who frightened her but wanted to protect her, and Jean who reasoned with her, but was prepared to use her and endanger not only her life, but her son's life too. If only Charles, who understood how vulnerable she was, could have been gentle with her, she would have obeyed him, feeling that he represented her husband. His greatest mistake was to disparage her longing for me, creating an uneasy space which sullied their relationship, a space which Jean cleverly filled with his assurances that I would acquiesce in what he wanted her to do.

You will ask, what about patriotism? What about making sacrifices for your country? In France during the war the issues weren't clear, and news was censored much more than in Britain where nearly everyone saw the war in terms of black and white. For the British, the only jarring factor was the alliance with Russia, a necessity which Churchill justified with stirring speeches. To many French people, Pétain was the patriot, the saviour who had extricated France from another horrible conflict. The "Free French" were officially traitors. Many of those who accepted the Vichy régime and the occupation of north France, looked upon them as an irritant which chafed consciences prepared to pay any price for peace. Most people were unaware of their existence.

Although Edmond was, by this time, only alive to Marie in their son, the presence of Charles might have enabled her to retain her reason. He represented the church – she was a Catholic by upbringing and dutifully religious by nature. But his anxiety to protect her made him more officious than he might have been, because he knew what the Nazis did to their enemies – supposed and otherwise. My parents were fortunate just to be sent away from the area. They might easily have been put in a concentration camp.

But torn between two men who hated one another, Marie had to make a choice. I don't think that Jean ever harassed her sexually. She would have recoiled immediately, putting his plans at risk. He was single-minded and ambitious, and although he realised that she was emotionally fragile, I doubt if he had the insight to weigh her use as an artist against her instability as a conspirator. She visited Caen and looked around with an artist's eye, absorbing detail and feeling at one with a task which suited her talents, and pleased Jean. His cause was mine – and even in a vague way her husband's – although she couldn't imagine how Edmond's interests could differ so radically from his brother's. She wasn't stupid, but she was lonely. She had to believe someone, and she was convinced that she was doing what I wanted. It is why, when she had nearly lost all sense of reality, she sent a message about the drawings which only I would understand.

"When are you next going to Caen?" asked Jean one day towards the end of 1943.

Marie was always agitated when they met. "Next week."

"You'll need paper and pencils. There's a doctor's surgery where you can go and draw after you have looked carefully at the fortifications. You can leave your work safely there."

She didn't reply that she had only agreed to look. He found that the easiest thing was to make a presumption, and then tell her what to do. She was too confused to argue. So Marie became an unwitting member of the Resistance movement in France. Once she had started a task she always took pride in doing it well. Jean was vigilant, and there were several Resistance workers in Caen making sure that she didn't behave too conspicuously. She would sit down and find someone beside her chatting and encouraging her. They never let her wander too close to the guns – or the Mairie…

By February 1944, the invasion was being planned in detail. It was just a question of time and preparation – and keeping the Nazis guessing where and when the allies would land. The capture of Caen was pivotal to their plans – in the end it didn't fall until six weeks after D Day, as the town was in the hands of a ruthless SS Commandant who believed in defending it to the last. Caen, beautiful Caen, with its half-timbered buildings and old-world charm, was flattened. My grandparents were killed in the bombardment, and their house obliterated. So the drawings, which were supposed to be a token of friendship, were important to the allies, and their safe delivery the responsibility of Colonel Grey and Marcus, who, like Jean, believed in short-cuts and blackmail. At least I knew that I had been manipulated.

Around Marie, the threads of conspiracy and betrayal were tightening. After her last assignment in Caen, she waited for André. Having been told to conceal the drawings, she did so with her usual attention to detail. She wrapped them in oilskin, and wedged them in a hollow in one of the wooden rails which André had carved in a corner of the cart. Jean had told her that they were important, that they were to go to England. As to how this would happen, she was sure that Jean would find a way of sending them to me. She had no knowledge of the presence of secret agents, nor even of the Resistance. She would go back home to give them to Jean, who was to meet her at the tree at seven. The doctor must have been relieved to see her go.

As she was leaving Caen, she saw a familiar figure on horseback, Charles, who also made trips to Caen every fortnight or so. He looked haughty and strained, and pulled up his horse in front of his sister-in-law.

"What are you doing here?"

"I come to Caen to shop. You know I do. Francis always needs new shoes or clothes."

"Go home and stay there. Send your maids to Caen for the shopping in the future."

Marie returned feeling deflated. Charles had been unusually unfriendly. She was glad that she would see Jean, who never talked to her like that. But Jean wasn't there at the tree at seven. Francis was in bed and she had already made preparations for an evening meal for two; she didn't want to see Charles, but she presumed he would come.

When Jean didn't arrive, she began to fret, and then loneliness besieged her mind and narrowed it, focussing on her love for me, anything rather than venturing outwards to the wider possibility of danger and reality. She must have held the package in her hand and wondered what to do with it. How was it to reach Anne in England? (She might even have smiled at a fanciful picture, imagining it floating across the Channel in its waterproof wrapping.) She must have thought of me, of the brass horse, of pulling against my arm as Francis' head peeped though her quivering legs, as she gasped with pain. She hid the drawings in the crevice and walked home. It is likely that she had already dismissed them from her thoughts, looking upon them as a sort of maths problem that had been solved: QED, "done and dusted", you might say.

Charles was agitated and beathless when he came in for supper.

"The Germans are on to something, and I'm sure that Belliot's involved. Serve him right – godless communist!"

"How do you know?"

"I've heard them talking. Now promise me, you haven't had anything to do with him?"

She looked into the distance and said, "Not any more."

"If you have they'll find out soon enough. Piot has already been arrested. They've got him up at Ronval."

"Not Bernard Piot! He's a fine man with an excellent brain. That's what Anne's parents always said."

"He's another one. A terrorist. They don't want the best for France, they want to establish a communist regime. That would be worse than having the Germans, who at least allow the church to go on as before." He paused, and continued more gently than she had ever known. "Marie, if you are involved, please let me take Francis and his nurse to the convent. I can't help you, but the Germans are ruthless with their enemies – and their children."

"Then you must take them," she said.

He looked at her and groaned. I know all this because he told Soeur Antoinette who took responsibility for Francis and his nanny. They dyed Francis' hair blonde and dressed him as a girl. It was Soeur Antoinette who made the decisions, and who would have gone to a concentration camp with them if they'd been discovered. She had been making plans for some time. They stayed at the back of the house where she gave music lessons, and the nanny had to wear the religious habit until the town was liberated in July. She was well rewarded for her courage, but for Soeur Antoinette the reward was much greater. I think it was the first time she felt truly alive.

They left in the cart which Charles had borrowed from André. The nanny was on the verge of tears, but one harsh word from Charles was enough to keep her quiet. They reached Quinon half an hour later. It was dark and they weren't seen.

But what of Marie? She probably wandered round the house in a dream-like trance. Charles had told her she must cut her hair and leave La Chenaie. When Jean arrived, he would have been breathless with fear; nearly all the members of his cell had been rounded up, but he wasn't with them because he had set out for the wood to collect the drawings. He had seen the soldiers pass and had to crouch behind a barrel until he knew that the path was clear. He asked her where the drawings were and when she told him that she had hidden them where the Nazis couldn't find them, he was relieved that they wouldn't be in their possession if they were caught. The British agents could pick them up later. In the meantime it was vital to get away. Jean cut her hair and they burnt it after she had swept it up carefully. They ran out into the darkness heading east towards Rouen.

Charles returned to La Chenaie the next day with the Commandant from Ronval. He questioned the maids, who were astonished at the disappearance of Mme de Valliet, her son and his nurse. They must have escaped with Belliot. The whole area was searched for a man with two women and a small boy, but they were never found.

Chapter 37 Spring 1944

Where was Marie? I tried not to weary Robert with my worries. He too was furious that I had been treated like a piece of flotsam, because I was vulnerable – and because I was French. Officially I was a British national, the wife of a junior, now decorated, officer in the army, who had escaped from the heavily guarded camp at Laufen in Austria. He had made use of the time to improve his German, and got away with another officer who was already fluent. There was an incident when Robert managed to frighten his fellow officers by imitating the guards – he had picked up the Austrian "o" sound instead of the dark "a", a little like Norman patois.

But there was little else that could spoil our happiness. I was free of ENSA – at least for the time being – and glad to be at home with him at last. We reasoned our way through our escapades until the danger receded in my mind, and I found a grudging satisfaction in having risked everything for the war effort. There was no point in being angry. We were sure Colonel Grey wouldn't be in touch again.

The worry about Marie had to be controlled but it was always there. I would forget it, and then my thoughts would fly to her as I looked at a picture or prepared a meal. Human beings can't endure much reality. I would imagine her in the hands of the Nazis. We didn't know much about the Gestapo (but the word "interrogation" was enough), only a little about the camps, and nothing of the slaughter of the Jews. I found myself shuddering with fear, and walking round the garden feeling selfish because I was trying to relieve my fears, not hers. But I couldn't let Robert suffer. He helped me to restore my old optimism with his cheerful humour and irresistible ability to laugh at himself and life around him.

"I'm glad you found room for one rose among this invasion of hens and vegetables."

"You'd miss them both if I hadn't dug up the flower beds."

"And who wrings the victim's neck when you want fresh chicken?"

"The gardener. I've done it once or twice."

"I think I'd prefer good clean fighting in the army. Did you get pecked?"

"No! The worst thing is plucking it afterwards!"

"Well – let me see who's for supper. What about that villainous-looking dark one in the corner?"

"She's a good layer. And you like fresh eggs for breakfast."

"What about keeping a pig too?"

"One wouldn't be enough and there isn't room for a family."

"Talking about families…"

"Wait and see!"

His large hands would stray towards my back and I would tremble with excitement. It was all part of his infectious happiness, as much as physical desire. He made everything fun. I would find myself laughing more than I had ever done before. The three week holiday had to include a weekend in Scotland which slightly curtailed our freedom, and I had to endure another evening of Hugh and Betty's insular conversation. We decided not to talk about my adventure in Normandy.

"So you've given up playing concerts for the troops?" said Betty. "You'll have time to look after your house properly now."

"My house is small and I have excellent help. I have a good gardener too," I replied.

"Anne grows every vegetable you can think of, and keeps hens too."

"We don't need to keep hens. There may be rationing, but Hugh's patients give us chickens and eggs."

"Meat is tightly rationed in London. It's very difficult to buy anything. If you keep chickens, you are given chicken feed instead of eggs," I added.

"Oh – down south …" Betty looked at us with grudging pity.

"Well, you'll be glad of good Scots roast beef here in the north. You don't need any fancy vegetables with Aberdeen Angus," said Hugh.

Emily did everything possible to make the meal festive, but I missed my vegetables and herbs. Betty refused to drink wine, and Hugh stuck to whisky, but in spite of the war, it was too important an occasion to drink water with the unadulterated rib of beef. Robert produced a bottle of vintage claret from the storeroom.

I was glad to get away and have two more nights with him before he went back to the army. The 51st Division had been reconstituted out of the 9th Division by the indefatigable General Wimberley, with most recruits from the same parts of Scotland as those who had been captured at St. Valéry. They were determined to avenge their fellow soldiers, languishing in German prisoner-of-war camps, and fought brilliantly with the Australians and New Zealanders in the Eighth Army at El Alamein, before thirty-nine days of fierce combat in Sicily. They had been shipped back to Britain to prepare for the invasion of France.

Robert rejoined the 5th/7th Gordons, who were training hard in the south of England. By the end of May I began to wonder if I was pregnant, but the signs were inconclusive and I presumed that I wasn't. It was disappointing for Robert, but we made plans for having children after the war. I wondered how I would fill my time without friends or family or concerts.

One evening I was at home when the door-bell rang. It was Tad and Paul.

"We've told your replacement to stay at home for the rest of the war. It was hopeless. We've persuaded the others that they don't want her either. What happened to you when you suddenly disappeared?" Tad had no time for health or the weather.

I told them about being parachuted into Normandy, and how the British Secret Service gave me only a fifty-fifty chance of survival.

"Well, come back to ENSA for light relief," said Paul. "The schedule's punishing but at least you know the repertoire, and they say that the end of the war is in sight."

"Any chance of doing something different?"

"Not likely. Perhaps if we went to Paris they'd let us play the Ravel."

"If we're playing that, I'd have to practise."

"If you've spent your time cooking and parachuting, you'll have to practise anyway." Tad was always direct.

I laughed. "I've been playing Bach ever since Robert went back to the army. At least my brain's in order."

"That's a start," said Tad. "Seriously, Anne, it'll be wonderful to play with you again."

A compliment from someone like Tadeusz really means something. I didn't need any more persuasion, and I found myself back on the ENSA treadmill, feeling more easily tired than before, but glad to be busy. I saw Robert once before June. He told me he had come across Edmond during field exercises.

He had fought in the West African colonies and the desert, under Général Leclerc. The summer of 1944 was the moment that all the Free French – still a small number of divisions – were longing for. I wonder now if Edmond had any idea how Normandy would devastated by the end of July, how towns and villages would be reduced to rubble in the name of freedom. When I look back, I have a little sympathy with the Vichy sympathisers who remembered north France as a wasteland in 1918.

"I met Edmond on a Dorset beach. He looked fit and well, but it was difficult to talk to him. Of course he asked after you."

"You didn't tell him about my adventure, did you?"

"No. He must be worried enough about the wife and son he left four and a half years ago. How much worse if he knew they had left La Chenaie!"

"It must have been hard for you not to mention them."

"I merely said that I hoped they were well. He doesn't even know your parents are in Paris."

A wave of nausea came over me. Where was Marie? Would I ever see her again? No, and I wouldn't see Robert either. The Second World War took them both away from me, only two among fifty million lives sacrificed for a nation's pride, and a clash of half-baked theories.

Chapter 38 Summer 1944

6 June 1944 has inspired films and books, D Day – Jour J for the French Resistance waiting by their radio transmitters for coded messages – the disgorging of thousands of British and Americans on to the Normandy beaches. The British and Canadians, well supplied with landing craft and amphibious tanks with mine-sweeping flails, met little opposition, but the Americans at Omaha beach suffered over two thousand casualties. Nearly four years to the day after the surrender of the Highlanders, the reconstituted 51st Division landed with the huge allied army to avenge the past on a nation that knew it was losing.

I have often wondered whether the drawings were of use to the battalions of the 51st Division who captured the defences on the east side of Caen. It was a difficult campaign for the Highlanders, responsible to several different commands, but the Gordons fought well and Robert distinguished himself, earning promotion from captain to major.

But dark clouds were gathering in our "commune", even though the end of the Occupation was in sight. To people who had accepted the Germans – and there were many of them – it must have seemed that the Anglo-Saxons were taking revenge for a conquest nearly a thousand years before. Their villages were flattened and their fields stank with the remains of the dead – man and beast.

Quinon was farther inland than the towns that were the worst hit by the invaders. Before the Canadians arrived, the Commandant made plans to retreat, but his soldiers didn't give up the Mairie without a fight. It was besieged and hailed with grenades and gunfire, while the invaders hid in the church and planned how to take it from behind. In the end the Germans came out waving a white flag, but the walls had been so damaged that they fell on top of three of them. The sisters from the convent tried to bandage the wounded of both sides, and to warn the people to keep away from the building. Another tall figure in a habit was helped by a little girl who fetched water from the pump.

It was at this moment that the curé roused himself from his torpor, finding the energy to minister to the dying, and saying prayers with men who lay crying for their mothers in English, French and German. A large nun with a capacity for taking command, opened a house where stretchers were laid side by side, while the local doctor went from one patient to the next, without morphine to relieve their sufferings. Soeur Antoinette was indefatigable, and Reverend Mother let her get on with it.

The next day a small boy was helping a woman who looked like a nurse.

"Où s'touve onke Char?" he asked.

"I don't know," replied the nurse. "Go and get some more water, Francis. Sick people are always thirsty. I must dress this wound again. Don't look."

Oncle Charles went back to Ronval riding as far as La Chenaie, and then walked up to the house that he had always known and loved. He wasn't aware of being followed, until he was climbing up towards the wood which separated the river and the orchard from the house. He started to run, but his pursuers were too fast. He fell down as though he had been tackled in rugby – he had played for Ampleforth – but this time it was in earnest. Rough hands bound his arms. He was dragged into the chapel on the east side of the house and locked inside.

"We'll come for you tomorrow," said Jean Belliot. André Roche stood guard outside, taking turns with someone else to make sure the prisoner didn't escape.

It was a time for settling old scores, a time without the rule of law, before the Canadians installed themselves at Ronval. Even they turned a blind eye to acts of revenge – collaborators who were found in a ditch gashed and hardly recognisable. Charles could expect no mercy. He had betrayed the Quinon Resistance cell. Their leader, Bernard Piot, had died courageously under torture, watched by the other two, who endured the first frenzy of pain, before gabbling incoherently about Marie, Jean and the drawings. They were taken outside and shot. All three bodies were dumped in an alley-way in Quinon, a reminder to the populace of what happened to traitors.

The revenge killings in France have been variously estimated as between 10,000 and 100,000, the real figure probably somewhere in between. Neighbour had traduced neighbour; the Jews had been deported and Resistance workers betrayed. The great French hero Jean Moulin had died like Bernard, horribly tortured, refusing to betray his friends. Bernard Piot, the sensitive idealist, suffered as much, but he too said nothing.

Jean knew that Charles had spied on him and the rest of the partisans. He had always hoped that the priest's desire to protect his sister-in-law would prevent him from betraying her associates, but he hadn't even recoiled from that. Jean had followed him when he made his fortnightly visits to Ronval, and watched him enter the headquarters of the Gestapo in Caen. Charles had been visiting the Commandant in Caen, when he met Marie taking the drawings back to La Chenaie.

Charles' means of supplying information to the Nazis had usually been through the rambling of worried women on his country visits, assuming his way into their confidence. He was with a junior officer when they had overheard a conversation between Bernard Piot and two of his fellow conspirators. With such proof the Commandant acted at once. Jean had escaped; he had come back thirsting for revenge.

Charles knocked on the door to get the attention of his jailor.

"May I have a pen and paper?" he asked.

"What do you want that for? It won't save your life."

"That's not what I'm asking for."

André conferred with another man, who went into the house and found writing materials. Everything had been left tidily, including the bureau where Marie, and Alice before her, had written her letters. Two pens lay neatly beside the inkwell, which was full.

They opened the door of the chapel, André held Charles fast while his companion put the pen, ink and paper on the altar. It was August and the nights were short. Charles wrote a letter to his brother, and placed it carefully in the recess where the paten for the Host had lain unused since 1940. Then he said Mass and waited for dawn.

I can't imagine what he must have endured that night. When I look back, I can see that the real victim of the war in our community was Charles. When Robert was killed, he died a hero, proud of what he was doing, surrounded by those who loved and respected him. Marie was finally shielded from fear by dreams and a cloak of fantasy in which I was approving of what she was doing. But the traitor doesn't have the luxury of his own approval or anyone else's. Guilt glares at him like the white lamp which is used to break down prisoners under interrogation. He can't pity himself, and he can't undo the suffering he has inflicted on finer men. He hopes that his own ordeal will be shorter, but he is in the hands of angry men with vengeance in their hearts. Charles was to be thrown to the mob. He must have known they were coming, from the distant roar as the sun was climbing into the sky to the east of Ronval. A shaft of dusty light on the crucifix might have reminded him he could expect no mercy.

They say there is safety in numbers, but there is also danger.

Collective anger feeds upon itself, drawing strength for acts of cruelty. The individual is subsumed into a monster with many heads and one intention – to kill, and in killing to satisfy its lust. But this mob had a leader, who had planned how to devour the victim. There was order in the ranks; the women screamed for vengeance, but the men knew what to do.

He was dragged down the path towards the river, over the bridge and up the path to the wood behind La Chenaie. André Roche was standing by the tree. Charles must have seen the noose as he struggled to keep his head up. He also knew that hanging isn't a merciful death – it was one in which the Nazis excelled, knowing how to prolong the death throes of the victim.

Yes, Charles was the real victim of our war, the war which destroyed our way of life, which swept away my husband and my friend. Had he gambled, like so many to the right of the political divide, that the Germans would restore the old hegemony of church and aristocracy? That is what the disciples of Bernard Piot suspected. They wanted a new way of life, a life that would be free and fair, where the privileges and wealth of the few would be shared by everyone. The last lap of the twentieth century has proved their dreams were empty, but the privations of the war and the loss of their companions made their ideas even more alluring. Not all the members of the mob were adherents of Bernard's philosophy. Some were supporters of the Resistance, but only a minority of the communist party. Others had simply followed the flow. They were all angered by four years of subjection to the Nazis, and they were outraged by the cruel death of a patriot. He had taught many of their children.

They hanged Charles from the tree where we had our swing, where Marie had hidden the horse for fear of theft, and the drawings as a present to me, the tree that I had risked my life to find in the dark. It was very old and, now that I too am old, I wonder if it hadn't witnessed other acts of violence. When it fell down in a storm in 1947, I wasn't sad. It belonged to my past. My children would have a swing, but it would hang from a different tree from the one where Charles died slowly.

They had learned from the Nazis to tie his legs together; they hoisted him up carefully, making sure that his neck didn't break. Then they stood and jeered as mobs have done since the beginning of time. They screamed the names of Bernard Piot and his accomplices. Someone may have shouted Marie's name – Oh God, I hope not! How she would have suffered if she had been there – but it's very likely that they did. Men and women – children too – experiencing in real and ghastly circumstances, that emptying of emotion which is the purpose of tragedy in the theatre. Perhaps they felt shame as they ate their evening meal. By then Charles was dead; his body was cut down by an old man and a handful of women in black and white, led by a round Irish lady who waited for her return to the convent to give way to her sorrow. She had known all along that Charles was in league with the Germans, that Jean and Bernard were working for the Resistance, and that Marie was their dupe. She had wanted to save them – even the communists. But she had only saved Francis and his nurse.

Chapter 39 Autumn 1944

It was a race between Seaforths and Camerons, two forward patrols fighting their way back to St Valéry on September 2. This time it was the Germans who were surrounded in Upper Normandy; the bulk of their army had retreated over the Seine; Paris had fallen. When the colonels of the Camerons, Lt-Col Derek Lang, and Lt-Col Walford of the Seaforths, who had both escaped in 1940, met in the Station Square, it was considered a dead heat. Five pipers from the original Battalion of Camerons played a "set", while the maire of St Valéry presented the colonels with bouquets of flowers.

Black Watch, Argylls and Gordons followed. They found four military cemeteries, which had been carefully tended by French civilians, each grave with a cross, many without a name. When you visit St Valéry now, you see stones bearing the inscription "Known only to God." Some Black Watch men came across a board with the notice "Honour the Black Watch Regiment who fought with courage in 1940." The German soldiers had not destroyed it. They admired the fighting spirit of the Scots, whatever their political masters did to civilians caught hiding Highlanders who had managed to get away.

General Rennie, who had also escaped in 1940, took up his headquarters in the same chateau at Cailleville, from where General Fortune had deployed his men four years earlier. The Gordons were to the east of the town. On September 3, the massed bands of the Division beat "Retreat" at Cailleville, before General Rennie delivered a moving address. He reminded the troops of the scene of carnage and humiliation in June 1940.

"That magnificent Division was sacrificed to keep the French in the war. True to Highland tradition, it remained to the last with our French allies, although it was within its capacity to withdraw and embark at Le Havre."

The Flowers of the Forest, a traditional Scots melody which mourns the loss of the "flower" of Scotland's army at Flodden in 1513, was played by the pipe-majors of the Division. General Rennie received a deputation from the town, the maire, the curé, and children with flowers, a tribute from a community which honoured the Scots who had fought for their freedom.

Robert could tell me little of this in his letters. I can imagine that he stood to attention, remembering Sergeant Fraser and the men of his platoon during that heart-breaking retreat from the Bresle to St Valéry. Macrae was still in prison; many of them were dead.

There was time to remember, but not to celebrate. Le Havre had to be captured. Robert fought through the forest of Montgeon towards the outskirts of the town, which was held by a determined General whose family had been killed in Berlin.

By the middle of September, I was sure that I was pregnant after all, and I wrote to Robert saying that I would leave ENSA after the next round of concerts. By chance we were to be sent to France. The last concert would in the Ecole Militaire. I was bursting out of my uniform, and I asked if we could wear concert clothes when we were in Paris. The authorities hesitated, but finally agreed.

It was the only way I could have travelled to France. The Channel was blocked with supplies being ferried from Britain to the allies, and the railways had almost ceased to exist. Those that hadn't been blown up by the Resistance were destroyed by the retreating Germans, and it was still almost impossible to send letters except through the army. I had tried writing to my parents at both La Chenaie and Paris, but the letters never arrived.

Coming back to Paris was an emotional experience for Paul and

Tad as well as for me. It had changed very little – although it had nearly been blown to bits by the Germans – and the sight of familiar places, so near the flat where we had first played trios, had a surreal quality. We did play the Ravel. I was exhausted, and very glad of all the work that I had put into the recording. I had forgotten how difficult it is.

Afterwards I rang the flat, wondering if my parents were there.

"Favoret," said my father's voice.

"Papa, is it really you?"

There was silence.

"Papa! It's Anne!"

"Who?"

"Anne!"

My mother took the telephone. "C'est qui à l'appareil?"

"Maman, c'est Anne. I'm in Paris – at the Ecole Militaire!"

"Is it really you, Anne?"

"Yes! I'm coming in five minutes."

I walked out on to the rue de la Motte Piquet, past the Champ de Mars with its memories of Robert and a volume of Beethoven Sonatas. I pressed the button which opened the door to the apartment block, and slowly climbed the stairs to my old flat. The last few steps were almost impossible to make. I was tired – and I had come home.

There was no need to ring the bell. They were there at the top of the steps. I fell fainting into my mother's arms. The maire of Quinon was speechless and in tears.

"How are you?" asked my mother, looking at my thickened waist. "You shouldn't be travelling around giving concerts!"

"I wouldn't be here if I didn't. But I've stopped now. I won't be going back to England."

"We leave for Quinon in a week. Your father will be maire again. They're going to give him a medal for his work with the Resistance in Paris. He'll have a car. It's the only way of travelling in France."

The conversation was stilted. We couldn't think clearly. My appearance was so unexpected. I had to tell Paul and Tad that I had found my parents, and that I wanted to stay in France. A replacement (whose playing met with Tad's grudging approval) had already been found. I gave Paul instructions for my house and the people who worked for me. They would be paid, and they would understand my change of plans; like everyone else they lived with the unexpected from day to day.

Gradually we told our different stories, or rather parts of them. Information fell like random leaves, in half-sentences. We needed to breathe the air of liberation after all the years of secrecy and distance; a coherent picture emerged very much later. My father had been put on a list of people suitable for administrative positions in post-war France. It had been compiled by Debré, a Gaullist agent, and son of a rabbi, who had remained in the Vichy government. We were always thinking of Marie and Francis. I didn't tell them about my escapade; it would only make them more worried. There was nothing to do but be patient, waiting in a state of limbo, of half-communication, for the car journey back to Quinon. Each longed to go home. Each was afraid of what we would find there.

We were driven by a gendarme who provided a little information. The Mairie had been wrecked, and makeshift offices set up in the state primary school. There was a deputy headmaster. Bernard Piot was dead. Did he have news of anyone else? The priest was dead. What had happened to the curé? Oh – he was all right – it was the young priest…de Valliet … yes – that was the name! What about

Ronval and La Chenaie – oh, those big houses? The Germans had used them, and now there were Canadians at Ronval. They had been told to get out of La Chenaie because the maire was coming back.

We were astonished and kept plying our driver with questions, but he either didn't want to communicate or didn't know. After Rouen we passed fields and villages devastated by the bombardment, and wondered to what extent Quinon had been ruined. Each us of was quietly relieved when we discovered that it was only the Mairie that had been destroyed. We were all thinking about Marie. The gendarme didn't know what had happened to her.

We got out of the car at the state school. Standing on the pavement, was the last person I expected to find there.

"Bonjour, M., Mme Favoret! Bonjour, Anne! " said Soeur Antoinette.

We left my father and walked slowly towards the convent.

It must have been one of the hardest tasks of her life. She told us very little, wisely knowing that we could only take one shock at a time. Marie was dead. Then she took us to the convent school, and called to a child in one of the maternelle classes. "Come, Francis! Here are Mamie and Tante Anne!" A young woman followed him. He looked at us, and then turned round and clung to her skirt.

"Bonjour, mademoiselle," said my mother. It was Francis' nurse.

Chapter 40 October – December 1944

It took several days to realise that we were back at La Chenaie, as we crept round the house in a whisper, trying to restore old habits and welcome Francis and Mlle Crochet. She had become attached to one of the Canadian soldiers who had been wounded in the battle for the Mairie. He had lain for days on a stretcher in Soeur Antoinette's music room, hovering between life and death, before being removed to the hospital in Bayeux, which had hardly been damaged by the invasion. It was the first town to be invested with a new préfet by General de Gaulle.

Whenever possible she went to visit him, and Francis grew attached to my mother and me. He slept badly, crying for "Nounou", "Onke Char", "Toinette" and imagining men in uniform with no legs, clutching his knees and saying that he would never be a soldier. Mlle Crochet must have been awake with him night after night when they were in the convent. It was exhausting.

Meanwhile the Canadians had left Ronval, and we had arranged for two of our maids to go over and clean it. Then we heard that Edmond, who was now the colonel of his regiment, was coming home after weeks in a military hospital. His leg had been wounded, and he would never walk again without a limp. I wondered if I would have to fill the same role with him as Soeur Antoinette had with us. (We still didn't know what had happened to Charles or Marie; all Soeur Antoinette had told us was that they were dead.)

We found piles of unopened letters addressed to Marie, sent almost daily since August; we tied them with ribbon, treating them with the reverence they deserved, waiting for Edmond's return. He arrived by car, obviously shaken by the news that his wife and brother were dead, or missing. I shall always be grateful that he already knew when I met him at the door of Ronval with Francis beside me. We had told him about "Papa" who loved him; Francis still asked for Maman and "Onke Char". When we told him that Papa and his uncle were brothers, he asked if Papa wore black too.

Edmond was pale and thin. We invited him to come back to La Chenaie, where I could care for him and his son. He had aged ten years since the beginning of the war, having fought in Africa and Italy, before being called back to Britain with General Leclerc. By the time the Free French had landed in France in August, the Gaullists were already taking over the administration in the north, although there was chaos and terror for months in the south, where the crimes of the SS and Milice were matched by the fury of retribution.

In Normandy, most people had been "soft collaborators", passively allowing life to continue under the Germans as before the war, without shortages of milk or bread or honey, cider or calvados. They lived well, and although other things were difficult to buy, there was little need to risk breaking the law. Communism tended to thrive among the urban poor; our own Bernard Piot was an intellectual whose parents had worked for a meagre wage in a factory outside Rouen. Bernard had undermined the war effort while Russia and Germany were allies, but worked hard for the Resistance after June 1941. Most resistants in Normandy and Brittany were firmly on the side of de Gaulle and the Free French, but even they were few in number.

Of course when Edmond came back I knew very little of the events that I have related. Bit by bit, I pieced the jig-saw together, mainly by talking to Soeur Antoinette, although she, who had always revelled in drama and loved to make herself heard, was reluctant to tell me much. It all came out gradually, and I was grateful that I could focus on the present without being disturbed by detailed knowledge of the recent past. The last piece of the puzzle, the revelation which made it possible to write this story, only fell into place a short time ago. But I am jumping ahead.

Edmond came to live at La Chenaie. He always talked about returning to his regiment, but he would never see active service again. In the meantime, he took pleasure in getting to know his son, who looked like his mother, with his thick dark hair and large blue eyes which had seen things that haunted them. My mother and I watched him carefully, wondering if he had inherited Marie's instability. I didn't think so, but he was acutely sensitive and had been scarred by the changes and upheavals of his early life. The memory of the German soldier lying among the ruins of the Mairie without a leg, made him imagine that Papa was going to lose his leg too.

When Edmond was well enough to walk, we took him out into the wood, where I was reminded that the story of my adventure in search of Marie's drawings was still a secret. I began to understand why Soeur Antoinette was unwilling to talk. We were all trying to restore normality, consigning to the past the events of a war which was over in France, but still raging in the Ardennes. Christmas was coming, and in January my baby would be born.

"I shall soon be able to walk over to Ronval," said Edmond. "The pain in my leg has gone and I shall be running in no time at all."

"Why go Ronval?" asked Francis.

"Because it's our home."

"No. Stay at Chenaie with Mamie and Papy and Tante Anne."

"What about Papa?" asked Edmond, picking up the little boy and holding him close to his chest.

"Papa stay at Chenaie too. Onke Char came every day."

Edmond's face clouded. "I want to know what happened to them both. No one seems able to tell me."

"We all have secrets in this war. You must have seen some terrible things when you were fighting."

"Yes, but the worst things happened to civilians – particularly the partisans in Italy." He stopped. He didn't want to relive the horrors of war, especially not in front of Francis.

"I shall go over next week. I want to see the old place before Christmas. What can I give you for Christmas, Francis? I shall ask the curé to celebrate Mass in the chapel. It would be a good time to open it again. Now – tell me what you want," he said, picking him up again.

"Jean Bello gave me a horse, but I had to give it back. It was made of wood. I have a brass horse but it's very small. I want a wooden one too."

We all fell silent. Francis was thinking of the disappointment of giving back his present, and we were searching in our minds for clues. Why had Jean given Francis a horse, and why had he been made to give it back? I decided to ask Mlle Crochet who was by now Mrs Marvin, but she also seemed uncommunicative. Then she left for Canada. How much she could have told me! I could have tried harder, because once I get hold of an idea I don't let go. The truth is that I didn't want to know. I was preoccupied with my parents, Francis, Edmond and the unborn baby, waiting daily for letters from Robert and trying to unclutter my life, when a new one was kicking hard inside me. Years later I went to North America because I wanted to write this book. It was difficult to find the former Mlle Crochet, because she had divorced Marvin, and married an American called Elmer Hackett. They lived in a large town house in Boston, ordered in the way that Marie would have run Ronval or La Chenaie. She was very helpful.

By this time Jean had received a medal like my father for work in the Resistance, but it didn't make him talkative. Yes, Mme de Valliet had been a member of the Resistance. She had been killed in an operation near St Valéry. She had left her child and his nurse safe in the convent. Times had been very difficult. Mme de Valliet had been a brave woman. It was all that he could tell us. He had already distanced himself from the communists, and my father was sure he would eventually be elected maire. He was popular and clever, and seemed to have a hold over our community, which was as unwilling as Jean to talk about the occupation. It was as if there were a wall of silence which only time would break down. I wasn't really sorry. I had enough to think about, wishing that Robert could also come home with a wounded leg; and we could all start our lives again.

His letters were cheerful – when they arrived – but vague about where he was. There was a rumour that the allies were being pushed back by a counter-attack across the Belgian border; but official news was always of events that had long flown past.

Did I have a good doctor and midwife? Would the hospital in Quinon be equipped for an emergency if there were complications? Was I looking after myself? He was glad that I was with my mother. He wished that he could be with me. I've kept all his letters. His anxiety for me and care for his men permeate them. But there are touches of humour which still delight me, and which I relive when I am with Mary Cummings (now Mcleod) and you, her sons, for whom I'm writing this book. She was born on New Year's Day 1945, at the start of the year which saw the end of tyranny in Western Europe. But the horrors of war, our war, weren't over.

Chapter 41 Christmas 1944 and New Year 1944/5

Edmond decided that Mass should be said in the chapel on the afternoon of Christmas Eve, and we invited the curé to join us afterwards for a festive *diner*. My father had begun to like, and even admire, the ageing priest who came to life when surrounded by wounded soldiers, behaving with dignity as he ministered to the dying. The maire had grown tolerant through living in humble circumstances; the priest had learned to overcome his fear.

Of course the curé knew what had happened to Charles. I'm sure that he intended to tell the colonel one day soon; I remember thinking there was a new strength and decisiveness about him, an inner confidence that trusted not only in God but in his own judgement too. Let Christmas, free of occupation, lighten the lives of the people of Quinon, let the seigneur spend the festival of goodwill with his son, and let the past rest for a moment.

So on Christmas Eve, my mother drove the curé to Ronval early, so that he could make preparations for the Mass. He went into the chapel which had been cleaned, looked for the paten in which he would consecrate the Host, and under it he found the letter. He was no fool. He knew exactly who had written it and what it contained. He took the letter and folded it in his pocket. Meanwhile my mother returned home to collect Edmond, Francis and me – my father refused to join us – and we heard Mass in the chapel where Marie and Edmond had been married.

It was a good Christmas. Francis had his wooden horse and

there were simple presents for everyone. Edmond was regaining his strength and making enquiries about Charles in Paris. He wondered whether he had gone back to Bavaria. He talked of finding Marie's grave in the spring, even though Jean was vague about it. We might contact some of the Resistance workers who had operated near St Valéry. Two of them had been decorated; it wouldn't be difficult to track them down.

After Christmas, as often happens, it turned cold. I stayed inside feeling tired much of the time, but Edmond seemed restless to be back at Ronval. We all understood his feelings, but wondered whether it wouldn't be better for Francis to stay with us. So on that fateful New Year's Eve he walked up to Ronval and went into the chapel to pray for Marie and Charles. The curé had put the letter back, but not quite where he had found it. Edmond could easily have missed it. The priest decided that he could no longer protect Edmond from the truth. He put it on top of the paten, not underneath it, having ascertained that no one would be cleaning there in the week between Christmas and New Year.

When Edmond saw the letter his first reaction was joy. Charles had come back and left him a letter! Then he read:

Ronval
2nd Aug. 1944

My dear brother,

Tomorrow I shall die and I deserve to. I have betrayed my country, the people of our community and your wife. I have no means of confessing to a priest, no access to absolution. All I can do is to confess to you and to God how greatly I have sinned.

It all started many years ago at school, or even before then, watching you admire those two girls as they came down to the river to bathe. They aroused feelings in you that I could never have. I almost envied you, because I realise that I didn't love women. In the sixth form at Ampleforth, I struck up a friendship with a younger boy, who admired me as much as I loved him. We were nearly caught once and I had to be vigilant. After I left he wrote to me. I wonder where he is now. He may be fighting in the British army.

When I decided to become a monk, I confessed that I was homosexual and was told that I must always abstain from any contact with young boys. I tried. I was ordained and plans were made for me to go out into the world. The monastery was threatened by the advancing power of the Nazis, but inside there was a solidarity of spirit which emanated from Father Anselm. We were determined to stand firm. Then a young baker came every day with fresh bread, and I got to know him. I realised that I was in danger, but I couldn't stop myself. Unfortunately for both of us we were discovered, and I was arrested by the Gestapo. I was taken to a concentration camp called Mathausen. I never heard of or saw my brothers again.

It was a place of indescribable suffering, and I was given a choice between staying there, or returning to France to give information about terrorist organisations – or any other subversive activities. I chose wrongly, and tomorrow I shall pay the price.

When I came back to Calvados, I was relieved to find that life had changed very little. The people of our community were fairly contented, as food was plentiful and few things were unavailable in the shops. I visited many families and found that passive cooperation was almost universal, and it seemed that I would escape the horror of betraying French men and women. Only one irregularity reached my attention; Favoret, who continued to be maire, was selling dairy products to the poor quartiers of Rouen and Paris at a low rate, and at slightly inflated prices to the Germans. To my satisfaction, nothing terrible happened to him. He and Mme Favoret left the area, and your wife took over responsibility for La Chenaie. By this time the Germans had installed their headquarters at Ronval. She organised an inventory of your things which I know they looked after carefully.

It was the first time that I had an opportunity to get to know Marie. I have always liked her. She is decisive, practical and the essence of a Frenchwoman, kind and fair to those who work for her, and observant of every detail of her household. I had only two reservations about her, a tendency to leave Francis to his nurse, and to sit vacantly looking into space. As I have always feared, she inherited instability from her father. She needs to be needed by strong people who love her, and to whom she can make herself useful. Sadly, without Mme Favoret, she was at the mercy of those who would manipulate her.

Believe me, I tried to protect her. When I found that Belliot was running errands for her I was suspicious. We all knew that he was in league with Piot, a self-confessed member of the *Parti Communiste*. I doubt if Belliot is a member. He's ambitious and will play the system for his advantage, and although he's sharp, I don't think he's got much time for ideas. But I know that there was a radio transmitter in the area, and that Belliot and his accomplices were in touch with the British and the Free French. What worried me most was that Belliot would persuade Marie to take part in dangerous activities, and make her think that in doing so she was supporting you. The nuns were worried that Belliot was a threat to her purity, but, although I encouraged them to keep an eye on her, I am sure that Belliot was too astute to allow his work for the Resistance to be complicated by an intrigue of that kind. Anyway Marie wouldn't have countenanced it. It worried her that she was forgetting you, and often looked at your photograph to remember what you look like.

I used to dine with her in the evening, and I'm afraid that I was too concerned about her to be a genial companion. When I found she sent Belliot to Caen to buy materials for drawing, I was angry with her. There were tears, and she said that neither you nor Mrs Cummings would speak to her like that. It was hard for me, because I was used to straightforward dealings between my brothers in Bavaria, not the gentleness that a soft woman like Marie expected. I can see why you love her, and I pray for her safety. In peace, surrounded by the love of her husband and friends, she should be all right.

But the British wanted drawings of the fortifications, and Marie has a brilliant photographic memory. She started visiting Caen. What her arrangements were I have no idea. I was only vaguely aware of what she was doing. Details emerged when Piot's accomplices were interrogated, but I can't give a coherent story.

I had to go to Caen regularly to report my findings to the Gestapo, and every ten days to Ronval, where I would give bits of information to the Commandant. He was a reasonable man, unlike the fanatics in Caen. Unfortunately they all had instructions to use violence to extract confessions. Several of the women in the community were aware of Piot's activities, although it was difficult to piece together anything concrete. Then, by chance, one of the officers at Ronval overheard a conversation between Piot and two of his accomplices. It was sufficient evidence to arrest them – and Belliot, who escaped. I presume that Marie went with him.

Soeur Antoinette was aware of much that was happening. She made arrangements to receive Francis and his nurse in the house where she gives music lessons. She kept them hidden during the last months of the war, disguising Francis as a girl and dying his hair. Soeur Antoinette's courage was unflinching. If they had been caught they would all have been deported, but if Marie had been with them they would have been shot. Nevertheless I deserve to die for this, if nothing else – not only did I betray your wife, but I put your son's life in danger too.

I asked Marie as gently as I could to cut her hair and leave. I would take care of Francis and his nurse. I don't know what happened to Marie. Belliot is back, full of his activities for the Resistance – I believe that Favoret worked for them in Paris too – and longing to avenge the deaths of Piot and the others.

I didn't see Bernard Piot die, but I saw his cruelly butchered body. He gave nothing away, and his example is with me as I face the mob tomorrow at dawn. God knows what they will do to me. The other two made rambling confessions and were taken out and shot.

I betrayed them all for what? There were times when I reasoned that fascism is preferable to communism, but both are illusions carried to horrible extremes by evil men. I should have died of exhaustion carrying boulders at Mathausen, not here at the hands of the French.

Soeur Antoinette begged me to go to Paris as soon as the allies invaded, but it was impossible. Would that I could confess to a priest and receive absolution! But even that is asking too much.

I don't know when you will read this. I hope that my last thoughts will be of you, Marie and Francis. Please pray for the repose of my soul.

Your loving brother,

Charles.

Edmond read and reread his brother's letter many times, at first with disbelief and then with mounting horror. As evening came and darkness filled the chapel he sat there, unable to accept the loss of his wife, his brother and the honour of his family. The night became frosty, the temperature dropped to well below zero and snow began to fall. Twenty-four hours later he was found half dead with cold.

Chapter 42 New Year's Day 1945

Mary Emily Cummings entered the world on New Year's Day with the brisk determination of the future captain of games. She upset the routine at La Chenaie for a morning that started early; the doctor and midwife trudged through a blizzard and arrived just in time; by 10.00 she was fast asleep in her cot. Her grandparents were too concerned about her to notice that Edmond hadn't returned from Ronval.

Poor Francis must have wondered whether Papa wouldn't disappear like "Onke Char", especially as Edmond didn't contact us later in the day. My mother rang the housekeeper at Ronval, who said that she had seen Col. de Valliet briefly the day before, but could add nothing more.

Although he hadn't slept much that night, my father drove carefully through the snow to register the birth of his granddaughter at the make-shift Mairie, and to contact someone who might give the news to a British officer fighting in Belgium. There was no way of ringing Scotland. He spent half a day trying different lines, taking more than one nip of calvados to drive away the cold. When he saw the curé in the street, he went out to tell him about little Mary and invited him to share the bottle, while he made another attempt to ring Paris.

"A girl – eh," said the curé. "Did the Major want a boy?"

"The Major will be pleased with this little lass! A fine pair of lungs she's got – and quite an appetite from what my wife tells me."

"Ah well. A sort of cousin for Francis. How's he taking it?"

"He slept downstairs to keep away – you know – from the stir. But he didn't sleep well, because his father didn't come home. We presumed he'd stayed up at Ronval on account of the snow, but when my wife rang this morning the housekeeper said she'd only seen him briefly yesterday afternoon."

"Monsieur, please take me to Ronval. I think I know where he is."

The curé looked at my father with an earnestness that wasn't lost on him.

"Could something be wrong?" asked my father.

"Yes, very wrong. We must go now."

No more needed to be said. My father was always decisive in an emergency and he trusted the curé. He had had enough of the telephone exchange, but he made a call to Ronval. There was no reply. They ploughed through the snow-covered roads and the curé went into the chapel. There, slumped on the floor with a letter in his hand, was Edmond. My father went straight to the housekeeper to find blankets, and they rubbed him until he was able to be dragged into the kitchen, which was the warmest corner of the house. It was obvious that Edmond was far from well; they rang the hospital in Bayeux to ask if they could take a case of severe hypothermia aggravated by a recent leg wound. By the evening Edmond was lying in a ward with several American and British soldiers, his mind wandering, and his leg giving him pain. The curé kept the letter.

Is there ever a good time for explanation? While I slept upstairs, with Mary in her cot, and Francis in a bed beside me, the curé told my parents the story of Quinon during the war. My mother had had some sleep that afternoon, but Papa was exhausted. They listened in disbelief.

"But why did he betray them when he wanted to protect Marie and Francis?" asked my mother.

"Blackmail, I should imagine. It's the way it's usually done." The curé was an astute man. Nothing would have induced him to read the letter, but he'd worked it out long ago. He hadn't witnessed the appalling sufferings of Bernard Piot, but he was moved as my father was by the courage that could withstand torture.

"Bernard Piot may have been a communist, but he was one of the idealists, unlike the thugs, malcontents and riff-raff that make up most of the party. He was one of the best, a hero who gave all for his fellow men. He didn't betray Marie or Jean," said the curé. My parents loved him for it. When it comes to human dignity, labels don't mean much.

"And Charles, what happened to him?" asked my mother.

The curé didn't flinch. "They hanged him. He's buried in the convent grounds. We didn't want to tell the colonel while he was recovering from his wound, and I wanted him to have Christmas in peace with Francis." He had already told them how he found and kept the letter. "I'll never know whether I did the right thing or not."

"You acted as I would have done – in the best interest of the people in your care," said my father.

A wail upstairs announced that little Mary was hungry. I changed her and fed her, and my mother came up to see us.

"Did you get through to Paris?" I asked.

"No one is connecting the calls. We'll try again tomorrow."

"Have you found Edmond?"

"He's had a relapse with his leg and is in hospital in Bayeux. I don't know when he'll be back."

"Is it serious?"

"I hope not. Now go back to sleep. It won't be long until she wakes again."

"Where was he?"

"At Ronval."

"Then he should have rung to tell us where he was."

"He…he was in the chapel."

Francis began to stir. "Papa, is Papa back?"

"We've found him. He's all right," I said, and he went back to sleep.

My mother tiptoed away, but I didn't go back to bed. I staggered slowly to the door, taking care not to wake the children, and walked stiffly to the top of the stairs, calling to my parents. I was surprised to see the curé with them. I asked questions which they were at first reluctant to answer; then it was my turn to listen in amazement.

"I know about blackmail," I said. I told them about my parachuting adventure.

You may wonder at this! Twelve hours after the birth of my daughter, I was listening to the saga of the war in Quinon, and filling in, not just details, but huge gaps myself. But this was during the war. People of my generation boast of the economies they made, and look down on the extravagance of a society which has its own reasons for distancing itself from the "throw-away" mentality of the sixties and seventies. Today we want to save the earth as much as ourselves. Our sense of care is global not personal. But in the war it was a different spirit, one of community and pride in saving, in "making do" and chuckling at our inventiveness and thrift. We were proud, but we were also courageous. We faced death daily and laughed when a new morning broke and we were still alive. It made us strong – and I confess a little condescending to the next generation, which didn't experience the "toughening of the fibres" which Soeur Antoinette felt young Anne Favoret needed. Dear Soeur Antoinette! You and Hitler made me as strong as an ox!

In another life I might have succumbed to depression, or lost my milk or become hysterical, but my confinement had been a lot less painful than when Marie gave birth to Francis. When I sat with Marie in labour, I had asked myself if I could endure so much, but I was stronger and it all happened comparatively quickly. Yes, I was stiff and sore and I was shattered that Charles had betrayed members of our community, but my principal concern was for Edmond and Francis. And not just for them. I had a husband who knew nothing of his daughter, and who was still fighting the German counter-attack between Marche and Laroche in Belgium.

Chapter 43 January – March 1945

It was a telegram that told Robert he had a daughter. He wrote back immediately, full of love for us both, and vague about his own activities. It was towards the end of the "Battle of the Bulge", when bad weather held back air support from the allies. It wasn't until mid-January that they were able to defeat Hitler's last attack.

I had to discover all this later, driven by love, and pride in Robert's service to his country and mine. Then there was his daughter constantly pestering me with questions that I couldn't answer, and finally grandchildren who wanted to know the whole story. In the meantime we were still at war, the future unclear, and I had two small children who depended on me, a merry baby who kicked like a footballer every time her legs were free, and a puzzled little boy.

We took him to see his father at the end of February, when Edmond's wound had healed and he was beginning to be more lucid. Nothing could have hurt him more than the revelations in Charles' letter. The doctors only allowed brief visits. It was obvious that more than his leg was afflicted, and for a time there was talk of sending him to a convalescent home. The parallel with poor Hervé was too strong. I talked to the doctors about Francis, and described our house as a place where both father and son were treated as members of the family. They agreed to allow him to return to La Chenaie at the beginning of March. He scarcely spoke of Ronval and made no mention of Charles. I think that it was the curé who told him what had happened in the early hours of August 3. He was a frequent visitor, contributing as much to the recovery of Edmond's mental health as did the stir of a house, where the needs of three generations were calmly supervised by my mother.

The mimosa was out and the sounds and smells of spring filled a March afternoon with the memories of childhood. I remembered working out the thirds that the cuckoo sings, when I was nine. There were plenty of them that afternoon, as oblivious of war as they were unscrupulous about getting other birds to raise their offspring.

"Cuckoo," sang Francis.

I laughed. "They change their call later when they've put their eggs in other birds' nests."

"Why?"

"Probably because they're satisfied."

"What do the other birds think?"

"They don't realise until it's too late."

"Are cuckoos bad birds?"

"In that way, yes."

"Are all Germans bad?"

"Of course not. They have bad leaders at the moment, but when the war's over they will have a different government, and the good people will be able to live in peace."

"Did the bad Germans kill my mother and Uncle Charles?"

"Yes, in a way they did, because they made it impossible for them to live as we do now."

"How did they kill them?"

"I don't know." What else could I tell a child? If he ever found out how Charles died I never knew about it. As for the death of his mother, it was still a mystery.

I heard Edmond behind me coming out on to the sunny terrace. He tired easily and slept a lot of the time.

"Francis," he asked, "what do you remember about them?"

"Oncle Charles was tall. He didn't smile and he read me stories, even when I was staying with Soeur Antoinette and my hair was yellow. Maman did smile. She had dark hair and read me stories too – and she drew pictures. The best was of a horse. She gave me the brass horse, but she made me give the wooden one back to Jean Belliot." He ran inside to fetch the brass horse.

Edmond sat with his head in his hands. "How can I start again?"

"You have to. Francis needs you. He's already lost Marie and Charles. You have to be strong and rise above the past. It's what they both would have wanted."

That evening, when I returned from a walk down by the river, still savouring the sight of pale green leaves and woodland flowers, I heard the piano being played. It was the rolling D major middle section of the Chopin Nocturne that had so entranced me all those years ago on our first visit to Ronval.

Francis was leaning against Edmond, as though he wanted to be part of his father's music. The nocturne finished. Francis sighed with contentment. It was bedtime. Papa would read him a story. Whenever I read to you, my grandchildren, it reminded me of Francis. The stories made Marie and Charles alive in his memory, and I don't think that anything can replace them in a world of television and computers.

The healing had begun. Edmond's urbanity and fine manners were steeled more by the drama of his family than the fighting in the war. He'd faced danger from the Saar to St Valéry, and West Africa to Paris, with equanimity, skill and intelligence. It was humiliation that had crippled him; now he had to overcome guilt and remorse, drawing spiritual strength from his talents, education and Catholic convictions. It is perhaps a gentle irony of this history that Charles relieved the curé of responsibility, which rebounded back on to him when Charles died, a responsibility which the curé exercised to comfort Charles' elder brother.

As soon as I could, I took the children to visit Soeur Antoinette who was as robust in her opinions as ever. I had visited her in the autumn, but she had looked ill and worn by all the events in which she had played such a crucial part. Now she was her usual plump assertive self. She was sure that I would spoil the children, that I had had enough of gadding about playing to soldiers, that I didn't help Mme Favoret enough, that the Mairie should be built elsewhere because the foundations had proved faulty, that I wasn't feeding the baby properly, because she was too thin and Francis was too pale. Even in the convent he had had a better colour. I said that he had stayed there in the summer, and that the winter had been severe – we had had snow – but it was my fault for not giving him enough fresh air.

When I changed the subject and thanked her again for all that she'd done for Francis and his nurse, she started on the Canadians, referring to them as Americans, and gave my shortcomings a rest. They had no manners. She was sure that Madeleine Crochet would hate America. Look what a mess they had made of the Mairie. It was useless to point out that the Mairie had been defended by the Germans, and that the Canadians had been told to capture it. Her moment of glory was over and she now had to obey Reverend Mother (not the same one as when we were children, but just as tight-lipped and officious). It must have been a penance for them both.

As I left she embraced me warmly. "It's good to see you, Anne. I pray daily for Major Cummings, and for all of you. That young lady will have character. Mark my words!" At least in this she was right.

Major Cummings reached the Rhine with the 51st Division, where amphibious troop carriers called "buffaloes" ferried the Gordons over the river on March 23 to the area west of a town called Rees. Although Robert's battalion lost only one officer and seven men, 1st Gordons faced stiff opposition. The 51st Division had to fight battle-hardened paratroopers tenaciously defending their Fatherland, even though the allied air-force had command of the skies. Thousands of paratroopers had been dropped north of the Rhine, in an operation which was reminiscent of D Day – in terms of danger and casualties. Winston Churchill had joined Montgomery, trying to control strategy and troop movements, running risks and eventually being told to get out of danger by an American general, as he stood on a bridge defended by snipers.

It was a sniper that killed Robert on March 26. It seems unfair that he should have achieved so much for France and Britain, escaped from Laufen and taken part in the liberation of St. Valéry, to be killed on the eve of victory. The 51st Division had lost their commander, General Rennie, on March 24, two days before.

The news reached London and then Scotland and finally Quinon. I was shopping in the market place when I heard someone ask for my address. I was handed a telegram which I read twice. I ran across the street, leaving my basket of provisions, into the arms of Soeur Antoinette. It was at moments like that when she forgot to be fractious; her wisdom and kindness surfaced from beneath a sea of frustration and restraint. She was born for big moments and important events, but she had been condemned to live with petty women and teach music to unmusical children.

"Ah, ma très chère Anne, la vie n'est jamais facile. Come, tell me what's happened. Has our dear Major been killed? Don't try to be strong – not this time. It's sometimes good to cry."

Chapter 44 1945 – 1948

I needed time to mourn, to allow the scars to heal and fade. Soeur Antoinette was right. It was good to cry. She offered to look after the children. My mother would take them into town when Mary was weaned, and leave them at the convent; one of the younger sisters would look after the baby while Soeur Antoinette read to Francis in English.

Edmond returned to Ronval, not wishing to impose upon my grief. Once his strength was restored he was invited to take an administrative post in Baden-Baden where his diplomatic skills, fluent English and knowledge of German helped to build relationships between the French and their allies, as well as our former enemies. I told my mother to assure him that I would look after Francis. There was no question of my returning to the concert platform. My life was here with two children who had lost a parent in the war, both full of questions, one resilient, the other marked by loss and trauma. He started to draw; I think that he managed to express much of his angst – the crumbling walls of the Mairie, the mutilated corpses and the pump where he had gone for water; and when he put down his crayons to stoop and look at a butterfly, I saw his mother, with her long dark hair, observing every detail of colour and pattern.

We twisted every bureaucratic arm to find and exhume Marie. With Charles there was no problem. My father was the maire, and the job was done professionally while the nuns were at Mass. A certificate registering that death had been incurred by strangulation was signed and filed at the Mairie. The curé read the service with a gentleness and forgiveness of one priest towards another that I shall never forget. Charles was buried at Ronval near the chapel where he had spent the last agonising night of his life.

To find Marie was another matter. Jean was uncooperative, although he told us that she had died near St Valéry. Two former Resistance workers eventually led us to a farmer who had found the body of a young woman dressed as a boy near a ditch; she had been buried by night so as not to attract the attention of the Germans. It was horrible but necessary, and in the end it was sensitively handled by the police of Seine-Maritime who recognised my father's authority and medal. I don't know how many forms he signed. Knowing France, I imagine that there were nearer fifty than twenty.

There was only one form which interested me. My father kept it carefully so that I could ask the same question as Francis had, after the conversation about the cuckoo. I wanted to know that she hadn't suffered, and when he told me that she had died from a bullet in the back of the neck, I was relieved. Soon after she was buried at Ronval beside Charles, Edmond left for Germany. I stayed at La Chenaie, often walking to Ronval with the children, and sometimes alone.

I took little Mary to Robert's mother in Scotland where we found a very lined old lady mourning the loss of her son. She reminded me of my own grandmother, whose face had been seared by Jean-Luc's death. Together we made plans to go to Germany to visit his grave. I met her without Mary at the beginning of 1946 at Reichswald Forest Cemetery near Kleve in Germany, where we spent a quiet day together, before travelling to Normandy where Emily took delight in finding that her grand-daughter was growing more and more like Robert. I promised to visit her every year – which I did until she died in 1963, after Mary had spent five happy years at Emily's old school in St Andrews. Mary was good at sport, an "all-rounder", popular and fun, like her father and grandmother. I'm not sure that I would have liked the school, but then I'm no more suited to living in a community than Soeur Antoinette. I like my space – and I would have wanted to play the piano.

1945 slipped into 1946 on Mary's first birthday and then into

1947. We were able to ring Emily in Scotland as international calls had become a little easier, although the French telephone system remained erratic for decades. And there were presents from Germany for both the children too. Francis was at the boys' Catholic school, conforming as his mother had done, a serious child who didn't always like the boisterous toddler who knocked over his toys and laughed at the huge joke of seeing them tumble down. Her worst crime was to steal the brass horse, which we gave back to Francis after scolding her so much that she almost cried.

At Easter of 1947 Edmond came back to Ronval, and walked over to La Chenaie every day. It was after the terrible storm when the tree fell down. Often I would go down to the river to meet him, as he limped across the bridge and up the familiar path, past the orchard and through the wood with its memories of childhood. I would walk close to him as we edged round the huge crater and uprooted sphere, earthen and bulbous. We both shuddered at the thought of August 1944. Soon André Roche would chop the branches for fire-wood.

"What does it feel like to be in Germany after this horrible war?" I asked.

"I find it helpful. There are many sophisticated people who hated what the Nazis were doing, but were afraid to speak out. It helps me to understand Charles."

"It's good that you can speak of him. Have you been to the monastery?"

"Oh yes. They were so kind. I didn't have to tell them much, and they said that he would have made a good monk and priest. They also reminded me that everyone has a weakness. And some choices are hard. I think I made the right choice in my life, but in doing so I abandoned my wife and son. It was a much harder choice that Charles was given."

"Have you ever thought that both of you chose to enter a community?"

He smiled. "Are you saying that we were deliberately abrogating responsibility?"

I was silent. After a moment he added, "Yes, I have thought that, but if it was weakness in me to follow family traditions and join the army, it was surely courageous of Charles to enter a community of men only, where his orientation would be exposed sooner or later."

"I worked with two very fine musicians during the war – and before it. They loved each other very much, and I shall never judge what they did to be wrong."

"You must let the Church guide you in that way." He paused. "But you asked about Germany and I am happy there – except that I miss you and the children."

"They are settled here. Francis no longer has nightmares. He doesn't always approve of Mary, but I think that her sense of fun is good for him – provided that it doesn't get out of hand. She can be very much like I was!"

"That can't be such a bad thing!"

"How do you know? I was always in trouble at school. Marie was the good one – like Francis. He has good concentration and his homework is impeccable. You should have seen my blots and smudges that the nuns held up in class for everyone to laugh at!"

"It didn't stop you playing the piano! Will Francis start soon?"

"Usually the best time to begin is at eight, when children learn to multiply, but he already tries to make out tunes on the piano, and I have given him a few lessons. I want him to start properly with Soeur Antoinette in September. By then he will be seven and a half."

"You should know! I play a lot now, especially when I'm alone in the evenings."

"That can't be often. If you are a sort of army diplomat you must have invitations to go everywhere."

"Yes, it can be tiresome. It's much easier if you're not a single man."

"But still easier than being a single woman!"

"Anne," he said, "when you have mourned so that it doesn't hurt any more, will you think of marrying again?"

I felt that I was going to cry and turned my head away from him.

"What is wrong?"

I breathed deeply, and let my words come out slowly. "You called me 'Anne'. You have always called me 'Madame', even when you were staying at La Chenaie. When you called me 'Anne' just now, it was like the time you called me '*vous*' – at the bridge – when I fell over. I still remember what you said: *Vous en avez du courage, Mademoiselle!*"

"I was right. You had a lot of courage. We had guns and you were both much smaller. You couldn't have been more than twelve."

He took my hand. "I shall always call you "*vous*". It would be out of character to call you anything else."

We walked on a few paces. He still held my hand. "Even if the answer is 'not yet', please give me some hope."

I looked at him. "Yes," I said.

We were married that summer of 1947. The children stayed with my parents for three weeks while we had a holiday in Italy, and they came with us to Germany for two years while Edmond continued to work for the French army. It's where our elder son Louis-Rémy was born. We called his younger brother Henri-Bernard. Bernard is not a family name, but he was born at Ronval, where a brave man died rather than betray Marie. What did it matter if he was a communist? As I have said, the human spirit transcends all these ideas and fancies.

Epilogue – 1999

The story is nearly finished, but there are loose threads to tie and a mystery to solve. I couldn't tell you until now, or at least until very recently, because what I suspected was only conjecture. And even if I had known, as I said at the beginning, I couldn't have written what follows for fear of causing distress. But those who might have been distressed are now beyond it. Edmond died and left me a widow for the second time in 1983, and Francis, who became a much-loved priest, died last year.

Six months ago I received a message from our curé, or rather a request to visit Jean Belliot in hospital. When my father retired from being maire of Quinon, Jean was elected in his place. He was just as popular and successful. His early dabbling with the *Parti Communiste* was forgotten, and he became as strong a Gaullist, and as staunch a republican as any Favoret. He never succeeded in buying our farm; but he owned the farm and land to the west of La Chenaie, and, working as manager in our family business, became prosperous and confident enough to learn that there is strength in kindness.

But there was little contact between him and Edmond, although I tried to ease things whenever they did meet. The past lay heavily between them. There was forgiveness, but the shadows of Marie, Charles and Bernard Piot still hung over us. It is one of the triumphs of Christianity that shadows like these can become benign, but they don't disappear in a flash of sunlight. Edmond's four years in Baden-Baden accustomed him to living with shadows which, in time, gave him strength and a strange sense of comfort after our marriage and the birth of our sons. How often I reasoned with him that they were all victims of war – most of all Charles! We both read more than we could bear about the Nazi camps, but neither of us saw one. Edmond had to forgive Charles his choice, but he also had to forgive Jean for killing him. He did. I remember them both planting a tree where the old oak had stood. It was a symbolic act, but it could never be the beginning of friendship. Too much was left unsaid and their personalities were so different.

I didn't dislike Jean as I had when I was a girl, and, although he knew I admired his skills as farmer and maire, I was still surprised that he wanted to speak to me. I reflected that, as he had never married, he would be lonely – and visits of that kind had become part of my life – just like Alice de Valliet. So I drove to Caen, always sad to see how much it had changed since I had lived there with Marie and my grandparents, to the modern nursing-home where old M. Belliot lay in a private room, the victim of a stroke. The nurse propped him up on pillows, and he seemed like a fly caught in a web of drips and machines with flickering needles. His speech was slow and he fought for breath, but he thanked me for coming and I sat beside him while he took time to form the words which were in his mind. He sat forward and took a deep breath.

"I cut her hair." He shuddered. "She swept it up and burnt it. We crept out of the house heading east and then north towards Rouen, where we could lose ourselves in the city. She wanted to come, to fall in with my plans, but then she would cry for you and for the child; I had to be firm with her, telling her that we were doing what you wanted. There were two Resistance contacts I had known before the war in Rouen – friends of Bernard – I hoped that I would be able to use their transmitter to contact the British. We had to move by night and hide in barns during the day; I had little sleep as I had to make sure that nobody found us. It took two weeks to reach Rouen. Marie was always obedient; if I asked her to be quiet she would crawl into a ball, and smear herself with dust so as to be as inconspicuous as possible.

"But by the time we met the Resistance workers in Rouen, she had forgotten why we were there. Before I contacted London I had to ask her where she had hidden the drawings. She sat looking into space saying over and over again "Horse in a swing, horse in a swing, Anne will know where they are." Then I realised that she had put them in the tree, and that the only person who would know where they were was you. So I sent the message and hoped that the British Intelligence would find you.

"I shouldn't have taken advantage of her – no, not in that way: she was married and she never loved me. But I shouldn't have told her that you wanted her to do the drawings. It was impossible to take photographs, and it was war – but she wouldn't have got involved if I hadn't persuaded her that you – and her husband – wanted her to." He sank back on his pillows, his face troubled; the effort to speak was exhausting him, but he tried again to perch himself forward so as to concentrate.

"After that we had a series of dangerous missions – blowing up railway lines and bridges. At first we took her with us, but she had no sense of danger or urgency, and we had to leave her behind. Then I thought of your holiday home in St Valéry and wondered if one of the maids would look after her in an attic. We knew the invasion was coming. It would surely not be long for her to remain hidden. I told her my idea and she immediately thought of practical ways of implementing it. She would dress as a boy and speak patois as she had done as a small child. She made a convincing boy, but I had to take the risk of travelling with her by train. It was very dangerous, even though we had false papers – but I doubt whether anyone would have recognised the châtelaine of Ronval in the ragged *gamin* who strode into the carriage ahead of me. I grew a moustache and walked with a slouch under a broad-brimmed hat.

"We got out of the train at St Valéry, and she followed me as I walked through the streets of burnt houses to your villa overlooking the harbour. It was full of Germans. Out of the corner of my eye I saw her slump down as I turned away from the place where she had expected to find a haven. I told her we must go back, but she began to cry. We bought some food and I took her up into the hills above St Valéry, looking for somewhere to spend the rest of the day. We walked towards Manneville. We were stopped once and asked to produce our papers, and then we trudged onwards to a barn where we waited until nightfall. I knew what I had to do. I couldn't leave her; having her with me became daily more risky. I knew what would happen to her – to us both – if we were discovered. They would have tortured us before they shot us. We crept out into the moonlight and walked towards a ditch. I had a small pistol in my trouser pocket."

His face twitched with pain, not the effects of his condition, which numbed rather than seared, but a hidden agony concealed for half a century. Even now he couldn't define it. Speech was too gross, too deeply imbedded to be dug out of his mind. He looked like a wounded animal. I thought of a hedgehog that Marie had found in a garden shed, its paw almost severed between the legs of a deckchair. And then I saw her lying in pain as she gave birth to Francis, her face uncomprehending, distorted, perhaps asking herself whether she wasn't too weak to bear the burden of another de Valliet.

"So you killed her. I have always thought that it was you, but I could never be sure. It must have been hard for you to live in the community with Francis, Edmond and me and my parents, knowing that you had killed both Charles and Marie."

"De Valliet was a traitor. He deserved to die – but Marie Millet was innocent." He looked at me. "Forgive me, Madame. I have never been able to forgive myself. I loved her. I still do."

He sank back again. There were tears in his eyes, but I don't think that he saw mine. I said, "Yes, I forgive you," and left.

French words and expressions in the text

à bientôt!	- see you soon
ami(e)	- friend – the (e) makes the word feminine
ancien régime	- former political structure – rule of the king and authority of aristocracy and the Church
Après un Rêve	- After a Dream – the name of a song (here adapted for cello) by Fauré
asile	- hospice
au revoir	- good-bye
bienvenue!	- welcome!
Bonjour!	- Good morning or afternoon
cadeau	- present
Calvados	- Lower Normandy – west of Le Havre and the River Seine
calvados	- distilled cider
capitaine	- captain (here in the army)
c'est beau, n'est-ce pas ?	- it's nice, isn't it ? Francis shortens to n'est pas
c'est qui à l'appareil?	- who's speaking? (literally "Who is at the contraption?")
c'est mon amie, comment va-t-elle?	- she's my friend, how is she?
chanter	- to sing
chantage	- blackmail

châtelaine	- lady of the manor
commune	- small administrative district, a town or collection of villages
dîner	- evening meal
concours	- competition
Conservatoire	- Music College
Ecole Militaire	- Military Academy (literally military school)
escalope de veau	- veal steak
fille du maire	- the mayor's daughter
gendarme	- policeman
gamin	- urchin
gars	- fellow, bloke
(un bon gars)	- a good lad
grande-dame	- a woman of social importance
haute-bourgeoisie	- upper middle class
la chasse	- (here) shooting – literally hunting
le patron	- the boss
Légion d'Honneur	- an award for public service instituted by Napoleon
ligne de recueil	- fall-back line
ligne de contact	- front line
lui	- (to) him or (to) her or (to) it
j'espère	- I hope
ma très chère Anne, la vie n'est jamais facile	- my dearest Anne, life is never easy
maire	- mayor
Mairie	- Town Hall
mais oui	- oh yes
Maman	- Mummy
Mamie	- Granny
manoir	- manor

maternelle	- kindergarten
mon vieux	- my friend – literally my old one
morte pour la patrie	- died for the country
mutilés de guerre	- war wounded
oncle	- uncle – Francis says "Onke Char" because he is too young to say "Oncle Charles".
Où se trouve?	- where is? (Francis shortens to "s'touve".)
nounou	- nanny
Papa	- Daddy
Papy	- Granddad
patois	- dialect
pont	- bridge
poilu	- hairy – the name given to the unshaven French soldiers in the trenches during the 1914 – 1918 war.
porte-cochère	- the wide door, formerly for carriages, opening on to the the paved area in front of a building
préfet	- administrator of a large community, presiding over the local maires
premier prix	- first prize or highest grade
pot-pourri	- here, a mixture of short pieces
quartiers	- areas of a town
Seine-Maritime	- Upper Normandy – east of the River Seine
- Soeur	- Sister
sorcière	- witch
soupe à l'oignon	- onion soup (made with grated cheese and bread)
tante	- aunt

truite meunière	- trout coated in flour and cooked in butter sauce with lemon
tu	- you (familiar)
un porto	- a glass of port (drunk as an aperitif in France)
un verre de vin	- a glass of wine
vieille France	- France before the Revolution
vin d'honneur	- celebratory glass of wine offered to a crowd of people
volontiers	- with pleasure
vous	- you (formal – courteous)
vous en avez du courage	– you are very brave

Scots words and expressions in the text

Auld Alliance	- Old Alliance – between Scotland and France, against England before 1746
fecht	- fight
killt	- exhausted, literally killed, dead-tired
ower	- over

Latin words and expressions in the text

sursum corda	- lift up your hearts
in nomine Patris et Filii et Spiritus Sancti	- in the name of the Father, and the Son and the Holy Ghost

German words used in the text

Oflag	- prisoner of war camp for officers
Stalag	- prisoner of war camp for ordinary soldiers

Stuka	- dive bomber

Musical expressions used in the text

andante	- music played at a moderately slow pace
arioso	- a song – here a song-like melody on which the last movement of op 111 by Beethoven is based
arabesque	- light-hearted piece
cadence	- ending of a phrase
chorale	- a hymn-like piece for choir
concerto	- a piece for a solo instrument accompanied by an orchestra
diminished seventh	- a chord
diminuendo	- becoming quieter
fugue	- piece with several lines which imitate one another
movement	- a complete piece which is part of a larger work
nocturne	- literally a "night" piece – generally slow and expressive
prelude	- literally pre-play – introduction; later just a short piece
primo	- literally "first" – the top or higher part in a piano duet
perfect pitch	- being able to identify the pitch of any note
op.	- opus – the way of cataloguing the works of a composer
rubato	- literally "robbing time" – expressive use of musical timing

scherzo	– a lively piece – often a movement of a larger work
set	– a performance of Scottish dance music in all rhythms and speeds: ie a reel, a Strathspey etc.
sonata	– a piece (usually in two, three or four movements) for one or two instruments
two part invention	– keyboard piece with two lines, one for the right, and one for the left hand
third	– distance of three notes (inclusive)

Sol-fa and Solfège

In the eleventh century a teacher and theorist called Guido d'Arezzo, working in France, devised a means of learning and identifying musical notes through a method using the terms ut, re, mi, fa, soh (sol), la. Te or si was added later and at some stage do(h) became interchangeable with ut. His ideas developed in two different ways which are incompatible with one another. The "movable" doh system identifies the first note of the major scale; the "fixed" system calls C - do, D - re etc. Each system has its advantages.

Sol-fa

The movable system is excellent for training the ear and learning harmony (combinations of notes); in the twentieth century it was adapted and developed for teaching by the Hungarian composer Kodály. Doh-Mi is always the same distance apart (four semi-tones) no matter what the notes may be. The disadvantage (if you are singing and identifying the notes at the same time) is that the doh has to change when the music changes key.

Solfège

The Latin countries use the "fixed do", whereby do-mi can – taken to an absurd extreme - be as much as six semi-tones apart e.g. C flat – E sharp – or even a unison (same note) i.e. C double sharp – E double flat. More practically and, in the eyes of the adherents of the other system just as unmusically, C can be C-sharp, E can be E flat. Thus there is no way of hearing the difference between the major and minor third, let alone the diminished third, C sharp – E flat. It bears no reference to harmony; it is just a way of identifying, saying and memorising notes. Players, particularly keyboard players, trained in this system develop good memories.

About the Author

Margaret Scott published her first poem inspired by Greek myths, told by her father, when she was seven. A year later at her second primary school she learned about the surrender of the 51st Highland Division at St Valéry en Caux when a French delegation came to Elgin where many of the soldiers who were captured had been recruited. The **memory** of being told about the fog which had descended over the seaside town and prevented embarkation **has always stayed with her**.

She has shared her love of history, poetry and music, with her husband for nearly forty years. When she retired from being Head of Keyboard at Uppingham School, she started to write novels, of which 'The Swing' is the first. **Many of the early episodes are based on her own experience**, especially lessons with her first charismatic piano teacher whom she remembers with great affection. **As she herself studied the piano in Paris, and lived there after her marriage, she describes the city and its unearthly beauty as a spiritual persona which is shared by all who know and love it.**

First and foremost a teacher, **Margaret's style is strong and direct,** and she has created a heroine who has the **determination** which is one of the author's family traits.

Recently Margaret has written a series of short stories. 'The first English Poem', which was awarded a prize by the Writers' Forum, is based on the legend of St Caedmon.

Lightning Source UK Ltd.
Milton Keynes UK
16 October 2009

145063UK00001B/9/P